ERIN GO BRAGH
II

ERIN GO BRAGH
II

The Middle Of An Era
1975-1982

Ruairi O' Cashel

This work of fiction periodically uses the names of real people who were involved in the most recent round of the Irish "Troubles." Their actions and conversations are purely fictional in this story. Readers familiar with the last forty years of the Twentieth Century in Irish History in the North of Ireland will recognize the names and the figures introduced that are or were real. But most of the characters are fictitious as is the story.

This book was printed in the United States of America.

Rev. date: 07/19/2013

To order additional copies of this book, contact:
Xlibris
1-888-795-4274
www.Xlibris.com
Orders@Xlibris.com
134166

Contents

Dedication

To all the Irish political prisoners who engaged in the 'Blanket Protest,' the 'Dirty Protest,' and 'Hunger Strikes,' men and women in both England and Ireland. I single out the 'Ten' who in 1981 gave their all for the cause of Irish freedom, the justice of the 'Five Demands,' and were victims of Prime Minister Thatcher's intransigence.

A special thanks to my Orange wife who has made suggestions and corrections. Any errors are mine and mine alone.

Introduction

We all missed Ireland. It had been more than a year and a half since we had all moved to Hartford, Michigan, to start new lives. Hartford was my hometown, and my best friend and brother-in-law Paul's as well. I had lived in Hartford my whole life; and he had lived here for the past fifteen years. But, our wives were new to Hartford, and America. They were Irish and they were missing Ireland as if it were oxygen itself.

My wife Barbrie and I had left Ireland a little more than a year ago, if not in a tare at least in a hurry. I had fled the North of Ireland with a cloud over my head. I had been a foreign graduate student first in Scotland and then at Queen's University in Belfast in the North of Ireland. Prior to leaving the United States, I had been contacted and then recruited by an agent of the Irish Republican Army, the "RA" as it is known in the North of Ireland. There was no need to designate it as the "Irish" Republican Army in Ireland.

During my time of study abroad, I had gotten directly involved with the Provisional wing of the IRA and their fight for freedom. I met my future wife through her sister, Eve, who was somewhat involved with the Republican Movement. Their brother Danny was actively involved with the Provisional "Army" and the latter two became well aware of my deepening involvement with Provisionals.

Before and after our marriage, my wife Barbrie, or Barb in 'American,' suspected I had been involved in some aspects of the Troubles but had no factual knowledge of my role and no real clue as to the actual nature of our departure for America other than to be with my recently widowed mother and her sister Eve who had recently moved to the USA. My beautiful wife did not suspect that our departure was in fact for me a hasty retreat out of Ireland.

My involvement in the Provisional wing of the IRA, the so-called "Secret Army," was hesitant at first but, over the course of a few years I was in up to my neck. The last week of my stay in 1973 was not just hectic, it had turned deadly. The last death I was directly involved with was the culmination of a series of unfortunate incidents that put me in over my head. I found it to my advantage to return home to the USA with all do haste. With my unsuspecting wife in tow my flight simply appeared to be a planned return to my country of origin.

My mother welcomed us with open arms as did Barb's sister Eve and her husband Paul. Eve and Paul had settled in western Michigan shortly before we arrived back home. The girls would get homesick at least every other month, but a trip to northern Michigan, or along the Lake Michigan shore line in the summer and fall, or snow skiing during the winter, or sojourns to Chicago even for just a day, usually distracted more than cured them for a while.

Just when I thought I had these distractions down to a science, a friend of my wife's was to show up for a short visit and my world turned up side down, or more to the point, it was to turn inside out.

A Visitor From The North

Vickie had been in touch with Barbrie because the two of them had taught together at a school in Belfast before we departed for America. Barb had a constant flow of correspondence from friends back in Belfast and there was no reason for her to single out Vickie to me any more than half a dozen other friends from Belfast. Several had gotten to Chicago and often Barb, Eve and I went over for a day or two to give them a taste of America and to show the "Irish friends" the "Windy City."

Barb would throw out a name or two and as often as not I didn't recognize the name, and in most cases I couldn't even put a face to the name I did recall. Whether I did or not I would accompany the girls for the Chicago rendezvous. Sometimes Paul, Eve's American husband and my very good friend would come along as well. We always had a grand time.

When Barb announced that a teaching friend from the school back in Belfast was coming over for a vacation and planned on visiting us if it was "Ok," I didn't give it a second thought. She was flying in and Barb planned on her staying with us for a week and then those of us who could would accompanying her back to Chicago for a couple of days before she was to fly out.

You can't imagine my surprise, shock and awe when none other than "Vickie" walked toward us in the airport at Chicago. I not only knew Vickie, but unbeknown to Barb, we had met under most unusual circumstances back in Belfast.

In Chicago neither Vickie nor I let on that before Barb and I left Belfast, Vickie and I had had an unforgettable encounter during that last week in Belfast a bit more than a year ago.

I had been at a farewell party put on by some of my Provie friends when a British Army raid in the Nationalist stronghold of west Belfast sent all of us partygoers on the run. I got separated from the rest and hid in Vickie's back garden while the Brits searched the neighborhood and then terrorized a family living next door to her. Vickie took pity on me, an innocent American student caught up in the "Troubles" in Belfast.

When trying to bring me back to the university district across town we were stopped by two Special Branch detectives, one of whom had taken a special interest in me from the minute I had made my first visit to the North of Ireland years earlier and had suspected me of IRA involvement. He had tailed me off and on for more than three years. As the two detectives were about to do me grave bodily harm, Vickie came to my rescue. In the process she crushed the legs and then shot and killed one of the men after I was forced to shoot and kill his partner.

In the aftermath of our escape, Vickie related a story I had heard years earlier from the Republican agent in Chicago who recruited me. This IRA friend told of a young Protestant girl back in Derry, many years earlier who had been savagely attacked by Protestant "B-Men" auxiliaries, who mistook her for a Catholic.

Vickie began explaining her background as I tried to comfort her over our unavoidable and unfortunate killing spree. She told her version of the very story I had heard years before in Chicago, paralleling my friend's version almost to a "t". But she further explained, starting with that incident she began to see the bigotry in the North of Ireland directed at the Catholic population in the six counties the Protestants called "Ulster." She nurtured and expanded her knowledge and understanding of the Protestant "bias" shown to Catholics over the years.

She had gone to university and took a teaching job in Belfast to escape her past in Derry, or as she had been taught to call it, "Londonderry." In the process she met and grew to like Catholic colleagues and in this process began to nurture not just a growing skepticism about the North, but in time found she had a deepening hatred of what the government of "Ulster" stood for. The unfortunate set of circumstances with the two government men earlier that night made it all came rushing back to her and she lashed out at what she had come to hate.

I explained that I had heard her story from an acquaintance in the late sixties, minus her name. What an extraordinary set of circumstances. As I explained my familiarity with her early history she also discovered I was the new husband of her teaching friend, Barbrie, from school.

We formed a pact of mutual silence about our Belfast encounter. My Belfast friend, Denny, checked on Vickie periodically to make sure she was coping with the tragic events she had shared with me. Barbrie and I were leaving for America and I never thought my past would walk back into my life in Chicago where I had first heard the story of the little Protestant girl who'd been mistaken for and treated like a Catholic.

Vickie lived up to our agreement on her visit with us here in the USA, she never said a thing about our encounter and the disastrous events of that night in Belfast. I watched and waited for something from her that would lead to my embarrassment. It did not come in Hartford. But the day before she was to return to Ireland while we were in Chicago, we found ourselves alone in a sandwich shop and cautiously we spoke of the unspeakable.

"Your friend Denny called on me a day after you and Barbrie left. He's a very nice guy. He has called in on me every so often ever since," Vickie said.

"Denny is the best, but he is also a troublemaker," I said and grinned. She smiled back.

"He said you were just in the wrong place at the wrong time. He told you to run that night and that got us all involved in an unfortunate set of circumstances.

He said as far as he knew you were just a graduate student from the USA. He's not only a trouble maker, he's also a good liar too," she grinned.

I let the last comment slide by as if I had missed it and inquired, "You are OK? I mean, no trouble with it all?"

"Oh, I'm fine. Your comments as you left that night made me feel better and as I thought about them they also made sense. You were right. Just because they had badges did not make them honorable, and they would have harmed us. Your friend Denny stops by or calls on me to make sure I'm fine every now and then. He is a character," she said smiling.

"I'm glad you are OK, and I appreciate your silence with Barb about it all. When I get around to telling her I don't know how I'll do it with out mentioning you and explaining we were victims of circumstances beyond our control."

Just then Barb and Eve returned and I observed, "Ah, you're back from the shoe store and both of you have bags I see. See Vickie, you should have gone with them instead of having to listen to me. They always sniff out the good deals."

Barb said there were good deals and that the next stop was at the Water Tower area where Vickie could get in on all the bargains. I just shook my head and smiled.

That night at supper at a little Italian restaurant, I finally said that I had a confession to make. I had thought about it all afternoon and while Vickie was still here, I thought I could come (partially) clean with Barb.

I confessed how surprised I was to see it was Vickie who got off the plane more than a week ago because we had actually met in Belfast the week of our departure for the USA. I explained the party, the Brits giving chase, Vickie hiding me and driving me to safety.

I conveniently left out the unpleasant details and the fact that we discovered that night back in Belfast that I was Barb's "American husband Rudy." I also said neither of us was sure of the other when we met here in Chicago. Her appearance was different with her hairstyle and coloring and I had kept my beard that I grew after I departed Vickie's house on the fateful night. I flippantly explained to Barb and Eve that I finally got around to broaching the subject only earlier "today."

We both expressed our surprise at realizing how ironic it was that Barb was our common denominator. What were the chances of that, back in Belfast or here in the USA?

Vickie said she was hesitant all week to ask me if I was indeed "the foreigner" from a year ago. I felt likewise, hesitating to ask her if she was "the helper" from a year ago. But here we were and we laughed earlier this afternoon at our discovery and admission, and we had a good laugh now. If Vickie was relieved, Barb seemed awed by it all, but Eve smiled and told me with her eyes she was only buying it as far as it was told, but her eyes also hinted that she suspected there was more.

Barb was not naïve, but she was trusting. Eve on the other hand had had a second, secret life back in Belfast, and she knew I also had secrets. I knew I would not have to wait long for Eve to grill me.

Later that night in the privacy of our hotel room, Barb asked in a serious voice, "Any more secrets you are keeping from me that are liable to pop up as a surprise, Rudy?"

"Barb, this was not a secret, it was a surprise," I lied by way of explanation. "I told you what had happened that night and that I had to stay at Denny's. I didn't mention Vicky driving me there because I didn't think it was that important. Honest. In all the commotion about being chased by the Brits, getting split off of Denny, us leaving for Hartford, that wee part of the story was lost."

"If you say so Rudy."

"Baby, that's the God's truth, so help me," I offered in my most sincere voice.

A half an hour later I was convinced that she was convinced of my story.

Disclosure

A couple of days after Vickie returned to Belfast, Barbrie and my mother were in Hartford at the market when Eve popped into the house catching me alone. She glanced around to establish our privacy.

"OK, innocent brother-in-law, what's the story with Vickie? I think the two of you were surprised to come face to face here, and your story was believable as far as it went. At least Barbrie is buying it. But I want it all."

I exhaled in a false bored disguise and said in as flat a voice as I could muster, "There's nothing more. You got it all in Chicago."

"If you won't tell me I'll get Barbrie to twist you, or even better your mom. She has her sources over there. Aye, she'll get the whole story."

There were times my sister-in-law was conniving, unscrupulous, devious and a pest. This was one of them. I had to come up with something, but the question was how much to confide in her. She was no snitch, and was trustworthy, but there were just some things that shouldn't be talked about.

My friend, Denny, back in Belfast knew but he passed on precious little info to anyone. He was discrete even to his comrades and commanding officer who he kept in the dark. It was all controlled and limited. Too much blabbering could come back and haunt and hurt a man, and his wife, and her sister. Denny was a pro and was careful. "Loose lips help the Brits," became a jibe during the Troubles with good reason.

I knew Eve would be relentless and that alone would bring the attention of Barb and my mom to the fact that something was up. I did not want to play that game. Before I got tired of it all, and had to answer to the inquiries of my wife and mother, I got angry and spilled the whole shebang, I thought I'd lay a ton of secret information on my sister-in-law. I had gotten her involved in a brilliant sting operation for the IRA. Maybe this was the least I could do to balance the scales.

"Eve, I'm going to break all the laws, rules and cautions that my friends in the RA taught me. I'm going to lay it all on you, and my life and my wife's life are now going to be in your hands," I said in a disgusted voice. (The IRA just referred to themselves as the "RA"; there was no need to specify "Irish.").

"Eve, you get arrested back in Ireland and put on the 'conveyor belt' of deprivation and torture used in prisons and detention centers by the British and their lackeys in the North to get you to talk, and what I'm going to tell you is just what they will want to hear and I'll never go back or I'll be arrested or killed.

"Hell they might try to expedite me from here to the North of Ireland. The Brits would just love to have you deliver to them the info I'm going to let you in on. Just this once I'm going to tell you, to put my life in your hands because I trust you, love you and your sister, and it's in the past. It's over and done with. I'm out of it now. Never again, and I'll not talk about it again either."

Eve looked more than surprised, more startled, maybe even shocked. But she did not protest or say that she didn't want to hear it. Usually we played this cat and mouse game. She suspected but never ever really knew. That was about to change.

"While I was a student in both Scotland and in Belfast I was involved with the Provies. You knew because of my involvement in your big time delivery, for the Movement. As time went on, I got more involved as they needed my expertise and as I started developing my own hush-hush double existence as student and IRA 'foreign' volunteer.

"At first I got packages from my mom to hand over to Mac Stick. Then I showed them how to smuggle in arms and explosives. Later I helped them acquire some explosives and arms from Eastern Europe. I also 'disposed' of a couple of bad actors in the UVF or UDA. I double-crossed a certain British officer who thought he was running me. As a matter of fact he was on to you and I steered him away, you might remember my mentioning a warning to you.

"Just before we left for Hartford I was at a farewell party when the British Army showed up. We all started running. I got split off from friends and I ended up in Vickie's garden. She helped a 'helpless Yank caught up in the Troubles'. She suspected I was more than I appeared to be, but she left things alone. She understands Barb is in the dark for the most part.

"Vickie was driving me back to my apartment when we were stopped by two undercover Special Branch guys, one of whom had tailed me and suspected me as IRA from my first weekend in Ireland years earlier. He was out to do the two of us harm. Vickie hadn't a clue what was really happening.

"There was a riot going on about four blocks away so these two goons could have their way with us. A scuffle broke out, I disarmed one of them and I had to shoot him and Vickie ran the second guy down and then shot him. Both were dead.

"I got her back to her place and had her report her car having been stolen. I talked to her to calm her down, but then she tells me about her past. As a wee Protestant in Derry, she was mistaken for a Catholic when she was ten years old or so and she had been beaten by B-Specials.

"Starting during recuperation and for years after she not only questioned the Loyalist-Unionist position on things in the North, she rejected the Protestant slant to it all. At the university she became an secret Nationalist sympathizer. She found she liked Catholics and things Irish. She wasn't a Republican for sure, but she was no longer a Loyalist lackey either. Working with your sister went a long way to convince her that her thinking and conversion was sound.

"Well it turned out that an Irish émigré in Chicago who recruited me for the Movement prior to my heading abroad for school, told me the same story.

He was from Derry and I don't know how he knew the story, but he did. When I told her about him and his version of the story, her story, we bonded. She trusted me and did not sick the Peelers on me nor did she ever tell a soul about our episode with the security goons.

"I had Denny check in with her shortly after that night, and he has regularly ever since.

"So there is the whole glorious and sordid story. Neither of us knew that Barb knew us both until a week or so ago. So that part is true.

"I was told that it was good that I was going home to the USA. There was some talk about a 'foreigner' being active in PIRA circles. So here I am, out of the way of harm deciding if I should and can ever go back to the North.

"I'm not scared about going back for myself, but I am nervous about your sister and you going back, especially if I go along with you. British intelligence doesn't just let thing like this go. So I have been somewhat vigilant. Nothing specific mind you, just a feeling every now and then.

"Hartford and western Michigan are small and I can spot the leopard. But in bigger settings like Chicago, I feel I may have lost my touch. I get jumpy. I start seeing things that probably aren't there. I don't want to tell your sister that I have a past that could cause us all hurt. But what's done is done, and it's on the record, and the Brits have memories, and records, and bureaucrats who keep checking things, sniffing around, running moles, listening, following up stories, that sort of thing.

"It was never that I didn't trust you, Eve, I do. I just didn't want to burden you with my baggage, make you vulnerable for my sake.

"But you pissed me off and now you are as bogged down as me. I know some of your secrets and working for the cause and now you know mine. Are you satisfied? Is your curiosity satisfied?" I asked.

I tried not to sound too sarcastic or demeaning.

Eve just sat there with her mouth partially open starring at me. Finally she managed, "Jaysus!"

After a substantial pause, Eve said, "I knew it. I knew you where in up beyond your ass. But you played it well. I'm fucken proud of you, I'm fucken proud to be related to you. You did good Rudy, and I know you are not telling me everything right now. But it's enough. Jaysus it's enough. Lets have a drink. It makes my little sordid secret really look little."

"No. Your secret, what you did for the Movement was huge. I believe it changed the course of the struggle. What you did was gigantic," I said. "You got our side a mole in MI5. That's huge!

"I'd rather that your sister not be told what I've just admitted to you. I think she would dwell on it and it might really upset her. She knows I did things for the RA, but she thinks it was coincidental and minor. I'd like to keep it that way . . . at least for a while longer," I pleaded.

"And you?" Eve asked. "All of what you did doesn't upset you. The lads back home have their mates to fall back on when they get to thinking too much. And the Brits and Loyalists do something stupid and the boys are confirmed in their involvement. But you are a loner now over here. It doesn't keep you up at night? Does Paul know? Do you confide in anyone?"

"No, I've not talked to Paul about any of it. I've not felt the need to talk to anyone about it. I suppose that if I ever did it would be you, here, I would turn to. But I have had no inclination, no bad dreams, qualms of conscience. I've had Denny who I could confide in over there. But you've got to remember, I brought my US Army experience to Ireland. That's what the RA needed from me in Ireland and used first and foremost. I also was involved in some nasty shit in Nam and I've lost no sleep over any of that either. I'm not a sentimentalist, and I don't get depressed. I get angry. My mother taught me that," I explained.

"Aye, your mother. She's an institution. After Barbrie I think your mother is my best friend. Oh, and Paul of course. But he's different, you know. I think you could confide in your mom. She'd be understanding," Eve reflected.

My mother, I thought. *Eve, if you only knew the half of it. My mother was directly involved if not responsible for most of my secret life in Ireland.*

History: The Modern Troubles From 1966 Through 1974

The modern 'Troubles' in Irish History had a ragged beginning, but the 50th Anniversary of the 1916 Easter Rebellion, 1966, is as good as any starting date. Some people in the Loyalist, Protestant, Unionist community in the North of Ireland, that they call 'Ulster,' were convinced that some if not most of the Nationalist, Catholic, Republican community were about to not just celebrate that 'Rising' but were going to sponsor a new rebellion.

Just as the terms Loyalist, Protestant, Unionist were not necessarily synonymous, neither were Nationalist, Catholic, Republican; but there was certainly some overlap in each community of these labels for some people.

The Loyalist community thought a revived 'Irish Republican Army' (IRA) would rebel in the hopes of bringing down the British supported system of government in the six counties that made up 'Northern Ireland,' or Ulster, as supporters called it. Nationalists referred to this rump of six counties of the original nine that made up the Historic 'Ulster,' as the 'North of Ireland.' This naming may seem pedantic, but it identifies what side of the divided community one identifies with.

In 1966 there was no Irish Republican Army to speak of, certainly not in the North of Ireland, but some Loyalists believed there was one, and they formed an 'Ulster Volunteer Force" (UVF) to preserve union with Britain and to protect Loyal Protestants. They then delivered preemptive strikes against perceived enemies of 'Ulster.' Loyalists had the sympathy in many quarters of the police, the 'Royal Ulster Constabulary' (RUC), so the Nationalist and Catholic community was under siege. In Belfast, Catholic neighborhoods were attacked and burned.

Some in the Nationalist Catholic community took to the streets with demonstrations over discrimination in voting and under-representation due to gerrymandering, discrimination in housing and employment. Many Loyalists were convinced these demonstrations were orchestrated by a handful of communist 'Official' IRA members headquartered down in Dublin which proved to be false. But in time the IRA reemerged in the North to protect the Nationalist Catholics.

By mid August of 1969, the UVF and RUC were joined by units of the British Military to combat the IRA, and theoretically protect Nationalists. Some members of the Nationalist community saw the British Military at first as protectors. But that label was dropped especially after 'Internment' was introduced by the British (the arrest without specific charges in many cases and without trials of Nationalists), and after 'Bloody Sunday' the British Army were called 'enemies,' (On January 30, 1972 the Paratroop Regiment killed thirteen unarmed Nationalists in Derry, and wounded seventeen more). These events turned the Nationalist Catholic community behind the IRA and solidified the IRA's claim of legitimacy.

Although a division existed (since 1969) within the IRA between the 'Officials' (a Marxist leaning faction), and a new 'Provisional' (PIRA or Provos or Provies) wing (seeing themselves as traditional 'Defenders' of the Nationalist community), the Loyalist community found the UVF challenged by another Loyalist group, the 'Ulster Defence Association'(UDA) in 1971. The Loyalist 'Ulster Unionist Party' was also challenged by the new 'Ulster Vanguard.'

The British government in London introduced 'Direct Rule' from London, replacing the Unionist controlled Stormont Home Rule system that existed since 1921. Loyalist dissatisfaction with perceived British lethargy in security matters against the IRA and prosecuting a Loyalist for the murder of RUC member, the Loyalists leaders called for a 'General Strike' in February of 1973. It temporarily crippled the six counties of the North in many public services.

The UDA had a sub-unit called the 'Ulster Freedom Fighters' (UFF) who were involved in a gruesome murder of the election agent of the leader of the Social Democratic and Labour Party (SDLP), a moderate non-violent Nationalist Constitutional party that participated in an election for a 'Northern Ireland Assembly' that would replace British 'Direct Rule' from London. Britain had corrected much of the gerrymandered districts that crippled Nationalist Catholic representation, so the SDLP became a key player in the new Northern Ireland Assembly.

In December of 1973 at Sunningdale Park in Berkshire, England, representatives from Britain, the Republic of Ireland, and the main parties from the North of Ireland (The UUP, the SDLP, and the middle of the road Alliance Party) met to discuss the 'Irish Dimension' in the North of Ireland. The firebrand ultra-Protestant Reactionary Reverand Ian Paisley condemned the conference. The conference was a bust, but Nationalists were hopeful that a United Ireland was on the horizon, while Unionists were obsessed with the notion that Britain was going to sell them out to the Irish Republic.

During the year 1973, the various factions of the paramilitary groups were very active with shootings (over 5000) and bombings (over 1500 with over 1000 actually exploding). Over 250 people are killed in 1973 and over 1400 people were charged with terrorist offences.

A General Election in the United Kingdom saw the Conservative Party Heath replaced by Labour's Harold Wilson. Nationalists had high hopes for the Labour Government since it had gone on record as early as the 1950s as saying major changes had to happen in the North of Ireland.

The Loyalists 'Ulster Worker's Council' called for another 'Strike,' and it was complemented with a series of bomb attacks in Dublin and Monaghan in the Republic of Ireland killing 27 people and injuring over 100. The UVF and UDA denied responsibility, but questions remained concerning their culpability.

Demonstrations by farmers at Stormont helped feed the Loyalist sense of accomplishment as they learned that the Executive of the new Assembly had collapsed. Loyalist sections of Belfast and outlaying areas openly celebrate the fall.

In Parkhurst maximum security prison, Frank Staggs and Michael Gaughan, two IRA prisoners, went on hunger strike, but were force-fed. The two Price sisters called off their hunger strike in Brixton Prison. The PIRA set off bombs at Westminster Hall and the Tower of London, also in Manchester and Birmingham. They also killed two judges in Belfast and set off two bombs at two pubs without the traditional warning, which was their usual practice, in Guildford, Surry, England.

Loyalists reacted and went on a sectarian killing spree. In October, the Maze Prison Republican prisoners burned their over crowded huts and the British Military was called in. Riots broke out at Magilligan and Armagh prisons and Nationalist areas of Belfast. Then in November, thirty-three Republican prisoners escaped through a tunnel, but one was shot and killed and the rest were recaptured.

Several Protestant ministers and PIRA men met at Feakle, County Clare to 'talk.' They discussed a cease-fire, and the PIRA declared one for December 22, 1974 to January 2, 1975.

Planning The Family Trip

It didn't come as a total surprise, but when Barbrie suggested that the four of us, and maybe my mother, go to Ireland for a visit it did stop me in my tracks for a moment.

It was only natural that Barb and Eve would take a holiday back in Ireland. But Eve and Paul, Barb and myself, and maybe "mom" all going to Ireland, I wondered if my mom would do it. There were a lot of people over in Ireland who obviously knew her, or of her.

Since dad died, she had tidied up things in Hartford. She stayed in the house and had no expenses to speak of: taxes, insurance and the monthly utility bills were all. She could afford to come with us to Ireland but, the question was would she come with us?

Whenever it came up in conversation I kept quiet and just smiled and nodded in agreement with Barb and Eve.

Mom's reaction was essentially that she would slow us down if she came along. They would all counter that she would not slow us down one iota.

Finally I offered, "Mom, since we won't be going on a tour in the usual sense of the word, how would you slow us down if we weren't going any where other than Belfast and Dublin?"

I thought she was waiting all along for my input to finally make up her mind. "I'll come along but only for a week or two. If you stay longer I'll come on home ahead of you," she qualified.

"We'll not be staying longer that ten to fourteen days, so we'll all be coming home together," Barb added.

"We can go up to Belfast for just a day or two, and we can visit you're family in County Down. It will all be grand."

I took a deep breath, looked at Eve, and thought, *I sure hope so.*

Everyone except "mom" was gainfully employed. Barb was teaching at a Catholic grade school and I was teaching full time at a local community college and moonlighting at a local university. Paul was working full time at an engineering company while Eve was working at the village library.

The biggest problem would be coordination calendars for the trip. Summer was the logical time for Barb and myself, although it would or could cramp Paul's schedule. Eve could manage the time off all right. Mom was available any time. She seemed pleased and flattered to have been included. Since we had months to prepare, we were all confident that we could pull it off without a glitch.

I had this little nagging concern gnawing at the back of my mind concerning a return to the North in light of my past, yet I kept reminding myself that we would be in and out before any one was the wiser. We'd fly into Dublin, and rent a car or take the train up to Belfast.

I immediately sent off a guarded and coded note to Denny. I hadn't been in contact with him in a couple of months and I figured a heads up could alert him to put feelers out to make sure that the trip would be safe for all concerned. We would come in about eight months time and I knew he couldn't predict the weather that far in advance, but he might be able to indicate if anything big was forecast on the horizon.

Within two weeks a letter from Denny gave the all-clear signal amid the banter about nice weather and clear skies. I felt confidant that plans could proceed with out much concern for my past rising up to bite me in the ass. But, I also knew that the weather in the North was neither nice nor clear as far as the IRA was concerned. I wondered if my mom's participation in the trip was as innocent as it appeared at face value, or did she have an ulterior motive? Was she playing them, and especially me?

History: 1975

Although the PIRA extends it's 'truce' beyond January 2, the British announce that 'H-blocks' were to be constructed in the Maze Prison, while a new prison was to be built in County Antrim at Maghaberry. The so-called Gardner Report recommended that the British Government drop 'special category' status for prisoners, treating 'political' prisoners as if they were common felonious criminal.

Seven "Incident Centers' staffed by Provisional Sinn Fein were set up in Nationalist areas during the 'truce' and known PIRA men, though active in the areas were not arrested by the British Army. Ruairi O Bradaigh, president of Provisional Sinn Fein, lauded the cooperation between the British Government and PIRA.

Margaret Thatcher, the new Conservative Party leader, appointed a close colleague, Airey Neave as the Conservative opposition spokesman on Northern Ireland. A feud broke out between the hard core Irish National Liberation Army and the 'Official' IRA, in addition to a feud between the UVF and the UDA resulted in gun battles and killings.

As the 'truce' ended, sectarian killings and bombings begin again in earnest. Four soldiers were killed in a bombing at their base at 'Forkhill, County Armagh in July while four Loyalists were killed at an Orange Hall in Newtownhamilton, County Armagh, by the PIRA using the name 'South Armagh Republican Action Force.' In November, three soldiers were killed at their observation post in South Armagh.

A bombing campaign cross the North of Ireland by PIRA saw UVF reprisals. A bloody feud between the 'Official' and PIRA broke out. PIRA, *in Derry, not only closed the 'Incident Center,' but blew up the building in which it was housed.*

Then violence was visited on Britain with killings and hostage taking in 1975, and there were 247 people killed from the 'Troubles' in that year alone.

The Pilgrimage To Ireland

The fall, winter and spring went by much faster than we anticipated. We budgeted very carefully and our only big expense was New Years in Chicago with Eve and Paul. Nineteen seventy six looked like a very promising year. The girls were getting whipped into a frenzy with Ireland on the schedule.

The closer the date got to the departure, the time seemed to fly bye. Even mom seemed to be getting excited. That in turn seemed to get Barbrie and Eve in a fever mode. I was finishing up exams and actually looked forward to a couple of weeks off before we were to leave. I got things done around the house and arranged for a local kid to mow lawns. Before I knew it, it was time to leave.

The Aer Lingus flight from Chicago to Dublin was both enjoyable and uneventful. The in-flight service was exceptional as always and the smooth ride was ushered along by a tail wind that put us on the ground twenty minutes ahead of schedule.

If only Dublin airport was as accommodating and user friendly. Stairs and narrow corridors were anything but welcoming. But our excitement of being back in Ireland could not be dampened by the inconvenience of the terminal and the long wait for our baggage.

The night flight had not lent itself to sustained sleep so we had planned to spend our arrival day and first night in Dublin. We had reservations at a centrally located hotel off O'Connell Street. After checking in to our accommodations, we walked along O'Connell Street to the General Post Office (or GPO to those in the know) so mom could stand there for several minutes, take it all in, and imagine.

The GPO saw some of the most dramatic events during Easter Week of the 1916 Rising. I don't think a trip to the Vatican and standing in the great square in front of Saint Peter's and behold the famous basilica with Bernini's columns and statues could have held any more meaning for my mother, a devout Irish Catholic. This place in the heart of Dublin was as sacred, as hallowed, and as much a shrine as any in the whole world, including Rome, to my mother.

None of us rushed her or spoke. Neither Barb nor Eve, Paul nor myself, would disturb my mother, so lost in her thoughts. Eventually, she approached the great fluted columns at the entry to the GPO and she reached out to touch one just below a bullet pockmark. It was like she was touching a holy sarcophagus. After some time, I approached her putting my arm around her shoulders and she looked up at me and said, "I won't make it. I won't be here for the hundredth anniversary of the '16.' But you will. Promise me you'll be here for it. Who knows, maybe the North will be united with the Free State and we'll be something of a 'Nation Once Again'."

A tear ran down her cheek. I pulled her toward me and squeezed her and said, "We'll all come back and be right here in 2016, with your grandchildren and great grand children in tow."

She looked up at me and then at Barbrie, as my wife came and hugged her. She asked, "Are you telling me something, some wonderful news I hope?"

"Aye, I am. We wanted to wait until we were here in Ireland to tell you, 'grandma'. Eve and Paul also have some news. According to the due dates we were first and they were copycats," I teased.

Eve chimed in, "We waited for them to get started since they are older and needed prodding."

"Like hell. Barbrie and I had to explain everything to them, well at least Eve. You know, those sheltered Irish Catholic schoolgirls. So shy, prudish and innocent. Barb had to have long chats with her. Paul was 'OK', but Eve . . ." I teased.

Paul was just shaking his head, while Eve was mumbling "Jaysus . . ." and winding up as if round two were ready to commence, when Barb said, "All right you two, behave yourselves. You are drawing attention to us out here."

Smiling and blushing a bit, she turned to mom and said, "We are about two weeks apart is all. In February, it will be grand."

"Indeed," mom said. "Jesus, Mary and Joseph. Let's celebrate. Let's head for Stephen's Green, I know the perfect place. Some lunch and a drink. Then we must go out to that wreck of a place, our Golgotha, Kilmainham Goal."

Everyone was so caught up in the moment, the announcements, celebration and excitement of it all: being in Ireland and the expected babies, that a greater revelation was missed. Mom knew exactly where places were here in Dublin. She'd been here before and she'd never shared that information with me.

I thought her world revolved around western Michigan with memorable vacation trips to Washington, DC, Chicago, Detroit, Upper Canada, Petoskey and the upper peninsula of Michigan, Boston, Miami, Wall Drugs, the Badlands, Cody, Wyoming, and Yellowstone National Park, and a canned tour of Europe from London, via Paris, Basle Switzerland, and Venice to Rome and an audience with the Pope at the Vatican.

In all the exhilaration, everyone except me missed the subtle but obvious fact that mom had clearly been here before. She was familiar with Dublin as only someone who had been here before could be. She had not intended to disclose this information but she got carried away with all the family news.

I decided to let this discovery slide by, at least for the moment. But I wondered to myself: *How many other secrets do you have, mom, and how many more surprises can I expect to discover on this seemingly innocent holiday?*

We lunched at a restaurant in a pub, some good Irish fare and drink, pub grub, before we took two cabs out to Kilmainhan Goal. It was in a sorry state and there was no admittance so we merely stood out in front. Again mom stood a bit off, alone in her solitude. She just stared at the jail that had housed so many Irish patriots from Robert Emmet, Parnell, the men and one woman of the 1916 Rising: Pearse, Connolly, Clark, Marklevicz and the rest.

She just stood there, looking at the front façade in its tattered state. It was as if she were transfixed. It was becoming obvious to me that the last four hours were not merely a destination but the start of a pilgrimage for my mother. With dad dead, she was finally free to do what she wanted to do and what she needed to do in the time remaining to her. Again I mused, *this is no mere holiday for her, its a religious journey of sorts. These places are shrines; she surely has been here before. Is this trip merely the last of her trips?*

"See the relief carving over the door—entwined snakes. During World War II the Nazis issued anti-partisan badges to their troops that also had entwined serpents. Interesting, don't you think. Oppressors using

The taxi pulled up as I exited the bar and I piled in. Five minutes later I was in familiar territory off Divis Street in the Nationalist Lower Falls area. Once inside the house he gave me a bear hug and said, "Fuck off. The beard's still a good disguise."

I asked if it was safe to speak?

"Aye. It's clean."

I said, "I could smell that fucking beard before I saw you go to the loo."

"Fuck off. But it's good to see you. How are youse?"

"I'm going to be a daddy in February. Barb's sister Eve, is expecting too."

"Jaysus, you got the both of them pregnant?"

"Fuck you, you wanker."

We both broke out laughing and hugged each other.

"My mother is with us. It's like a pilgrimage for her. We went to a few of the key sights in Dublin. She'd just stand there, and it wasn't so much her gazing at the places, but I could sense and feel her experiencing it all. It was really something.

"I waited to tell mom we were expecting untill we were here in Ireland. When I told her I was to be a daddy and that I was just here as a visitor, that things had changed for me since the last time I was here, she said that according to her sources things indeed had changed, and for the worse."

Denny exhaled deeply and said, "She's right. The Brits have rebounded in the past two years to the point where if the truth were known, they now have the upper hand. Locally, many of the lads have been scooped up including Adams and 'Darkie'. It has brought things to something of a stand still. There was a real strategy while the 'Dark' was in charge of operations, as you know full well.

"It's not just the leadership, it's a big feckin part of the Army that are in the 'Kesh.' Long Kesh Prison is an old British Army camp about ten miles south of Belfast now used as a prison for political prisoners. Others are in Crumlin Road Prison here in Belfast, towards the top of the good old Shankill, 'THE' key Loyalist road and area in west Belfast, just a stones throw from the Falls. We drove by the prison, do you remember? They finally closed down their prison ship in Belfast Lough. But it's still like we are just treading water.

"There are some people who would like to talk to you. Nothing involving you here, mind. But you could help procure some stuff back home. They will fill you in on the particulars."

I said as forcefully as I could, "Nothing here and nothing that can be traced back to me in America."

"Aye. I'll fill them in on the new circumstances and explain your conditions. They will understand," Denny assured me.

"Let me get you back now and I'll be in touch to gather you up for a meeting. Now where's my beard?" Denny asked.

"I think I saw it leave by the front door and now it's probably crawling along the gutter," I smiled.

"Why do I never get tired of telling you to 'fuck off'?" Denny asked with a smile.

———————————

In less than ten minutes I was walking into the establishment where Eve and Barbrie were holding court with their friends. Paul was chatting with Vickie who had joined the celebration during my absence.

My mother seemed to be enjoying herself considering the time. There was a last call before closing up.

Barbrie said, "Aye he's back just in time to buy the last round."

I nodded agreement, went over to her, kissed her on the forehead and said, "So you did miss me."

"Your mother was quite concerned."

"Did she not know I am about my Nation's business?" I implored in my most Biblical tone.

"I'm sure she will ask you about it," Barbrie countered as she returned to the banter with her friends.

With the early return of Professor Smyth's colleague, we had to move to new lodgings. The Hotel Europa was open for business and had vacancies—it would be the most bombed hotel in Europe over the next few years (PIRA's economic warfare).

True to form, the next morning at breakfast, mom asked where I had disappeared to last night for a time? "Oh, just an old friend. I'll want you to meet him in the next day or two. A real character. I suspect you will like him a lot. He was a Provisional. He knows some important people. You'll enjoy talking to him. We'll just have to find a safe place to have private conversations, if you know what I mean?"

"He was or is in the Army?" mom asked.
"Yes. So I do not have to tell you we'll have to be careful."
Mom just smiled and nodded.

———————————————

Barbrie, Eve and Paul planned to spend time at Barbrie's old school to talk to students about America and to see some of the teachers who hadn't made it to the party two nights before.

Denny arranged for a meeting with some friends while the girls and Paul were at the school. I told Barbrie that I wanted mom to meet Denny and some of the others while they were busy at the school and that we would all meet at Queen's for a late lunch with Professor Smyth and possibly Professor Jones.

The cab ride with Denny driving was a typical ride to ditch any tails. Mom and I were out of his cab and into another, then dropped off at a front door and out a back door and back with Denny with traffic purposely bottled up in back of us as we drove off for the warren off the Falls.

The address was new to me but the lay out was familiar as most of the row houses are of a similar pattern in the Nationalist and Loyalist ghettos: living room and kitchen down, two bedrooms and a toilet up. As we entered there was a surprise in store for both mom and myself.

"Kathryn, you look lovely. The years have been good to you," Sean Keenan said as he stepped forward and hugged my mother.

I just stood there open mouthed. Sean finally stepped back and said causally, "Good to see you Mr. Castle. You always seem to be surrounded with beautiful Irish women."

"Yes, most of the time," I managed. "But I have been surrounded by some particularly ugly types on occasion. However, the Irish women I do associate with just happen to be beautiful."

He laughed and said, "I do remember out in Donegal. Denny did relate how some ugly types at the border surrounded you, but I thought they were males. As I recall you handled yourself very well."

"All's well that ends well," I said as I smiled.

"What's this?" my mom asked.

Before I could deflect the question Sean said, "Just another chapter in the legend of Rudy Castle to those who know, and another incident to those who do not know about the myth of the 'foreigner' working with the IRA. Would you agree, Rudy?"

"Well, with myths and legends like these floating around, any foreigner might not feel safe in Ireland," I exhorted.

"But you are among friends here, is that not so Denny?"

"Aye it is. And friends who are indebted to you, and who honor your family, and have need of you again," Denny commented.

"I am only here in Ireland a week more with my mother and pregnant wife. When I left a year ago the leadership of the RA was locked up and the Movement in shambles because of touts, infiltration by the Brits, and possibly traitors. Have things changed to the point that careless talk can be thrown about with no fear of arrests?" I pleaded.

"Rudy look around, you know these people from before. They are solid, I will vouch for any and all of them . . . ." Denny said as he gestured.

"I don't fear my brothers, but those not seen who might be listening and watching. Denny, you yourself taught me . . . ."

My mother cut me off. "Rudy, do not waste your caution and energy here among friends who have obviously secured this place for themselves and us their guests.

"Some times Sean, I have to remind him of his manners. I know he never let his guard down in Vietnam, and Denny taught him to be vigilant here, that's how he returned to me safe and sound with a fine Irish wife. And he will tell me later tonight that one cannot be too careful, but there are limits," mom explained.

"I understand. Rudy, we here are to be trusted," Sean pleaded. "We do need you again my friend. Well, your expertise. I'm here because we are so thin in the leadership because of what you yourself described.

"But before business, let's catch up on some recent craic and return to some old times." Sean launched off on remembrances with my mother: "Kathryn, do you recall . . . ? Kathryn, remember . . . ?

Kathryn what was the name of . . . ? Kathryn who was it that . . . ?"

We all relaxed and Sean and my mother chatted at length about the good old days. To my surprise my mother had traveled to Ireland through Canada several times in the 1930s for contacts in Chicago and in Canada. She had delivered money and information from America to what was left of the IRA in the 30s and in early 1940.

Sean explained, "As war in Asia was threatening Britain's colonies and commonwealth, and as war in Europe seemed unavoidable with a resurgent Germany, the IRA hoped to take advantage of England's preoccupation with the Japanese in the Far East and Germany on the Continent. And your mother delivered hope, among other things, to the Irish cause.

"Kathryn had met many of the heroes of the 1916 Rising who were still alive and involved in the Movement and those who would lead the IRA in a new Rising. Her nickname, or code name, was 'Hope.' No wonder, she engendered the 'Hope' of Nationalist Ireland now during the new Troubles. She had been active during the late fifties and early sixties also, the so-called IRA's 'Border Campaign' called 'Operation Harvest.'

"It had turned out to be a bust, but Kathryn had done her bit back in Michigan collecting money and delivering it along with messages from certain people in Chicago to be delivered to Ireland for the 'cause of Irish freedom.' New people had replaced her but every one remembered the American girl, 'Hope was her nickname,' who delivered hope in her own right, rain or shine. She was, and still is a legend."

My mind began to pick up the rest of the tale. At the end of the 1960s she had encouraged me to follow in her footsteps as she had followed in her father's footstps, a veteran of "1916". As I thought about the past couple of years I now saw that she more than encouraged my participation in the "cause of Irish freedom," she enlisted me in that cause.

If this trip was a pilgrimage for my mother it was a total learning experience for me. A hundred loose ends were being tied up. But then Sean said very quietly to my mother, "I haven't forgotten a certain matter concerning your father that you asked me to look into many years ago Kathryn. I am still pursuing it when I can."

I wondered what this was all about. When I asked her about it later she said she'd explain it to me when we had more time,.

But back to the present, after another hour or so of reminiscences for Sean and mom, I reminded her about our luncheon date with Paul and the girls at Queen's. Denny drove and Sean rode along. While being driven to the university, Sean explained the need of my expertise.

It was somewhat annoying to me that Sean kept addressing my mother rather than me. But I was after all Kathryn's son, her only son, and only her son!

"Kathryn, thanks to an un-named source who happens to be with us today, we have come into possession of large quantities of plastic explosive. It is so much easier to handle than dynamite and more compact than some of the fertilizer mixes available. What we need are not timers, but radio controlled trigger devises. Apparently they are available in America, but draw a lot of attention if sent to Ireland. We need the devises and a way of getting them into Ireland. We might have a source for securing the objects, but we don't know yet if our man in Florida can obtain sets. We hope to know any time now.

"In the mean time, we want to set up a program to make sure they can be delivered without drawing attention to them or us.

"Kathryn, your son here, Rudy, is something of a wizard at getting things into Ireland so I am told, We are so hoping he can solve this new puzzle for us. It would be so reassuring to us all if we would have your assurance that it is feasible and that you have a plan in mind Rudy," Sean concluded.

Mom just looked at me, sitting up in the front with Denny, from the back seat of the taxi where she sat with Sean. I looked at Denny, back to my mother, then to Sean and said, "I am Kathryn's son, and with me 'Hope blooms Eternal.' My code name will be 'Eternal,' OK?"

My mother responded, "Rudy, don't be impudent. I'm going to knock you into the middle of next week. You won't know if you are on foot or horseback."

Every one of us in the taxi broke out laughing. Before she could react I said, "Some times she has to remind me of my manners. Some times I let my guard down and it gets me in trouble . . . ."

This time even mom laughed. She shook her head and said for Sean's and Denny's information, "When I get my hands on him there are going to be two hits, when I hit him and he hits the floor."

"I know Kathryn sent you Brown Bread when you were a student here with aluminum foil packets baked in the bread. Money, notes, what have you. Your family is a legend for getting things through. And like mother, like son," Sean said. "We know you'll try your best."

We all laughed again. As mom and I got out of the taxi I turned to Sean and said, "I've got some thing in mind. I'll know by tomorrow if it's feasible. I'll contact Denny tomorrow with good news of a plan, I **hope**." I stressed the "hope."

As they drove off they watched me running ahead and away from my mom, the two of us laughing and taunting each other.

"They're more like old friends than mother and son. They are two for the books. Denny, do you think he really has a plan already?"

"Your man there, aye, he has a plan alright, and I have no doubt he already has most of the details worked out. He only needs to identify the problem and he is on it like a soaking rain on a field. He once told me, 'If humans have created an obstacle, humans can solve the dilemma. There is no substitute for brains.'"

"His da made him take foreign language and math every semester in school, both in high school and college. His da said the two subjects would help him survive. Rudy believes it, from his experiences in Vietnam and here in Ireland. He speaks several foreign languages and his mind is as sharp as a mathematicians," Denny said.

Old Games

Jones couldn't make the luncheon but hoped to touch base with us after the meal. That was all right with me. Jones had tipped his hat when I was a student that he was involved with Special Branch and the British Military Intelligence as an informer and contact. I could claim that I tried to see him, but if I failed, so much the better in reality.

Smyth was waiting at his office with Eve and Barb when mom and I showed up out of breath from our game of tag on the way into the building. Needless to say we drew some odd looks. But our laughter put every one at ease.

Smyth and my mother got on very well and took an indisputable liking to each other and again I sensed that her reputation preceded her. Smyth was not simply cordial, he clearly was in "awh" of mom.

Their chat was not merely polite but genuinely friendly, and when he learned of the expectant babies we were all talking at once. He knew Eve better than Barbie from her university days, but through me he certainly felt he knew Barbie well enough.

The pub was between the university and my old boarding room. When it became apparent that Jones wasn't going to join us, Smyth said he needed to run along to his office for a while to catch up on some work. I suggested that the rest of us call on old Barnaby, my former landlord, whose boarding house was not that far away.

Barnaby was very gracious considering we were unannounced and caught him by surprise. He also got on surprisingly well with my mother considering their contrary political views, assumptions and experiences.

After about an hour, we were back at Smyth's office when I told him I had a few ideas to bounce off him and asked if he and his wife could meet us for a drink after supper at the Europa Hotel. He said he and his wife could be there about eight.

We caught a cab ride back to the hotel where the girls took a rest for about an hour. Later, we went for a walk down by the Victorian City Hall and found the city center full of uniforms and quite inhospitable.

We drew long looks from both the RUC and British Military. I asked my mom, "Gee, I wonder what Berlin looked like in late 1945?"

In the spirit of William Blake who once said "Hell is a city much like London," or something to that effect, mom answered, "Belfast in 1975 is a city much like Berlin in 1944." I appreciated mom's wit even if the girls missed it.

We met some more of Barbrie and Eve's friends for a drink about five-thirty that evening.

After dinner the Smyths joined us for desert and drinks. Mrs. Smyth had a little some thing for the two expecting mothers. The four women were totally absorbed with talk of motherhood. I said to Paul, "Sorry to desert you for a couple of minutes, but business." He nodded understanding.

Smyth and I went to the bar near a speaker broadcasting Beetle's tunes when I said, "I've been asked to deliver some sensitive timing equipment to some friends of ours.

"My plan would be to send to the university here some oceanographic measuring devices that you and I planned on using for our research on piracy along the coast. Our mutual interest and collaboration and all of that sort of thing.

"I will ship the hardware on ahead of my arrival, but at precisely the time of my showing up, they will mysteriously be stolen from the university storage area where you have placed them.

"I will make arrangements for more of the delicate devices to be shipped over immediately. Yet unfortunately these will be lost to thieves as well, and I will order more.

"I figure we will be able to get enough in for a year's worth of operations and plenty for our engineers to dabble with preparing for copy cat imitations of their own. The RA will be in business for years to come."

"I can arrange everything from this end. I'll send you an invitation in a month or two to join me on this wet field study and request the equipment," Smyth said as he smiled.

"It's a brilliant idea Rudy."

"Thanks. Your invitation will be good because I will be able to blame you for my return here when it takes place. Barb won't like it, but I will be able to explain that it will be the 'opportunity of a life time,'" I suggested.

"Oh great, I get blamed," Smyth feigned hurt.

"Aye, it's the price for doing business with an American colleague with an Irish wife. I'll let our friends know we have a plan. But I'll be very cautious about who knows and advise them to take care about who is informed. The fewer the number in the know the better. I will not go into the details. I'm just going to say I have a plan. You, Denny, and me; that's it on the particulars. We cannot be too careful.

"The Movement has been penetrated and I want to protect you and your family as well as mine. Denny is like a brother, so he is in on the plan too. Ok?"

He smiled and nodded his agreement and consent.

We returned to the women and they were still sharing information, questions and answers about childcare. Paul was on his third jar.

The next day I informed Denny that my plan was in place. I explained that the fewer who knew of a plan, let alone the actual details of the plan, the better.

Denny agreed and said he'd inform Sean and reiterate the need for silence.

I asked Denny out right if he was all right with being on the outside for now? He said of course.

I said I hoped that would be his answer, and explained that I'd tell him why in a minute.

I suggested a short walk and as we walked away from the hotel amid the crowd and noise, I informed him of the plan. He merely smiled and said, "Brilliant."

I told him I wasn't testing him, just playing with him earlier when I asked him if he was OK with being left out for a time. "Not every one would accept being marginalized," I said. "How could I leave you out? You've got the beard."

He smiled and shot back, "Fuck off."

I suggested he not pass the plan on to anyone. He just looked at me and said, "Okie dokie."

"It will be our secret. You, Smyth and me," I said conspiratorially.

He asked, "Not Sean?"

"Tell him I told you I had a plan but that I refused to tell you specifics. Tell him Kathryn's son has turned into a paranoid asshole. We'll see if he goes to my mother to get me to explain what I have in mind. Curiosity killed the cat, in this case KAThryn's son.

"I think that people who need to know more than they need to know are potentially a problem and suffer from a character flaw. I'm not saying anyone in particular fits the bill, but lets play with this a bit."

"Rudy, Rudy. What are you up to?" Denny asked. Has this come from some one on the Army Council or some other notable?"

"No. It's probably nothing, but we'll see. Let me play my game. You said the RA has been penetrated. Lets see who is overly inquisitive. We've got a plan and we have woven a trap for some mole. Two for the price of one," I explained.

Again, Denny whispered, "Brilliant. It's fucken brilliant. A wee bit Machiavellian, but brilliant."

"I don't know if it's brilliant, but it might flush out some scum."

Family Reunion

Taking my leave of Denny I gathered up my mother and Barbrie, Eve and Paul and we headed for Saintfield in County Down. I don't know how, but Denny had gotten a "rent a car" for us. It was Saturday, market day, but the whole family would be there. My grand father's daughter, Kathryn, would attract them all like a hundred watt bulb would attract moths just after dusk.

I had spent a Saturday with granda's family a few years ago, and made good on my promise to return with my mother who had left with her da so many years ago. They complemented my effort because they were all here at the old farmhouse that I found easily.

The patriarch Richard and his slightly younger brother Eddy, and his son Eddy, and his son Eddy "The Third" were waiting for us as we pulled into the yard.

Richard and Eddy's sisters Edna, Irene and Emma were all smiles as we exited the car. At first they were hesitant if not reserved. It had been this same way when I had visited years before, but their warmth and hospitality exploded on the scene within minutes of my arrival back then. The joke was, would I, could I, remember all the names that were introduced to me back then.

I spent much of that day embarrassing myself by asking the names of people, "the man over by the stove", or "the door", or "in the red shirt." I kept saying I was so out numbered; they only had to remember one name, "Rudy." I had at least twenty to remember.

Now the numbers were a bit more even, so as I slid out of the driver's seat and smiled at all my relatives I said laud enough for all to hear, "The prodigal colonial boy has returned with his mother and his wife and his sister-in-law and her husband. Now we'll see who remembers all the names."

They must have heard the roar of laughter back in Belfast twenty some miles away. They came in a rush for my mother, they surrounded me, and they came for Barb, Eve and Paul, and swept us all into the house.

After half an hour of introductions, and re-introductions we settled down in the kitchen around the huge table I remembered from my previous visit. My mother was the center of attention.

She recounted the Diaspora of her parents, her brother and sister and herself from Ireland first to Canada and then to the USA. She spoke of her parents longing for Ireland. She addressed their deaths and her sister Dorothy's death. Every face that was not wet with tears was as solemn and serious as a priest at the graveside. I noticed Barbrie, Eve and Paul were also caught up in the emotions as mom's saga unfolded. No one but myself had ever heard the sorrowful tale she told. She had to stop several times to compose herself, and aunt Emma came and sat next to her, hugged her, and held mom's hand.

I had all I could do to keep my composure. After nearly an hour of this long sad tale of tears, I knew we were ready for a change of pace.

To change the mood I suggested that mom talk of her brother Frank, who was still alive and well and his family, which she did. Then I produced packets of popcorn, chewing gum, peanut butter and photos of every one from the family in America, both living and dead.

Just before lunch I made a more formal introduction of my Irish wife Barbrie and her sister Eve from Belfast and Eve's American husband, Paul, my best friend from Hartford. Eddy "The Third's" wife was a Barb and also pregnant. "If the child is a boy he will not be the "Fourth," she said emphatically to everyone's applause. "If it is a girl she will be another Emma," she exclaimed. Some one said, "The second." Everyone exploded in laughter. With all of these expectations the young girls broke off and headed into the sitting room to discuss parenting.

While the aunts started to load up the table with a buffet that would have arrested the famine of 1846 for quite some time to be sure, I stayed with mom and encouraged Richard, Eddy and the aunts to bring us up to date on the family, living and dead that were of my grand parent and my mother's generation. At times their recollections were very somber.

I produced a bottle of Kentucky bourbon and another of American whiskey and so what had at times become close to a wake became more of a living occasion of reunion and celebration. They had Jameson whiskey, which I preferred. Even with all the food, I was feeling no pain and suggested that we might have to stay a night or two or three before I would be in any shape to drive back to Belfast.

This announcement was greeted with approval by everyone. I kept repeating, "I'm only kidding, I'm only kidding," over and over in slurred fashion to everyone's delight.

Periodically the talk became serious about the recently unfolding Troubles, the family's dilemma of being Protestant but also being non-sectarian United Irishmen at heart. This was a family secret that I was entrusted with some years before. The family here in Down was loyal to the notion of a united non-sectarian Ireland, as Theobald Wolf Tone had envisioned it in the 1790s. But their Protestant neighbors expected them to assert an anti-Catholic loyalism to the Crown, to openly side with the Union with Britain, and to show a militant Protestant allegiance to the Northern Irish Stormont regime.

The younger generation was being assailed at school for being neutral. All of this pressure was causing a serious dilemma with the family. The youth of the family might have to be rescued by shipping them off to Canada to live with family there who knew their circumstances here in the North.

Mom was clearly moved and cried for their misery and committed herself to their well being. She reiterated my offer of a couple of years earlier; "If any one needs asylum they are welcome in Hartford, Michigan."

"Thanks" was extended to my mother, and sincere appreciation to this invitation was given. She and they all knew she meant it.

Barbrie, Eve and Paul were now full-fledged members of the family and privy to one of the greatest family secrets. If Paul was over whelmed the two girls were awestruck by these revelations. They knew we had a Protestant side of the family, but that knowledge was simply academic and foreign up to this point. Now they confronted the reality and the complexity of our family and they were humbled by it all, especially by my mother's compassion and love.

By the time we headed for Belfast we were all emotionally drained and physically exhausted.

After dropping the women and Paul off at the hotel, I headed for a parking area. It was then that I spotted the shadows. Two of them, obviously G-men working for the Special Branch of the Royal Ulster Constabulary.

After locking the car I slowly headed for the hotel when they approached me. With no formality they simply said, "Mr. Castle, a word."

"And who is it who wants this word?" I asked sarcastically.

"Is there any doubt in your mind who wants this word?"

"There is a lot of doubt about who wants this word. Has harassment now extended from one segment of the local community to foreign visitors?"

As I started to walk away one of them said, "Don't make this difficult. We can have a chat here or we can bring you in to headquarters."

"You and what army?"

As I continued to move toward the hotel they caught up with me, one on each side. "We are not going to ask you again," one said.

The other retorted, "As a matter of fact, we are not asking you. We are telling you to stop and answer some questions."

We were nearly at the hotel entrance and a doorman and security officer were watching now.

I said, "These two Bozos are hassling me. Would you get them off me and call the police?"

They pulled out their identification and said, "We are the police."

"Well, this is the first I heard of it and they did not identify themselves to me earlier."

Every one just stood there for a moment. I finally said I was tired from touring County Down with my family and that I was heading up to my room.

"Mr. Castle, we do want a word with you," the one who was in charge finally said. The doorman and hotel security man clearly deferred to him. He motioned to a set of chairs in the lobby. We went over, sat down and he leaned close and started his spiel.

"I am Ian Partridge and this is my partner David Potter. We are from Special Branch. We were informed that you might be able to help us. We understand that you were very cooperative and helpful to a certain Major in the British Military a few years ago. We hope you are still so inclined.

"The two Conlon girl's you are traveling with have a brother who is sought by Her Majesties security forces, If he tries to contact them, or if they try to contact him, we expect you to contact us. We understand you worked for British Military when you were here before and we would like to think you would extend this courtesy to us now," he said.

I folded my arms on my chest. Then I raised my right hand to my chin, putting my thumb and for finger to my lips. I studied him, his face, and his clear authoritarian posture and finally said, "The Conlon women are now married, one to me. Her name is Barb Castle. Both women are in the process of becoming American citizens.

"As to my brother-in-law, whom I've never formally met, we have no knowledge as to his whereabouts. None of us have any plans to contact him. As to his plans about contacting us, I have no knowledge. If contact is made it will be a complete surprise to us and I have no intention of contacting you about it either. Is that clear?

"What I did for the British Military was done out of comradely courtesy, soldier to soldier. They never asked me to spy on my future family. They showed some class.

"But you boys can fuck off. As my mammy would say, youse can eat shite, drink gas, step barefoot on broken glass, and die in a fucken fire. Now good night, and good riddance."

Frankly I was relieved they did not prevent me from going to my room, and they apparently did not follow me to my room. I am not sure what I would have done in either eventuality but, what came to mind bordered on mayhem.

I wondered who put them on to me and wondered further if they really thought I would inform them if my brother-in-law, Danny Conlon, contacted any of us. I hoped my bluntness set the record straight for Special Branch.

"Gee, what took you so long, we were starting to get worried?" mom inquired.

"I had a reunion of a different sort, an unfriendly reunion. I got stopped by Special Branch."

"Oh Rudy," Barbrie said in an overly concerned tone. "Are you all right? What did they want?"

"They were telling me that they are going to tail me, us, if they aren't doing it already. They also expect me to let them know if any contact is made with your brother Danny."

"Jaysus, Mary and Joseph, what did you tell them Rudy?" mom asked.

I smiled and said, "I told them to fuck off, to eat shit, to drink gas, step on broken glass, and to die in a fucken fire. I gave them all of your blessings mom."

"Nice. But remember you are in mixed company here with Barbrie. Mind your manners," mom scolded. "We will all have to watch out for our selves. Did you notice any thing unusual today, this morning or this evening going or coming from Saintfield?"

"No. Not a thing, and I was mildly vigilant. I will of course be on high alert now. Tomorrow I need to talk about business with Denny."

"Well, there is nothing we can do about it now so let's go to bed," mom instructed. "We will tell Eve and Paul in the morning. No use in waking them and getting them riled up tonight."

When Partridge and Potter left the Hotel they discussed at length my hostile response to their demand of contacting them should Danny Conlon contact anyone in our party.

"The man has a serious attitude issue. He was plainly hostile to us. He'll not inform us of anything. And now he knows we will be watching him and his family for any communication by Danny Conlon," Potter complained.

"I hope we didn't do more harm than good by talking to him. We certainly tipped our hand and he will tell the family to be extra careful. This did not go well at all," Partridge said as he rubbed his forehead with his hand.

Twenty minutes later, back at headquarters the two Special Branch men reported to their superior of the botched contact with Rudy Castle. They explained both the rude rejection of any cooperation and the hostile attitude exhibited to the Special Branch men.

"Was he threatening?" the supervisor asked.

Partridge answered, "No, not really. That is, nothing specifically directed at us in particular. But he made it clear that he would not inform on his brother-in-law. He had a bad attitude toward us in general."

"From what I gathered, he was very helpful to British Military Intelligence when he was a student here. Of course that was prior to marrying one of the Conlon girls," the superior muttered.

Partridge added, "He mentioned something about helping the Brits. He said it was comradely courtesy, one soldier to another. Clearly he does not extend that courtesy to the police."

"He also said that the military didn't ask him to spy on his girlfriend and her family," Potter added.

"Hmm. Mr. Castle is drawing fine lines here, but what he says makes sense in its own way. He was willing to work for the British Army on the one hand, and they didn't direct him to spy on his girlfriend's family. I wonder what he did for British Military Intelligence?" the supervisor mused.

"I'll put some people on Mr. Castle while he remains here in Ulster. Not you two, he'll be watching for you. But who knows, maybe he'll inadvertently inform us of things by what he does and who he meets, the sort of things that we would want to know."

The next morning at breakfast I brought Paul and Eve up to date on the previous nights doings. I didn't want to alarm them, just to inform them of the bad company they were keeping being in my company.

Eve was incensed to think that the RUC would think that any of us would tell them of being contacted by brother Danny. If Eve was angry, Barbrie was simply concerned.

I told the "Conlon girls" not to worry that we had only today left in the North. Referring to Eve as a "Conlon girl" really wound her up. I couldn't wait until we headed to the city center where we would be stopped by security personal at checkpoints. I knew she would put on a special performance.

We left the hotel after breakfast and walked over toward Donegall Square and city hall. Amid the security forces there were only a few shoppers, discouraged by not only the threat of violence, but by the periodic security searches.

We had to pass through two security checks and Eve was true to form. At the first she handed over her coat to a soldier and as squaddies scrutinized her bulging stomach she asked, "Would you be wanting to probe my belly with a bayonet? This isn't Africa where you did that sort of thing."

At the next stop the RUC were actually quite civil but that did not deter Eve: "This child will be born in America and will not have to put up with this degrading treatment. I tell all my friends back in the US about this sort of routine. I bet your lovely Queen wouldn't tolerate this sort of treatment for her family. I'm supposedly a British citizen and this is what it comes down to. Shame on you. Shame on you all."

I thought, *Well, it could have been worse, from both sides.*

It was our last day in Belfast and technically we had nothing in mind as to an agenda. Denny was to catch up with us about noon for lunch at a pub off of Donegal Place.

As we all took a table toward the rear of the establishment, I noticed two sets of obvious G-men come in taking up positions at the bar and at a table for two in the center of the place. They were clearly watching our party. I quietly informed every one of the situation and told them to ignore Denny when he came in.

When Denny sauntered in I gave him the sign that all was not well. He took a turn at the bar and as I went up and ordered a round I slipped him a note of explanation. He understood and he avoided us. He downed his ginger ale, looked around, then at his watch. He shook his head, mumbled something not quite under his breath and left in a huff.

My back was to him but I was watching everything from a small mirror on the wall along the back the table positioned between Barb and mom. I not only caught Denny's routine and departure but the identity of the two G-men who tailed him as he left.

I continued to watch via the mirror as the two RUC men exited the public house, stood out front for a few seconds, registered that Denny was nowhere in sight and that they had already lost him. Each took off running in a different direction quite befuddled to Denny's satisfaction, their annoyance and my enjoyment.

He was standing directly across the street from the entrance to the pub with his fake beard, glasses, and goofy hat looking directly through the window at me. I couldn't see the smile but I felt it, he tipped his hat, took a bow and calmly walked down the street.

I could also imagine him saying in his fake British accent, "Elementary, Castle, elementary old boy."

After lunch the girls had some place to show mom and Paul as I took my leave for the hotel. The other two G-men were my shadows back to the hotel. I was only in the room about half an hour when the knock at the door announced room service. My physical build look alike swiftly entered the room quickly shed his uniform which I promptly put on. Stepping into the corridor I apologized in my best Irish accent for delivering the papers to the wrong room on the wrong floor and mustered a hasty retreat "upstairs to the correct room. "My apologies, sir."

Once in the stairwell, I shed the hotel attire, donned an old sweater, fake glasses and hat. I walked right out the through the lobby past the two G-men and into Denny's waiting taxi.

Before Denny could beat me to it I snapped off, "Elementary, Denny, indeed elementary. And I look a hell of a lot better in these glasses and cap then you do in yours."

"Up yours you do."

"I must admit your routine at the pub was brilliant," I said by way of a compliment. "The tip of the hat, the bow. Simply sterling."

"What did I do to bring out all of this negative attention? Do you think they suspect something of my visit? Did some one rat me out? Some tout?"

"I don't know Rudy. I'll be sure to keep an ear open for anything. Maybe that British Colonel of yours pointed then on to you," Denny suggested.

"Hell, I'm sure he's long gone. I'm wondering if our little cat and mouse game has already trapped a fucken tout at work," I said.

We were at the university before Denny had a chance to reply to this suggestion. I was off to see my friend Professor Smyth for final details on our plans. I told Denny I would take a real taxi back to the hotel.

"We will need a lift to the train station in the morning though. We are off at 11:00 if you can finagle it. We can say our goodbyes then."

"Aye, I'll be out in front at 9:30. In the mean time, I will discretely inquire if any one has any idea why the G-men are so interested in youse. I got a feeling that it's more than your relationship to Danny Conlon."

I gave him the keys and money for the rented car. I stepped out of his taxi, feigned paying my fare and saw him pull off down the road. I slowly sauntered along the sidewalk fumbling with my billfold, but carefully scrutinizing the street and car traffic. I had a pocket-sized mirror in the billfold so I could see what was going on behind me as well as in front of me. An old army trick from Saigon. No one seemed to be tailing him or me as far as I could tell.

Smyth and I got a drink in the university cafeteria and under the cover of a steady drone of a hundred conversations from academics, we went over everything one more time. I reiterated that only three of us were in the know, but that I had attracted some unwanted attention in the past twenty-four hours. I advised him to be very careful.

Still wearing my cap and glasses, I exited the university after scrutinizing everyone near the door, inside and out, and headed for the street and hailed a taxi for a lift back to the hotel.

The next morning Denny picked us up right on time and we were off without a hitch. We said our goodbyes to Denny in the rolling cab. I left him an envelope with a "Thank You" card and some money. While unloading the bags from the boot, he said no one had any ideas about who turned the dogs on me. He said he would continue to pursue it though.

Everything was in order at the train station. The "girls" were nostalgic about leaving Belfast, but also relieved to be going "home" at the same time. I knew exactly how they felt. Paul was the only one who seemed oblivious to the tension the rest of us felt. His carefree attitude calmed all of us down once we were settled on the train.

As for mom, she just calmly took everything in and showed neither a concerned nor contented expression on her face. Later she said she just studied the crowd at the station from a relaxed spot while drinking some tea and carrying on a nonchalant conversation with some strangers on the platform where she spotted at least two G-men. I suspected they were the same two that I saw but decided to ignore, hoping not to add to the tension.

When we were well on our way to Dublin mom said, "Rudy, you are going to have to be careful, even when we get home."

Home In Hartford

The trip back to Hartford was as uneventful as the past weeks had been eventful. What bothered me like a haunting prophecy was mom's warning as we were leaving Belfast that I had to be careful, "even when we get home."

About a week after our return, I caught her alone in the kitchen of her house and inquired, "Your warning to take care, even here, was that an intuition, or based on a tip from some one, or what?"

"About fifty percent of each," she answered. "I spoke to Sean by phone the morning before we left and passed on to him the stories of the G-men hassling you. He said he would check into it for me. I called him again from a pay phone in the terminal just before we left Belfast. He said your man Denny was also asking around but striking out as well.

"He said he had nothing specific but the RUC's activity must indicate something. He told me to tell you to be extra-careful, even here. The Brits spied on us in the late 50s and early 60's during 'Operation Harvest.' I never found out if it was on their own, you know Canada isn't that far away, or if it was with the cooperation of that creep Hoover and the FBI.

"I wouldn't put it past Hoover to be in bed with the Brits on spying on Irish sympathizers and supporters here in the US. He strikes me as a bit queer in every sense of the word, like all the British uppers from their boy's boarding schools. That's probably where it started, some secret liaison."

"Jaysus, mom! Are you going fey on me now? Your imagination is running wild. Slow down. If they have mikes here in the house your just feeding em," I said with a smile.

"No, I'm just saying there are probably a lot of links between bed fellows that shouldn't be ignored," she said. "Any way, be careful Rudy with what ever you are up to, understand. You keep me informed as best you can and I'll let you know if I learn anything. That's all. OK?"

"Aye, of course," I answered, studying her posture and expression. I saw a casual stance but a serious stare at me while she pealed the potatoes for the evening meal.

I contacted a man in Chicago named Daemon; I had an old acquaintance named Sean McDuffy check on him. He was solid and squeaky clean according to Sean. "Under the radar of US authorities, and reliable with the Movement to a fault. He could be trusted with the nails to the true cross," Sean said.

Sean had recruited me some years before for the Provisional wing of the IRA just as I was leaving for graduate school, first in Scotland, then in the North of Ireland. If Sean said the contact was pure sterling, he was pure sterling.

Daemon made the contact with somebody in Florida who would not only supply the IRA with a new generation of explosive triggering devices but also with instructions on how to build them from simple, inexpensive, discrete, and everyday materials that would not draw attention from security people when purchased. He even offered to instruct any one from the movement who could get to the USA.

Daemon said the Florida technician would need some time to assemble the devices, especially if they were to pass as oceanographic equipment. A couple of further requirements were that the detonators could be easily shed of their unnecessary disguises before their use in the North of Ireland and that no trace to either an American or Queen's University source could be found on the material prior to or after their use.

The Florida man was supposed to have muttered some thing to the effect, "Hell, no problem. I can have them look like they were manufactured in China or Cuba if you want me to. All I need is time. If these boys have time I can do any thing with the devices."

The fact of the matter was that we did not have all the time in the world. We were on a schedule, and we were seriously behind already.

New Games

It was nearly half a year later before I heard from Daemon, in the late spring of 1977. The materials were in Chicago and ready for delivery.

"Jaysus, I thought your man was spooked and the whole project was a bust. I haven't heard anything from any body for half a year," I told him. "Have your man sit tight for a while since my contact in Ireland isn't ready for the delivery. We'll probably have to start from scratch on this project."

Sean collected the materials two weeks later and passed them along to his friend Paul, my brother-in-law. Paul stored them in my mother's Michigan cellar behind a padlocked door.

It was another two months before Professor Smyth from Queen's University contacted me about some new opportunities to explore some medieval and early modern places along the north coast of Ireland possibly used for smuggling. He had secured a grant for the two of us to conduct research. Some technical oceanographic equipment would need to be purchased and the US had experience and expertise in this area through exploring sunken treasure in the Caribbean looking for Spanish and Aztec gold.

I contacted Shedd Aquarium in Chicago for information on the type of equipment we would need to do for our exploring and research along the north Atlantic coast of Ireland. They were very helpful and put me in contact with oceanographic instrument contractors in Florida, Texas and California. I established a legitimate paper trail that would leave no doubt as to our bona fide academic endeavor.

We were on the way. I contacted the federal government's export office to ensure that the oceanographic equipment could be legally exported to Queen's University, Belfast, Northern Ireland.

Everything was in order and the shipping would go from the US to Ireland by the end of the month. Customs officials would scrutinize it both here and in Ireland, but we were sufficiently assured that the oceanographic equipment was certain of being delivered on time for the summer season of diving.

Professor Smyth was informed and said he was excited to hear the good news. He also informed me that he had given all the proper authorities in the North of Ireland a heads up on our plan. He explained that it was a continuation of work we had started some years earlier. He was referred to both security and environmental offices in Belfast where he filled out the necessary preliminary paper work, but was guaranteed that there would be no problems concerning our fieldwork.

Depending on how much money Smyth was granted would determine if the material I had secured would be sent by air or sea. Since we had received a substantial stipend from both the university and the cultural ministry, we had plenty for air transport so all I had to do was get the instruments to New York and Aer Lingus would shuttle them to Dublin for pick up by Smyth and some eager graduate students from the university.

In late August 1977, my mother happily agreed to watch our daughter Eoffa, and Eve and Paul's daughter Bairbre, (whom they simply called Barb) so the four of us could deliver our shipment in person to the Aer Lingus terminal in New York and spend a couple of days in New York on a mini vacation. The time in the Big Apple was expensive and fun. We thoroughly enjoyed ourselves, but after three days we all missed the wee ones so we hurried back to Michigan, tired, broke, excited to have gone, and ready for the routine of family life once again.

The very evening we returned Smyth called from Belfast to report that the merchandise was safe and sound at the university. He said every thing went like clock work. The only delay was at the border going into the North of Ireland. But his paper work was all in order, so after a quick look by the security forces at the "frontier" as Smyth cryptically called it, they were in and everything and everybody was as safe and sound as anything could be in Belfast as 1977 was nearing the midway point.

I was in Belfast for a week in October 1977 to prepare for our fieldwork and research that would begin in earnest the summer of 1978 when "disaster" struck. All of our oceanographic equipment was "stolen" from the storage room at Queen's University. Smyth bore the brunt of the RUC investigation. They interrogated him hourly the first few days. After about a week, the investigators only cornered him for half an hour or so every other day.

I got off with only a few sessions from the RUC. I guess they figured that being an American who just recently arrived on the scene I was both ignorant of the theft, and innocent. But I was reacquainted with two old chums from Special Branch, sergeant Ian Partridge and his partner David Potter. They didn't give a damn about the theft of the oceanographic equipment. They were back in old territory. They ask if I knew where Danny Conlon was? Had he tried to contact me while I was here in Belfast? How about back in America? Had I heard from him back there?

"Like I would tell you. But let me ask you, do you think he stole the equipment so he could contact me or that I would contact him, you know through sonar?"

They were not amused. They said they would be in touch.

I said, "If you touched me I'll break your arms off and beat you with the bloody ends. If you don't believe me ask a certain Major from the British Army whose name might be available to your boss, or his boss. You guys are not of sufficient rank to be privy to such national secret information. But the Major can vouch for my skills and demeanor if threatened."

On a more serious note, all I kept repeating to the RUC was that Smyth was devastated by the loss. It would set our research back by several months. He picked up on this same theme and after they would hammer him with questions, usually ending with, "Who and why do you suppose would want oceanographic equipment?" he would retort, "I was hoping you would figure that out."

With my prompting he also began to sow seeds of questionable police investigation by asking, "How did the crooks know we had the equipment?" "How did the bad guys know where it was stored?" "Where could these people use this equipment except along the coast or in loughs here in Ireland, in and around the UK, or Europe. Had the RUC heard anything?"

His questions were making the G-men so uncomfortable that I think it was a leading factor in ending the questioning of Smyth.

After a couple of weeks, we pursued the next phase of our plan by informing the university that I would return to the US and try to secure a replacement shipment of equipment. The university said they would come up with some monies from insurance on the loss, and I promised to seek out stipends and grants back home to cover expenses.

Deadly Family Favors

Three days before I planned to travel down to Dublin for my return to Hartford, a student showed up at Smyth's office door asking for me. Smyth thought it was odd that a student would come to his office and ask for me. But the young man did not seem to pose any threat, so he decided to give me the message and a warning: "Be careful with this guy, Rudy. There is something odd about this."

He had the student wait in his office while he retrieved me, with his warning, from the faculty mail office just down the hall.

I was more than curious about a student asking to see me. As I entered the office I immediately recognized the longhaired bespectacled student, it was none other than my brother-in-law Danny Conlon, Provisional IRA sniper extraordinaire, wanted so badly by the British and Northern Irish Security forces.

I had Smyth close the door, put my finger over my lips, then hugged him and whispered, "Are you fucking nuts?"

All I got was that famous Conlon grin that Barb, Eve and Danny would flash at both opportune and inopportune times. I came up with a fake name for the "student" and we all slipped out to the student cafeteria. On the way I explained to Smyth who my student was, and Danny said that Denny would be around to pick us up in half an hour.

"You and Denny in cahoots now," I asked Danny? "Starting your own wing of the RA?"

"Aye, sort of. The Brits and RUC are tracking us down like fucken roaches. They're getting their info from inside the RA somewhere, from someone. Denny's one of the few I can trust here in Belfast any more."

"Denny and I picked up on these leaks some time back. The "Dark" told us about it and before I left with your sisters it was obvious. When your sisters and I were here a few months ago we sensed it and Denny and I tried to lay a trap or two. All we seemed to get was reassurance that someone was leaking information. Did you get anything more Denny?"

"No. I would have told you if I had found out anything more," Denny said irritatingly.

"Denny, you mugger, don't be sore. I just thought in the rush of things you were waiting to fill me in, when the time was right. So come on, I know you'd tell anything and everything," I said apologetically.

"We have a more pressing issue now," Denny said. "Your man here seems to be on everybody's hit list. He's planning to slip into the Free State and present himself at a very public meeting so as to be seen there. Down there we can get him in and out without complications. We want his mug seen by every one so as to place him there. This is where you come in Rudy. We need one of your talents to operate here in the North at exactly the same time.

"I know sniping is not your forte, but I know you can and have done it, maybe some time ago, but you know how to do it. How is your shooting, Rudy?"

I smiled and said, "In the Fall, hunting deer is some thing of a secular religious cult in Michigan. It's not long range like in the western states of the US, but we sight in and keep our skills sharp in preparing for deer season. Paul and I hunted deer last fall so I'm somewhat in the groove. So what do you have in mind for me?"

"Danny here is the premier RA sniper in the North of late and this has marked him. He is awfully vulnerable do to his special talent.

"If you could bring down a few legitimate targets here in the North while he is known to be in the South, it would not only confuse the hell out of the Brits and RUC, it would lighten the pressure on Danny, and it would reach out and tap a couple of real pieces of crud. One is a prison guard who is a terror to our people in the Kesh. The other is a Special Branch bully. They are both legit targets that deserve being hit. We have their routine down pat and have some lairs you could use to zero in on them.

We can also get you out and into the Free State before they know what hit them"

"This last part would complicate things since I'm here officially so I would have to leave from here, you know what I mean?" I asked.

"I also have two Special Branch shadows who tail me every time I show up here in the North. Staying away from them will be no easy task. They shadow me constantly. I'll have to come up with some plan to make them think that they have me under surveillance while I'm at work. I've got something in mind already. Denny can help me with the details."

"Aye, right," Denny observed. "I'll help in any way you want. Does this mean you'll do it.?"

As Danny just stood there I said, "Of course, he's family" as I grabbed him by the back of the neck and reached for Denny and pulled the two of them in for a quick hug.

"I will be leaving soon so we'll have to make haste. I've got three days is all. So Danny you'll have to take off now to make it South while Denny can show me the locale and the target."

After a quick farewell, my brother-in-law was off for South Armagh and the way into the Twenty-six Counties of the South for his "public" appearances in the Republic. Denny showed me around to the killing grounds in his Black Taxi.

I explained to Denny my plan for disappearing in plain sight so I could carry off the assignment to help Danny Conlon. I would need the man who switched hotel garb with me more than half a year ago in the Europa Hotel so I could get out and about with Special Branch thinking I was still in my room.

The Provie was a pretty close look alike to me and I was banking on Special Branch being convinced that I was where I wasn't.

I wanted them to think I was was at the Redemtorist Clonard Monastery off the Falls. My look alike would be in the toilet a head of time when I very visibly walked in and asked for a day of religious retreat. I would enter the toilet, give him my identification, cap and jacket, and have him return to the registration area and ask for a day of reflection. He would sign me in, make a donation, and retreat to the sanctuary of the chapel to pray and meditate . . . in private and seclusion.

In the mean time, I would be driven away in a delivery van and delivered to Denny some blocks away for our days work.

Denny had suggested the Special Branch G-man as our first target. His name was George Thomas and he lived in the area of east Belfast. We decided his home turf would be too difficult and risky for the shoot. I opted for a stike at his work place.

Denny had a photo of our target; we also knew the Special Branch Headquarters where our man would be found. Our black taxi blended in well and we cruised the neighborhood. After an hour of watching and waiting, Thomas casually walked out of the station, got in a car and headed toward the ferry dock.

Denny and I switched the taxi for a car that had recently been requisitioned for this job and had been put on stand-by for our operation. The switch went smoothly. We followed our target to the parking lot at the port. He went into the terminal building and emerged about ten minutes later and walked into a bullet fired from inside our car, out the rear passenger side window.

We were moving in traffic for about a kilometer and then we swung off on a side road, ditched the car and were picked up by a taxi that had been circling the neighborhood for half an hour. Within half an hour the K 98 Mauser, similar to one I hunted with back in Michigan, was handed off and stashed, I was dropped off at the university wearing my disguise of fake eye glasses, beard, and duncher. Denny said he'd stop by in an hour or two.

Although everything went like clockwork, I found I was nervous as I waited in Smyth's office. I was intently listening to every sound outside in the hallway, and time just dragged. I was hoping Smyth would show up and our conversation would calm me and help the time speed up.

I heard a familiar shuffle out side the door, some hesitation and then the two knocks, pause, followed by a third. I flung the door open startling Denny who said, "Jaysus, youse ok?"

"Aye, where you been? I was getting lonely and jumpy."

"Youse were?

"Aye, the new Rudy has a family now and he thinks differently. He worries something can go wrong," I explained.

"I'd never let anything happen to youse, you know that."

"I do. But with all the turmoil as of late, I almost feel I'm living on borrowed time. For Danny, I'll do this. But Denny, I don't know if I would for anyone else besides you . . . and Danny. I'm getting too old for this shit."

"Do you want to call this next one off?" Denny asked.

"No, no, but I'd like to get it behind me as soon as possible."

"Okie dokie. Lets go for a drive."

"The screw, that's what we call prison guards, like in your gangster movies, should be heading home about now, right? His name is Davis Terry, and he deserves a slow death, but we haven't the time. Lets get to the cross road and wait for the bastard. We'll wait along the Lisburn Road in that pull off we'd stopped at the yesterday."

"They gave me the same Mauser, just to make the point . . . . There technically will be a major connection between the earlier incident today and this one, especially in hindsight. Both will have 'Danny Conlon' written all over them," Denny explained.

Denny had walked back up the road a hundred yard, and was checking the side of the roadway as if looking for a hubcap or something. He was wearing his fake beard for good luck.

Some luck, a RUC vehicle came along and asked if he needed assistance for anything. In his best east Belfast accent he said no bother, "Just a wheel cover, if I don't find it, so be it."

They drove on, and as they passed by they noted the license, make of car, and myself the passenger. I was just hoping they would not stop to query me. I was edgy enough. Thankfully they didn't. I had also slipped on Denny's fake eyeglasses as a disguise.

Later Denny used the agreed upon signal and stepped well out of the line of fire. Denny had picked out a perfect spot for the ambush. A clear line of fire, the ability to see if any other traffic was coming alone, and ample room for Terry's vehicle to leave the road and possibly plow through underbrush before coming to a halt, swallowed up by vegetation.

There were no other cars on the side of the road and none coming along toward or behind the target car. I retrieved the rifle, stepped out of the vehicle and rested the gun on the roof. Davis Terry drove into his death at about fifty kilometers per hour.

His car carried on for about a hundred feet in a straight line past me as I was storing the gun. Denny ran up he said, "Did you hit him?"

"Aye"

"Where's he going then?"

Just then Terry's vehicle turned off the highway into a patch of overgrowth and was swallowed up as if it were following a script. Denny and I looked at each other and we both smiled.

"You asked where he was going? I'd say to hell by way of Dundonald Cemetery."

There was still no traffic in either direction. What luck. We got in our car and we drove by as both of us crammed our necks checking to see if there was any movement in or from the car. Terry was as still as a corpse in a hearse.

We just looked at each other and this time we laughed as I said, "This is for you Danny. Hopefully this will put them off of you." I looked at Denny, "For family."

"For family and the movement, these two were deserving of death, and you were merciful to do them so professionally. No pain, no suffering on this side of death. But if there is a hell, I know they'll suffer now for eternity for the evil they've done.

"You are a good man Rudy Castle, a good man. You're brother-in-law is lucky to have you in the family," Denny concluded.

"At least I'm a good shot. Hopefully that will serve Danny well, and the Army."

An hour later I was delivered to Clonard Monastery in the back of a dry cleaning van. I found the chapel and my look alike; we swapped clothing and ID. As I walked out the entrance my imposter rode out in the van right past my Special Branch shadows.

I approached Partridge and Potter and said I felt very much at peace after a day of contemplation, solitude, and isolation. I recommended that they consider the same for their peace of mind. I asked if they could give me lift back to my hotel since I was sure they would stake that out too. They actually obliged me. I thought to myself, my actions today were actually civilizing the Special Branch and tomorrow would be a better day for all that I had done today!

The evening news was spouting that an "Ace IRA sniper had struck down two victims in two separate attacks with deadly accuracy." They ventured it was the work of a well-known IRA marksman.

The next morning the news pondered the same problem that the security forces were confused over: the suspected IRA sniper ace Danny

Conlon in the two assassinations from yesterday had been seen in public down in the Republic yesterday at approximately the same time as the shootings.

The two assassinations from yesterday had his signature written all over them, but it could not have been him because of his public appearances in and around Dublin at the same time as the deaths in and near Belfast. Confusion reigned as a cold drizzle engulfed the North of Ireland.

The room was crowded yet chilly, like a morgue. Deaths were not the issue, but murder was. And this sort of professional killing was offered by only a chosen few in the North of Ireland. This meeting in Belfast was not to his liking. Professional hits on the crown's men were always upsetting. The two recent murders were especially so.

The chief investigator asked, "Ok, who in the hell was it? Who can imitate Conlon in shooting like this? Where we wrong about Conlon, or is there a second man with his accuracy and audacity? Well gentlemen, I'm waiting."

None of the assembled officers offered an opinion or any analysis. They were as speechless as the chief was agitated.

"It couldn't be Conlon, period. He was seen very publicly in Glassniven Cemetery giving a speech yesterday at the time of our shootings. Then who is it? Anyone got any bloody suggestions? Any speculation on somebody who could make something like this happen? South Armagh has some snipers, but this is unlikely to be one of them. They stick to their own killing grounds and their own turf. Well, anyone?"

He waited for an answer from a crowd whose eyes were cast down as at a funeral, contemplating the death of a close friend and wishing to avoid the eye contact of the deceased person's spouse. No one had a clue. But if it wasn't Conlon, someone was out there with a rifle, skills, guts and he was Provisional IRA. That fact made everyone edgy, very edgy.

"Let's start over and comb the areas, witnesses to any thing out of the normal. Look for anyone not appearing to be a local or in a normal situation. A patrol saw two men along the Lisburn Road at about the time of Terry's' death, but one was looking for a wheel cover. Later it was discovered that the vehicle they had matched the description of one reported stolen, and it has not been found yet.

"The patrol officers can't describe the two men other than the fact that one of them had a beard, and an east Belfast accent. Probably, both the beard and the accent were fakes," the chief inspector offered. "So get out there and find more to work with, I want this man and his friend found and if they are the ones, which I suspect they are, I want them thoroughly punished."

Ian Partridge turned to David Potter and said, "If Rudy Castle leaves for the Republic in the next day or two I'll bet he will meet up with his brother-in-law. We should get the OK to tail him down there. At the very least get the Guarda to get on Conlon and try to bag Castle if the two of them are together. We are all supposed to be cooperating with each other now."

"Aye, I just have this feeling that those two have been working together all along. One is in a cemetery and the other in a monastery while two people of ours are killed by excellent shots. Both of the victims were moving targets. It's got Conlon written all over it, but he was down in Dublin with the whole country watching him. His appearance was a show, a set up, all scripted like a movie.

"When Castle was in the American army, he wasn't a sniper was he? Wouldn't that be something," Potter commented?

"I'll ask the chief if he can check that out. But Castle was at Clonard yesterday, all day. It couldn't have been him. It couldn't, could it?

"I'll tell you what, you go check on Castle this morning. I'll check in with you later. I'm going to Clonard to make sure he was there all day," Partridge said.

But later that day Potter had lost Castle, and Partridge said the priests claimed Castle was in the Chapel the whole day. No lunch, only went to the toilet once. He was seen going in and coming back to the Chapel. "That's a dead end," Partridge said.

"Castle wasn't a US Army sniper either," Potter exclaimed. "But the chief found out he was a crack shot, he has marksmen awards, but he was no sniper."

Partridge could only purse his lips, squint his eyes and mumble, "Hmm."

The problem of 'Who?' remained.

History: 1976-1977

Political killings continued in the North, though they were routinely referred to as 'sectarian murders.' There was still constant talk and concern over 'internment,' 'British Troop withdrawals,' and the fact that the PIRA were no closer to a United Ireland than they were in 1969.

Frank Stagg died in Wakefield Prison; rioting and bomb attacks exploded in Belfast and Derry. The ending of 'special-category status' added fuel to the fire.

Harold Wilson announced his retirement as his minister for Northern Ireland announced a new policy of 'Police Primacy,' putting the RUC in the lead of security forces. The British Government's 'Prevention of Terrorism Act' allowing detention for a week without charges and expulsion from the UK, went into effect. The scaling down of British Military presence continued as did discussions with the IRA and the UDA and UVF on how to end the conflict.

Nine Irish Republican Socialist Party members tunneled out of the Maze Prison while eight SAS soldiers were arrested after crossing the border into the Republic. Political/Sectarian violence continued, while the British ambassador to Eire, Christopher Ewart-Biggs, was killed in his car as a mine exploded under it giving new meaning to the verse in an Irish blessing that "the road rise to greet you . . . ."

Republican rallies commemorated the anniversary of 'internment,' and Maire Drumme, a vice-president of Sinn Fein warned that by dropping 'special-category status,' the British would see Belfast, other towns, including some in England "come down," "stone by stone".

After British soldiers killed the driver of a car with gunmen in it, the car crashed over the sidewalk killing three children from one family, the youngest only six months while in his pram. The children's aunts, Mairead Corrigan, and Betty Williams, founded the 'Women's Peace Movement' [later renamed the 'Peace People'].

The European Commission on Human Rights found that Britain's 'deep interrogation' treatment of IRA prisoners was against the European Conventions on Human Rights. The Irish Republic brought the case to the Commission who agreed Britain was using not only inhuman and degrading measures, but also torture.

When the PIRA man, Kieran Nugent, the first convicted on terrorism not to be afforded 'special-category' status was sent to the 'H Blocks' at the Maze Prison [named because of their shape], he refused to wear the prison uniform as worn by non-terrorist criminals [called 'ordinary decent criminals' or ODCs]. He wrapped himself in his blanket in protest, and thus began the 'Blanket Protest' that eventually evolved into the 'Hunger-Strikes.'

In late October, Maire Drumm was shot and killed in her bed in Belfast's Mater Hospital by Loyalist gunmen. She was one of 297 deaths arising from the Troubles in 1976.

At the beginning of 1977 the West End of London was on the receiving end of seven bombs, and an English manager and Scottish businessman were killed in the North. The United Unionist Action Council, led by Paisley and supported by the UDA, called for a 'strike' to protest government security policy (twenty six members of the UVF were jailed and sentenced to over 700 years). The RUC, supported by 1,200 newly arrived British soldiers, dismantled over 300 roadblocks. Twenty-three people are arrested, three killed and 41 officers injured. But, lack of popular support and stronger reaction by the government results in the 'strike's' failure.

Captain Robert Nairac, a veteran British army officer, posing as a 'local' was recognized as a 'spy' by the IRA in South Armagh. He was kidnapped and heard from no more.

Nine UVF members from Coleraine were imprisoned for over a hundred years, as the RUC was successful in breaking up UVF gangs. The British Government announced that it would withdrawal some troops while the RUC would increase by as much as 6,500 members, and the Ulster Defence Regiment (similar to the National Guard in the USA), would have 2,500 full-time members.

A feud between the Official and Provisional IRA resulted in four deaths. Fire bombs in Belfast and Lisburn resulted in one million pounds sterling worth of damage. In spite of IRA efforts to prevent the visit, the Queen paid a two-day visit to the North as part of her silver jubilee. The next month, September, there were no civilian deaths caused by the Troubles.

Betty Williams and Mairead Corrigan, founders of the 'Peace People' it was announced would receive the Nobel Peace prize. A British Government spokesman announced, "The tide has turned against the terrorists and the message for 1978 is one of real hope." One hundred and twelve people died in 1977 from the Troubles.

———————————————————

Unfriendly Visitors

By the end of October, I was home in Hartford with my family. I explained that things were going from bad to worse on the project along the Antrim County coast and that since the ordinary thieves or the UVF or somebody was stealing our equipment the whole project was in mothballs.

"We can't get a break. The RUC is leaning on Smyth like he has something to do with the theft. This is his big project and he has stuck his neck out twice to get funding and all. It's bad enough it's fallen through, but the RUC suspect him of having the equipment stolen. They even grilled me. They are desperate and they aren't grabbing at straws.

"Oh, before I forget to tell you, there were two sensational sniper operations in and around Belfast just before I left. They got a Special Branch G-man, and a prison guard. Both first class assholes, pardon my French, from what I heard from Denny.

"You 'Conlon girls' will want to know that a certain very wanted super sniper, Danny Conlon, was not in the North, but was very publicly seen in Glassniven Cemetery in Dublin at the time of the shootings," I reported.

As my mother reprimanded me for using such course and vulgar language in front of ladies, Barb stood up gesturing with her hands saying, "What does this mean? What does it mean for Danny?"

Before I could explain, Eve gave me a sideway glance and said, "If Danny didn't do it, the Brits and the RUC have got to rethink all the other shootings they laid at the foot of our brother. If they were extraordinary shots, there is someone besides Danny Conlon who's out there targeting Loyalist ass . . . assets. The pressure will come off Danny a bit and a whole new search will be under way for Mr. X. Right, Rudy?"

"Couldn't have said it better myself," I admitted. "As for pressure being relaxed on Danny, I doubt it, but they can't lay these two at his feet. They'll never let up on Danny Conlon, but now they have a whole new set of problems to sift through. You've got to love it. The RUC and British Military will be up burning the midnight oil trying to solve this one."

Everyone just sat there in silence for a long minute. Then my mother said, "Is there any speculation on who this mystery shooter could be?"

I shook my head "no" and shrugged my shoulders, "Not according to Denny. I think he might have indicated if he knew. But he didn't. He did think the authorities will have to rethink all the shots they attributed to Danny though."

Everyone just had a puzzled but satisfied look on their face, except Eve who stared at me and silently mouthed "Thanks."

Then my mother said, "I think I'll thaw some of that venison Rudy shot last fall for some spaghetti sauce."

Eve said, "That would be appropriate. A good welcome home for our own super shooter and hunter, Rudy."

Barb and my daughter Eoffa continued to sit by me on the couch, while Eve's husband Paul played with his daughter Barbrie. Out in the kitchen I could hear the muffled undertones of discussion that I knew was speculating on the sniper who relieved some of the pressure on the Conlon sister's brother, Danny, THE super sniper in the north of Ireland, my brother-in-law. I would hear more from the kitchen help on this matter I was sure in the coming days.

It was two days after my return from Ireland, Barb, the baby and my mother were shopping at the supermarket when Eve and baby Barbrie stopped by.

"You just missed them. They all left for the market not a minute ago," I said.

"I'm not interested in shopping just now Rudy, I want to thank you again for what you did in the North, for Danny, and the Movement of course. If they were real assholes as you say they were, regardless of who got them, they deserved being killed."

Eve gave me a hug and a kiss.

"Jaysus, your child is going to be confused and scandalized by her mother's language and actions and carrying on. Now behave yourself. And hush those **dangerous** accusations and **unwarranted** judgments. The wrong people could hear them and draw damaging conclusions," I warned.

"Do you honestly think they are snooping around and listening in Hartford, Michigan? Come on Rudy, hardly. Do you think they followed you home and now are zeroing in on you? Are you afraid that the RUC or British Intel is on to you? You're not getting paranoid on us are you Rudy?"

I shook my head and offered, "I think those people are capable of anything. Word has it that the security forces pass names along to the Ulster Volunteer Force or the Ulster Defense Association and they do the dirty work that the official security forces don't feel they can get too close to. Its 'collusion,' pure and simple, and the North is full of it while the nationalist community is targeted day in and day out."

"And you think they could show up here? How could they penetrate a private home? The local cops and sheriffs department are going to help them, huh?" Eve mocked.

"If somebody had the right credentials from the British Embassy and Chicago Legation, they might be able to bluff their way past local police. You know, to help trace down international criminals and terrorists hiding right here in western Michigan. Aye, I think it could happen. Denny warned me to keep a lid on any and every thing concerned with the North of Ireland. I believe and trust him," I offered.

"Well, I think you are a little paranoid. Or maybe now that you are confused with Danny Conlon maybe you are getting a feeling of self-importance," Eve mocked.

"How can I feel so self important when only two or three people know the truth of who the new sniper really was? Maybe he's not new at all, maybe brother Danny has been living off this man's laurels all this time," I countered.

"Rudy, you can fuck off, you wanker. We all know who the real marksman is in the family."

"Aye, and I must have hit the bull's eye nerve to have you get so worked up Eve Conlon."

Before she could retaliate, the sound of a car came up the drive. "You are saved by another Conlon, Rudy. And thanks again for what you did.

In spite of your faults you are a good man, and I'm glad to have you in the family," Eve said with a grin.

With that I hoped we put it all to rest. Was I naïve, for now it was my mother's turn. I could get no rest.

After dinner, Eve, Paul and baby Barbrie were heading home and Barb was putting baby Eoffa to bed upstairs, my mom handed me a drying towel out in the kitchen and we went to work on the super dishes. We'd be undisturbed for a while so she started in hushed tones.

"Is there anything you wish to add to your news about the theft of the oceanographic equipment and the shootings of the G-man and the prison guard?

I assume the special equipment is a cover for some technical equipment the Army needs? Yes, as I recall that was part of your plan dating back to our wonderful trip up North. And the assassinations were not just warranted and justified, but helpful to your brother-in-law. You certainly pack a lot into your excursions Rudy," mom said in a serious tone.

"I'm hardly at liberty to say much more than I already have on any of this. You have probably already heard from your sources so I'll let it go at that, unless you have some specific questions. I'd like to move out on the porch or into the yard," I said with a smile.

"Why the caution? Are you concerned about bugs?"

"Actually yes," I admitted as we went out on the front lawn. "Denny warned me back at the end of our trip and again just last week before I came home. Nothing specific, but he cautioned to be careful. The Brits and the RUC can and have mounted operations to trace, harass, and extradite people back to the UK when they can. I don't want to become a statistic for the Brits getting their man.

"Eve thinks I'm paranoid. She quizzed me this afternoon just before you came home from the store.

She knows just enough to be dangerous. Remember back in Belfast? I got her out of the North for her own good. Paul thinks I planned it all for her happiness and his. That was only part of it.

"I love that girl in spite of her wild side, but just because she's here doesn't eliminate the caution we all must exercise," I explained.

Mom smiled and said, "Wise words from a natural born Irish Rebel leader."

"Jaysus mom, you can be as bad as Eve. I know you love Barb like a daughter. But I also know you not only love Eve, you really like Eve from a Rebel standpoint. I suspect she's told you some stuff from her past. She was pretty well entrenched and did some pretty heroic stuff. But I never know what to expect from her when she opens her mouth. Remember her antics on the trip?

"It's not that she doesn't know what's going on, it's timing and there are some things that should not be talked about, asked about, or brought up. She could drive me to drink.

"She is like a Celtic female warrior of old. She's dangerous, to friend and foe alike. She is a tornado, or better a hurricane, 'Hurricane Eve.'"

"She led you to Barb and you led her to Paul. All's well that ends well."

"I just hope Paul forgives me," I said with a smile.

It was a month later and I was at the college when I got the call. I had just concluded a class, talked with some students, and was opening my office door when the phone rang.

Barb was on the line and she was hysterical. She was shouting, "They shot him. They shot him."

"Jaysus Barb, who shot who?"

"Paul! They shot Paul. They just shot him. Right outside the house, in the drive, from a moving car," she shouted.

"Is he alive?"

"Yes. He's on the way to the hospital in Kalamazoo."

I took a deep breath, "Is my mother there?"

"No. she's gone with Eve. I have little Barbrie."

"Now listen to me. Calm down, pack up the babies and go to the Caster's house. Tell them you are so upset that you could use some company while every one is with Paul. They surely are aware of what went on, right?"

"Aye."

"Leave the lights on but lock the door. Cut through the back yard and stay away from the windows. I will call the Caster's as soon as I find out what's what at the hospital."

"Rudy, who'd do such a thing?"

"I don't know, but I am sure it was not an accident. We must take precautions to be on the safe side, you understand? I don't want you alone. I love you girls, and I'll call soon," I said as I hung up the phone.

I then called the sheriff's department and asked for Bob Lawlor, an old school friend and a deputy. I asked him to drive by the house since my wife was alone with the kids at the neighbors. He said he planned to and asked if I had seen Paul yet. I explained that I was just heading to the hospital, but that I'd let him know what was up.

Hartford was a small community and everyone knew everyone. This incident would have everyone in a tailspin. People were shot in hunting accidents every once in a while, but not from a moving car while standing in a friend's driveway.

It suddenly hit me, "while standing in a friend's driveway!" Was Paul mistaken for me? We were about the same height, build and weight. We might very well be mistaken for one another. In this case, Paul could have been mistaken for me.

At the hospital I was happy to learn that Paul had a flesh wound. When the medical help all vacated the room and we were assured some semblance of privacy I asked Paul what he saw of the attacker, the vehicle, the kind of weapon. Did he or they say anything, or yell anything? All things that the police would have already asked I was sure.

Eve and my mother paid special attention to my tone more than the questions themselves. They did not interrupt when I tried to get Paul to recall more than the sketchy information he reported.

I asked him about license plate colors, was the driver in control of the car as they sped off?

On these last two questions Paul thought a moment and described unusual license plate colors: white, not Michigan blue. Also he said as he lay in the drive he noticed that the car, a late model white Chevy, swerved as it left and gravitated to the left side of the road as it barreled away.

Eve and mom were as curious about these last questions as the answers. But they remained silent and they saw me squint, bite my lower lip, and finally say, "Not Michigan, Illinois or Indiana licenses. The swerving could be from unfamiliarity with a big American car, and staying on the left side of the road could be a habit brought here from Britain or the North of Ireland."

"Jaysus, what are you saying Rudy? Are you saying what I think you are saying?" Eve asked accusingly.

"Rudy, do you think someone came all the way here purposely to shoot Paul from over there?" my mother inquired.

"Why Paul for God's sake?" Eve demanded.

"Yes Rudy, why Paul?" mom followed with a scowl.

We were interrupted by a nurse who asked us to step out of the room for a few minutes so she could do her work. Paul was feeling the effects of the sedative and was nodding off to sleep. The three of us headed for a lounge. With no one else around to interrupt us, we continued the conversation.

I started off with, "You were asking why Paul of all people? I couldn't agree with you more. Why Paul, in my driveway, about my height, my weight and my size? Maybe some one thought Paul was me. That makes perfect sense considering where I was and what I was involved in only a short time ago."

"Sweet Jaysus, that actually makes sense," Eve acknowledged after a long pause.

"I hate to admit it but it makes more sense than somebody, anybody, shooting poor Paul," mom added.

"Barb is next door at the Castor's with the girls. Eve, I'm bringing mom home to be with them, I'm going to make some calls and I'll be back as soon as I can. Are you alright with that Eve?"

"Yes, of course."

When we got back to Hartford I called Bob Lawlor at the sheriff's department to say Paul was doing well with only a flesh wound. I also asked he could see to it that a patrol car cruised by our house periodically over the next few days. He said he would indeed schedule drive bys, and mom said that he personally cruised by several times a day over the next several weeks and stopped in to visit periodically. Hartford took this assault on one of its own personally, and the sheriff's department responded with diligent concern and commitment. A sense of security began to return.

Mom got a hold of an old Irish friend from the old sod, Tom McCormack, who came straight over to the house. He was armed and he was old IRA. I filled him in as to what happened and my speculation as to who was the real target. He understood and told me not to worry about my kin here at the house.

Then I called Denny in Belfast and explained what happened "in my driveway", also suggesting that possibly it was a mistake in identity. I was sure Denny got the inference and I was also sure he would be on it in

Belfast. He would get any info to me through secure channels as soon as he unearthed something.

Next I called an old acquaintance, actually a friend of Paul's, living in Chicago. Sean had recruited me years earlier to work for the Provisional IRA. He would want to know what happened to Paul, and that he was OK. I mentioned the possible Canadian plates on the car, the driver's problem in handling the vehicle when speeding away and the fact that the car stayed on the left side of the road for some distance.

He said "interesting," and that he'd put feelers out here in the USA, Canada, and in the North concerning what happened.

Besides the facts, I expanded on my take of what really happened. He just listened at first. Then he interjected that he thought my analysis was probably correct considering what he was hearing of my exploits as of late. He said he'd be in touch and rang off. In "touch" meant he'd be here in person, and soon.

A day later Sean from Chicago showed up. I told him Paul had been discharged from the hospital. While I drove him to Paul's house, he brought me up to speed on Loyalist activity in North America.

"They are low key but pretty active in Canada. There are Orange Lodges in cities like Ottawa, Toronto, London, Kitchener, Chatham and Windsor. I contacted some friends in these cities and asked them to listen about and to report anything of interest," Sean informed me.

"Do you think I'm being overly suspicious, or paranoid about this?

"Actually, no. Your suspicions are probably spot on, but I want to wait until my "ears" in Canada get back with me. I also have some lads in the North collecting some craic on what's about. It will take a day or two, but they are good, accurate and precise in their Intel and reporting. We'll get what we need to know before we decide what action to take," Sean explained.

"Brendan would have a plan developing already."

"The Dark would, to be sure," Sean reflected. "And knowing you Rudy, I suspect you are scheming some too."

"Aye, but I'll wait to be sure. Here we are at Paul and Eve's place. He'll be happy to see you. I don't know how much he suspects and how much Eve has shared with him, so go easy. I'll let you out and cruise the block for a lap or two. Can't be too careful now."

"Good on you Rudy, Paul's lucky to have a friend like you."

"But maybe that friendship got him shot and nearly killed," I said as I slowly drove off observing everything I could along the street, in the yards, and between the houses.

Sean stayed at our house, actually mom's house, and he and mom's old IRA friend Tom McCormack who was still staying at the house, got on famously.

A day later at breakfast, I told mom in front of the two Irishmen, "We'll be having trouble getting these two to leave. They'll conspire to sensing trouble right here in Hartford that will necessitate the 'Army,' namely them, being present for some time."

"Rudy, mind you manners. These men are honest and true son's of Eire," mom scolded in jest.

"They are 3,500 miles from Ireland and to hear them the Brits are at the outskirts of Hartford and Special Branch has infiltrated every house in the village. Everything is about to go under with the exception of this building, especially the kitchen which will be held to the last round," I joked.

Tom chimed in, "Speaking of rounds, is it too early for a bit of Jameson's?"

"Jaysus, mom, what did I tell you. They are here for the duration."

Sean countered, "But the question is, for the duration of what?"

Everyone laughed as I scowled and shook my head.

At that point the phone rang and it was for Sean.

Sean's "ears" in Canada had some interesting news. Two men from the North, probably Belfast by their accents, had been heard and observed in and around Ottawa over the past week or so but had dropped off the radar in the last couple of days.

They had been visiting Orange Lodges trying to raise funds for "victims of IRA violence back in Ulster."

They had spoken at some rallies in Orange clubs that had been reported in the local Ottawa news circles.

The two Loyalists from the North were identified as George McVeigh and Billy Douglas, both related to men in the Ulster Defense Association (UDA), who were murdered in 1975 by rival Loyalists.

The obvious question was, what was their relationship to me? Had I crossed paths with them and was this a personal grudge, or were they sent by the UDA?

"Aye, that question will only be answered by the "ears" in Belfast, and that may take some time," Sean indicated.

"It's afternoon in Belfast, right? I'll make a call to my man there and just see if he has heard anything."

Denny picked up after only two rings and cryptically said to the enquiry of Seamus being there, "Sorry. No one here by that name."

Ten minutes later Denny was on another phone somewhere in the Falls area of West Belfast. "Jaysus I had a premonition it was you on the wire. Nothing yet in concrete from here. Any thing from youse?"

"Aye, Paul is home and doing great, but will the names George McVeigh and Billy Douglas be of help to you there? They have relatives known to be active in UDA circles. These two are in Canada to drum up money for Loyalist victims in the North. But they have dropped out of sight for the past few days. I'm willing to bet I am also on their agenda. I can't figure out how I crossed paths with them. Possibly they've been sent here by the UDA to deal with me. I'm wondering if it concerns past transgressions or more recent sins. This last part is as important as to whether these are the triggermen sent to hit me. You know what I mean?"

"Look, Rudy, before you go off hunting these wankers, let me get on this info and I'll get back to youse ASAP," Denny pleaded.

"Aye, I will be close to the phone except on Mondays, Wednesdays, and Fridays from 7 AM until about 16:00. Those days and hours are my teaching and office hour schedule at the college. I'll be waiting Denny. Bye the way, fuck your fake beard. And thanks Denny." I hung up before he could retaliate against my beard comment, but I could feel the love and imagine Denny's smile.

———————————

Two days latter Denny called and in a coded conversation said to call him back ASAP. I drove all the way to Kalamazoo before calling him on a public phone on the Falls Road.

"Youse have the right names of the likely people who got your man, and it appears they were after youse. Be careful Rudy and bring backup, youse understand?"

"Aye. I'll be in touch."

I drove back to Hartford. Talked to both mom and Barbrie in the back yard. I packed an overnight grip and headed to Detroit.

Mom's men were waiting for me late the next morning with a untraceable non-descript Plymouth. I was instructed to back into a garage and to lock my car. "It will be watched over." The two men then shook my hand and uttered something about good hunting." I just nodded and headed for the bridge to Windsor, Ontario.

I had no problems at the border, just returned a nod and was headed for Chatham. Mom had relatives in and around Chatham but I thought it best not to disturb them with the business I was about to unleash. No one needed to know about this sordid business but me.

I drove around the small city of Chatham and killed time untill it was getting on to evening. About dusk I went to a bar and inquired about the local Orange club. I had donations from Ohio and needed to locate the Belfast men before they headed back to "Ulster."

The bar keep was very helpful and called the lodge to let them and the Ulstermen know I was coming. I was coming alright: two 45s and a 9mm for back up. It turned out to be neither a lodge nor a club house, but another bar where I was to meet the lads.

As I donned my fake glasses and beard, thinking that Denny would have been so proud of me, I noticed that the parking lot was virtually vacant. "Good, only two cars," I thought as I strolled into the establishment, resplendent with Union Jack flags and a large picture of the Queen and the Queen Mother.

"Ulster forever. Where are the lads from Ulster?" I asked in a Belfast accent.

The barman pointed and the two of them turned toward me grinning and returning my greeting, "Ulster for . . . ." I blazed away and they went down in a heap. I pointed with a 45 at the barkeep and said in my best Belfast accent, "Erin go bragh. If youse and your family want to see another week, you lay behind the bar and don't move for fifteen minutes, or youse are all dead. I'll come back and get youse all."

I calmly walked out to the car, turned and squeezed off a round back into the bar, got in the vehicle and with lights off I headed back into Chatham, but half a mile up the road I turned and headed west for Detroit, the Tunnel to the USA, and home to my family in Hartford.

In an hour or so East Belfast would be getting the word that retaliation had been swift, accurate and deadly. "Fuck em!"

The border crossing into Detroit went without incident and the long drive across Michigan was going to be tiring but exhilarating at the same time. I was satisfied that I had avenged Paul's shooting, I was excited to be able to report to those who needed to know that both justice and vengeance were handed out. Some would simply want to hear that I had avenged Paul's shooting, others would see it as meeting out justice for an innocent's being shot, while others would simply smile and not quiver over semantics, it would be all the same to them—vengeance, justice, who the hell cares what you call it as long as it was done and over with and the guilty were dead.

Quite frankly I settled with the latter attitude and was satisfied and smug that it all went so smoothly. I did wonder how soon there would be the obvious questions sent my way by both Canadian and Michigan, and possibly US Federal authorities.

I had dumped the car in Detroit and set it ablaze as instructed. I had piled into my own vehicle and pulled out of the garage where it had been stashed. I didn't bother to look around to see if there was anyone watching. There may have been but I didn't need to see anyone and didn't care to dawdle. All I cared about was motion. I cautiously began to drive west out of Detroit.

It had been a couple of hours now and I wondered how long I could go without exhaustion and carelessness catching up with me. I could not afford to stop at a motel any more than I could afford to doze off and get in an accident. I had an alibi for Hartford and to be spotted anywhere else would be trouble.

I didn't have to stop for gas until I was in Jackson. I got out of the car wearing the fake glasses as a precaution and asked the attendant if I could pull off to the side and catch a few winks. He was friendly enough and said sure.

I backed along side of the garage so my license wouldn't be obvious and slept for about two hours.

I tooted as I pulled out and the Sunoco attendant waived. A couple more hours and home.

I drove directly into the garage and pulled the Illinois licenses and hid them, replacing them with my Michigan plates. As I turned around Barbrie, little Eoffa and my mother were all coming in the garage with concerned faces. I just smiled, and even in the darkened garage they registered my satisfaction with a job well done.

They gave a collective sigh of relief, and as we all emerged into the yard, Paul, Eve and Barbrie came from the house with expectant expressions, and registering our nods gave broad smiles of relief and satisfaction.

As we sat in the back yard and drank cold beer, I gave them the run down of the previous days work. They were all pleased, proud, and relieved it was over.

In back of my smile I couldn't help but wonder of it was really "over." I had my doubts.

The following day I contacted Denny and passed the news along. He responded, "Och, Jaysus, don't we already know. Those boys to the east are besides themselves. There will be a reaction Rudy. Youse best lay low for some time. They are in a fowl mood."

"Give me a heads up if you hear anything specific. I'll try to stay out of sight as best I can but there is only so much I can do without drawing a lot of attention to myself."

"Just be careful Rudy. I'll be in touch."

To everyone's surprise we heard nothing from the authorities about the demise of the two Ulstermen. Nothing. Not a word. *Alls well that ends well,* I thought. But I still had this nagging sense that it wasn't over yet. Thanksgiving was upon us and I had so much to be thankful for, not the least of which was that Paul was back on his feet and was clearly feeling well.

A New Year And New Enemies

Christmas and New Years came and went, and still there were no warnings. When Spring was upon us and everyone was just feeling relaxed the call came.

Denny was all business, "Rudy, you remember your suspicion about a tout working for the RA? You had us set a trap with certain merchandise? Well the trap has sprung. It turned out to a man right here in the Falls who met you a time or two during both of your visits, Sean Green. You remember him?

"During this latest one he was asking all kinds of questions that didn't raise much suspicion at first. But then your man Smyth spotted him around some students inquiring about Smyth's work with youse and the oceanographic equipment.

"Lights flashed and bells went off and I started to watch the man. I got help from our internal security, and we almost had the bastard. Problem was, he was on to us and he's gone. Probably over in England.

"But I think he may be the one that passed your name on to the RUC, Special Branch, and then to the paramilitaries.

"You flushed the wanker but he returned the favor and they are on to you. We'll keep looking for him here and we've passed on info to folks in Boston who will pass it along on your side of the world.

"Between what went on in Canada and now this discovery, you may be a special object of interest. We have picked up that some hot heads want to send a special group over to pay you a return visit.

"They clearly sent the first team. They don't suspect that you got to them because they apparently think they wounded you and there was no way you could have done the Canadian job. But the rumor is that they want to finish the original job. Two possibly three of them. Youse have to be careful, ready and focused Rudy. These boys are on a mission."

I thanked Denny for all the great news. He said as he learned more I'd learn more. He also said my brother-in-law said, "Hello, thanks, and to take care of yourself and his sisters and their babies, and Paul."

Denny concluded by saying that my brother-in-law and his friends would keep an eye out for Seamus Green.

I immediately informed all the family members and asked mom to arrange out of town stays for the women in my life. There were objections but I passed on that I was the intended target, and that although I was not associated with the Canadian targets I was still a priority because of a tout associating me with clandestine stuff in the North.

Reluctantly the women, except for mom, visited relatives in Chicago, Grand Rapids, and Battle Creek. All locations only an hour or two away and hence close enough for me to visit on days off. We all wondered, "How long will we have to wait for this to blow over, or blow up?" We hadn't long to wait.

The Special Branch chief who was in charge of this 'interview' was Mr. Ronald Poole, "Ronnie" to his friends, none of whom worked in Special Branch. At work he was simply "Poole."

The RUC had a turncoat walk in to a police station and offer a lorry full of information on local Provisionals and PIRA operations. His motives were important for Poole to understand, for they would help convince him to believe or not believe what the man was offering and that he was legit.

"I know you told the RUC officer why you decided to provide Her Majesties Government with vital information, but I would like to hear it myself from you. So, would you mind telling me why you are willing to provide such valuable information to us?"

"As I said before, they passed me over time and time again, to move up the chain of command. They bypassed me for one wanker after another. I'm sick of it. I was good enough to trust with handling weapons, but not leading men. I'm sick and tired of them making me just wait around."

"The 'they' is the IRA?"

"Aye, the Provies," the traitor said in a clearly irritated voice.

Poole nodded understanding, and continued his questioning, "You're full name and where you live please."

"Sean Patrick Green. Originally from Cupar Street in Clonard. Now I just live here and there in the same neighborhood."

"How long have you been a member of the Provisionals?" Poole continued.

"About six years, or close enough. I was recruited by 'em, so I was. They said I was young and obviously had talent, being educated and all. I completed St. Dominic's School," Sean Patrick Green said rather proudly.

"Were you just a soldier for the PIRA?"

"Aye, at first, but then I was put in the quartermasters unit handling weapons. But over the years I also spent some time with organization and planning."

"By planning do you mean you planned operations?"

"Aye. But I was part of a team. I worked for, well, er with Brendan Hughes, who you have in the Kesh. I tried to stay low the past couple of years while more and more of us was being picked up and put away.

With so many in the Kesh, I figured I would move up to greater authority. But they just kept playing me along, never really recognizing my talent and moving me along. Well, fuck em. They pissed on me long enough. I'm getting even now."

Poole studied the man. He was not only irritated but also getting nervous and agitated. Using some psychology, Poole said, "I appreciate you being patient with me and all these questions. But it's the procedure. So bare with me a bit longer.

"What can you tell me about any plans the Provies are putting into play or are thinking about?"

Green, without hesitation, offered, "There is something going on with new bombs. They have been waiting for some new detonators or firing mechanisms. I was not in on the planning or the operation to get them, but they are coming in from abroad. I think probably from America.

"This American who went to school here, at Queen's some years ago, has a friend at the university and I think they planned getting the new works for bombs into the country. His name, the American is Rudy Castle. He was thick with Hughes back then. Although I never saw them planning anything, they often argued about the way the war was going."

Poole asked, "What do you mean they argued about the war and how it was going?"

"Castle was not in favor of killing civilians, with bombs. He would argue with Hughes about the morality and negative press it created. But they were friends though. They respected each other."

Poole was thinking, *Green on the one hand is telling me that Castle* **might** *be tied to bringing in new bombing devices, and on the other hand he argued about setting off indiscriminate bombs. Maybe Castle has changed course or feels by helping the IRA he can focus their bombing campaign in a new direction. This does not fit.*

"Castle and his family were back here recently. He married a Belfast girl . . . ." Before Poole could complete the sentence Green finished it for him.

"Aye, Danny Conlon's sister, don't we all know."

"And you are pretty sure Castle is tied into this new bomb program?" Poole pressed.

"No, not one hundred percent. I heard things about new bombing stuff, the ignitions. I know it wasn't locally made. I know Castle was mixed up with the Provies some years ago. I mean I never talked to him specific about it, nor did I ever see the man doing operations with them or bombing. But he had a reputation as an American ex-service man with a lot of experience from Viet Nam.

"A lot of bombs are going off all over the North and even in England. They seem to be of a new generation, wouldn't you say?" Keen asked.

"Who was his friend at Queen's?"

"I don't know. But he was a professor of his as I recall. I'm sure you can check that out."

"Well Mr. Green, tell me more about some other PIRA projects and people."

And with that Green went off on new people and projects he was privy to, but he for some reason he failed to mention Denny. So Denny was still in the clear, at least for now.

Poole was still thinking about Castle in the back of his mind as he listened to Green expose other people and plans involving the IRA.

Poole was one of the few outside Military Intelligence and MI5 who knew that Castle had worked for the British Military when he was a student. So you'd expect him to try and get close to the IRA or somebody who knew IRA members. But that's different than being IRA. He was successful and delivered for the British Military.

His cooperation clearly did not extend to the RUC or Special Branch. He had made that very apparent. But could he be tied up with explosives?

Much of Green's testimony seemed to be based on speculation. Nothing concrete. But still. If British security couldn't touch Castle over in America, maybe the UDA or UFF could get to him.

Poole thought to himself, *Call it collusion, call it what you will, but we Brits have always felt the end justifies the means. If we can't get to Castle officially, we will get him unofficially. Loyalist paramilitaries can and have been useful and used for the greater good of the British Empire.*

As Churchill said, well what he meant was, since we write the history books we edit history to look good. If we can't get to Castle directly, we have ways to get to him indirectly. The important thing is to get to him. Sacrifice one, no matter how, for the greater good.

Special Branch would check on Castle's friend Smyth. Green didn't know his name, but Poole did. They'd been down that road before and Poole questioned whether there were fresh tracks on that road or not. He didn't want to waste time, money and personnel by following a dead end.

But Castle always seemed to be in the thick of things. Hmm, Castle.

———————————

History: 1978

At the beginning of 1978, an article in the 'New Statesman,' claimed that Roy Mason, the British Secretary of State for Northern Ireland, was making headway against the IRA: "It may be that he has broken the fighting capacity of the Provisional IRA."

By February when a incendiary bomb killed twelve and injures twenty-three at the La Mon House Hotel in Castlereagh, County Down, there followed over a hundred bombings in the North so far in 1978.

Gerry Adams was charged with being an IRA member, but released seven months later due to insufficient evidence, while a prominent Provisional, Francis Hughes, was arrested after a gun fight.

Ambushes of the RUC in Crossmaglen saw retaliation by the RUC and British Army. The Catholic Archbishop of Armagh, Tomas O Fiaich said that British withdrawal from Ireland was necessary (Ian Paisley refers to O Fiach as "the IRA's bishop from Crossmaglen"). O Fiaich visited the Maze Prison (Long Kesh or H-blocks) where 300 Republican prisoners were not only on the 'blanket protest' refusing to wear prison garb, but many were also involved in the 'dirty protest' where they smeared their excrement on their cell walls. They were protesting denial of 'special-category status for those convicted of terrorist offences, creating conditions physically repulsive. They matched what the security forces created by their new rules, creating an environment not fit for animals, let alone humans.

On the tenth anniversary of the Derry riots that saw civil rights evolve into definite sectarian conflict as far as the Loyalists were concerned, Derry again saw violence as a Sinn Fein demonstration marched through the Protestant Waterside area of the city. A bomb on the Belfast-Dublin train exploded killing a woman and injured two other passengers.

The PIRA experienced declining support from the Catholic-Nationalist segments of the population; they formed small semi-independent 'cell' units for greater security. A misplaced British Army intelligence document stated that the IRA may be loosing popular support, but their ranks have "intelligent" and "experienced" members who are NOT the "mindless hooligans" often portrayed by the British, and that the cell reorganization is "less vulnerable to penetration by informers."

In November, PIRA began a bombing campaign with car bombs; fifty bombs exploded in one week in November, 1978, signaling that the PIRA was far from "broken." Bombs exploded across the North of Ireland and in Liverpool, Bristol, Manchester, Southampton and Coventry. Also, prison guards were targeted with the Deputy Governor of the Maze Prison, Albert Miles, being shot dead.

In December several thousand police patroled in London to discourage a PIRA bombing campaign prior to Christmas. Three soldiers were machine gunned to death in Crossmaglen while shoppers did Christmas shopping.

Eighty-one deaths attributed to the Troubles occurred in 1978, but there were 755 shootings, 655 bombs planted with 455 exploding and 115 incendiaries.

Warnings

A month after talking to Denny I got an urgent message to contact him "ASAP" on a secure line. The news was what I had been waiting for and it was not good. Three hard men from the UVF were on their way to Canada. I could expect them any day.

Just when it seemed to be coming to a head I got a call from out of the blue from an old Vietnam army buddy who was working for the Pentagon in Washington. He was restricted to a wheelchair because of a VC or NVR mortar round. I had carried him to an evacuation area and visited him once in Saigon and once again in California. We had stayed in touch intermittently, and he suspected my involvement in some clandestine stuff in the North of Ireland, but was savvy enough not to talk "out loud" and inquire about it in a "public" fashion.

So when I got his call quite frankly I was surprised, and his cryptic message had "urgency" spelled all over it.

"Rudy. Its Jack, what's up with you?"

"Jack, great to hear from you. Just raising my family and teaching. What's with you? Still living off the US government I hope."

"Oh yeah," he shot back. "But I need some help from you. I'm writing an article about some shit we did up North along the DMZ, and I need you to confirm some stuff. Any chance you are going to be here, soon? We need to confer ASAP. This info cannot wait. How about it?"

"Well, weekends are cheap flights, how about bright and early Saturday morning? Where will I meet up with you?"

"At my place. Washington is beautiful this time of the year, cherry blossoms and all. Well I'm glad you can help me out and can make it. Good, good, good. See you then."

Jack ended with another cryptic ending, "Good, good, good." Back in Nam that relayed just the opposite: "Three goods = Bad fucking shit."

Secondly, we weren't up North by the so call "DMZ Dumb Mother's Zone." He was making it clearly unclear to anyone listening that we needed to talk, but not about Nam. "Up North" could only mean one thing, the North of Ireland.

After talking to my mother and letting her know what was going on, I drove to Chicago and caught a cheap flight into DC, landing about 10:00 local time. I caught a cab to Jack's place. After greetings, he said "Let's go."

Out the door he went, down the ramp to the sidewalk and down the block. I just tagged along as Jack whirled along in his motorized wheelchair. He started the conversation by explaining, "Outside is better. More noise to disturb any listeners."

"Listeners?" I quizzed.

"Rudy, your name started showing up on my desk some years back. It seems that British Military Intelligence, Scotland Yard, Special Branch, and the RUC all wanted a background check on you. Apparently you did something for one or all of them?

"Well, any way, I did the background check on you and apparently you passed with flying colors because some Brit major wanted to have a special commendation put in your file from Her Majesties government or Armed Forces.

"Good going, I suppose, and congrats. Then a couple of weeks ago the Michigan State Police filed a report saying that possibly some Protestant Loyalist paramilitaries tried to shoot you and hit your your brother-in-law.

"Care to comment?"

"Jaysus. They were shooting at me? They weren't after Paul. Well that's good because we just couldn't figure out why anyone would go after Paul.

"Actually, I'm not sure why any one would want to shoot me either. Why do the Michigan State Police think it was me they were after?"

"To that question I haven't a clue or answer, Rudy."

"Well that is disturbing. Can you press the Michigan State Police on their suspicion, Jack?

"And let me explain the Brit connection. Years ago I was in Scotland and then the North of Ireland in grad school when a Major in the British Army asked me to work for them. The problem was that through my mother my loyalties were with the guys I was supposed to spy on, the Provisional IRA. So the long and short of it was that I was a double agent really working for the Provies.

"I usually passed on info to the Brits about criminals, Loyalists, the 'Official IRA,' as you know both rivals to the Provies. The Brits thought I was a 'hero.' I protected the Provies. That's about the gist of it," I explained. "But mums still the word, OK?"

Jack said, "OK." Then asked, "And more recently?"

"I took my family to the North a while ago. Then I helped an old prof to obtain some oceanographic equipment. Some of it got stolen and there were accusations that it was going to be used by paramilitaries in explosive devises I guess. I don't know how in hell you could do that. It would be easier to just use alarm clocks or something like that.

"Then some guys shot my best friend in my driveway a few months ago, just before Thanksgiving. Now you get me here and here I am."

"Sit on the bench here. I've got to tell you a few things. I've got to be careful, that's why the walk and talk," Jack said. "Pretend to show a fly dive by a jet with your hand like fliers do, and point out spots hit. like pilots did in Nam."

With my right hand flattened out I raised it up and then had it swoop down and then climb up again to the left. With my left hand I pointed three times, snapping it with my index finger as if shooting.

"Just like a fly boy, Rudy. Anyone would think we were reliving some strafing in Nam. That's my cover story for seeing you, remember?"

"Aye, but I feel like a fool doing these hand gestures," I said.

"And that's how we fool anyone suspicious," Jack said quietly. He shook his head and didn't smile. Rather he looked dead serious.

"Rudy, this is so far off the record I could probably be executed, not just fired for what I'm about to tell you."

"Surely you're kidding."

"Nope. Here goes. A friend in another department who tracks unsavory types gave me some 'hush-hush' at lunch Thursday. I called you later because it was really disturbing.

"They, his department, is tracking some nasties from Northern Ireland, members of the Ulster Defense Association. They have landed in Canada. According to sources they are two for sure and possibly a third guy here to do several things. First, to retrieve some money, two of their brethren collected some months ago for Loyalist causes in Ulster. Apparently the two brethren were shot and killed in a bar in Canada recently. You know anything about that?"

"No. This is the first I've heard of it. Was it in the news?"

"I doubt it here in the US. Second, is to find the guy who killed their friends. He's from the US, possibly Ohio, but has an Irish accent.

"And third, apparently to kill you."

"To kill me? Why me? Your people know this?"

"Yeah. They got wind of it over in Ulster from a snitch. The guy has never been wrong. You were named as some one the earlier two guys were to have killed, but obviously they just 'wounded' you.

"Why didn't you tell me you had been wounded Rudy?"

"Because I wasn't. My brother-in-law was shot in my driveway. We assumed he was the target. None of us had any idea of why anyone would shoot Paul, but it was him who was shot. The local sheriff's department is still working on it.

"But now you are telling me two guys from the North of Ireland shot him. His wife and mine, sisters, are both from the North of Ireland, and she was involved in the Nationalist Movement over there. But it wasn't him they were after, you're telling me it was me they were after?"

Jack looked around and whispered, "Ya. And at least two more are coming to finish the job."

"But who got to the first two," I asked sincerely?

"Nobody has a clue. It wasn't you was it, Rudy?"

"Hell no, I was protecting my sister-in-law and her baby from whoever shot her husband, my friend."

"OK, but you, besides whoever did it to their buddies, are on their list this time around," Jack warned. "The Michigan State police have pieced some of the recent stuff together and now an unnamed agency of the US government says there is a continuation of an assassination attempt in the wind.

"I'll see what I can drum up on the Michigan State Police. It won't be easy, but I'll gently probe my friend. If and when I get anything substantial I will be in touch. You've got to keep your head down Rudy."

I returned home Sunday about noon and as everyone gathered, we moved outside into the back yard. I had called my mother on Saturday and told her to collect everybody because I had some good news to share.

Once we were out of the house, I explained that it was not Paul who was the target but me. There was a mixture of both relief and concern as one might expect.

Next I explained how both the Michigan State Police had now come to this conclusion and a security agency of the US Government. I said I knew how the feds got their tip but explained that how the State Police got theirs was a mystery.

I said a new Loyalist team was on the way here to deal with me among other things. I asked Paul and Eve if mom, Barbrie and little Eoffa could stay at their place for a while, while I made preparations for the uninvited guests.

My mother refused to leave the house and Barbrie was concerned in general about my safety. I explained that I would have to face the assassins now or forever be looking over my shoulder. Reluctantly, she agreed to go to Eve and Paul's place and lay low until it was resolved.

After they had left, mom and I settled into a routine: we kept the lights down low, we stayed away from the windows, and I strung some string and cans around the perimeter of the house. I took a different route to the college and back every day.

Five days later, on Friday morning, the shot rang out loud and clear. From the front porch the shot shattered the window to the dining room and came directly at my head. The shooter saw the blood splatter from the head shot sprayed the wall in back of me along with skull fragments as my body crumpled to the floor.

There was no doubt in the shooters' mind that this part of the mission was accomplished. He wiped down the gun and threw it from the car into a swamp about two miles down the road. The two men in the get away vehicle headed east for Kalamazoo. The shooter and his partner would switch cars there, and then they would head for Detroit where two separate autos would be used to enter Canada.

The shooter thought, *It was a clean hit, and if Rudy Castle was involved with the Republican Movement and hence guilty of war against the Crown, and Her Majesty's governments both in Whitehall and Stormont, and it's loyal citizens, it ended this morning. Let any and all know that justice was served and that no one could escape Loyalist judgment. "Ulster forever!"*

Word of this killing would travel through both Loyalist and Republican communities worldwide, but especially in Ulster. "God save the Queen!"

I had been standing at the end of the dining room table and as I was returning the drained orange juice glass to the table when I caught a glimpse of the shooter as he zeroed in on me from the porch.

I instinctively tucked my head in as I dropped and snapped my head to the left. I swear that I felt the bullet pass by the back of my head.

As I rolled left behind the side chairs for obstruction and protection, I was aware that the china jam container blew apart and splattered strawberry jam against the back of the cupboard as the fine dust of the shattered container clouded ever so finely the air above me.

My mother was shrieking from the kitchen and I heard three more shots follow below the table to the spot where my body would have been if I had been hit by the first round. But I was off to the side of the table and I heard the assailant run across the porch, down the steps and into the waiting car.

They were at the end of the driveway when I stood up and said to my mother, "Damn, that was close. But I'm OK. I'm not hit. The bastards missed."

"I've got the make and color," she said. "Get a gun. I'll call Barbrie and tell her we are on the chase and that she can come back here. Let's go."

In two minutes we were off. I hadn't had time to think through what we were doing. Mom was all commands and motion. In three minutes we were out the driveway, mom at the wheel, me feeding the clips of my two 45s and the backup 9mm.

There was a fair amount of traffic on the road. Being a Friday morning people were on their way to work. I wasn't confident we would find them. They might have headed toward Chicago, or just some place to lay low for a while. But half way to Kalamazoo she said, "There they are, about half a mile up ahead. Too much traffic to do anything now. We'll just tag along."

"Mom . . . ."

"Don't 'mom' me Rudy! I've done this before, I'm not squeamish about this and I'm good at tailing 'Prod Pups' like these guys. So don't lecture me or try to reason with me. I've forgotten more of this sort of thing than you can imagine. So let me concentrate on the matters at hand and you sit there and come up with a plan."

"Don't go sectarian on me mom. The bastards are Loyalists, not 'Protestant pups'."

I sat there all right, but I couldn't think of a plan at first. About half an hour later, they had switched cars on the far side of Kalamazoo and kept heading east.

"I suspect they have a full tank of gas and we have just over half a tank. This could be tricky," mom explained. "Have you got a plan yet?"

"I'm working on it."

We continued on for about an hour and mom said, "I have to stop for gas."

"OK. Let's do it."

To our astonishment our assailants pulled off just in front of us and were intent on lunch. Mom and I just smiled at each other. "What luck," I said.

"Of the Irish," mom responded.

"Rudy, I'm going in too, and get some coffee and a sandwich. You get gas. They won't recognize me, so hurry back but stay in the car. I'll get you a drink and a sandwich."

After gassing up, I returned and parked off to the side. I walked along side their car and placed two nails I found at the gas station in the treads of their tires so when they backed out it would just be a matter of time before they had a flat tire.

Mom joined me just moments later, and five minutes later the Loyalist gunmen were back on the road. Within fifteen minutes, they were on the side of the road with a flat tire.

We pulled up in front of their car. The sun was rising right in their faces as mom stepped out of our car to offer help. As they were explaining that they had things in hand, I had exited on the roadside and came along side their car and circled behind. With a 45 drawn in front of me, shielding it from passing traffic coming up behind us, and the two cars hiding it from west bound traffic, I told the men to spread and rest along the side of their car. Mom searched them and found no weapons. We waited for a break in the traffic and at the right moment we had them enter the trunk of our car.

We tied their hands behind them, closed the trunk, and headed for US 23 toward Toledo, Ohio. It only took two and a half hour later and we were on a deserted road just north of Toledo along Lake Eire.

We kept the radio on during the ride so mom and I could talk over the next step. I told mom I fully intended to shot them after questioning them. All she responded was, "Aye, it's only right and just."

At dusk we got our captives out of the car and mom cut their hands free. I moved them right to the shoreline.

Before I could interrogate them, mom stepped forward brandishing the 9 mm Berretta and asked the one to the right, "You shoot at my son here and try to kill him. Who sent you? What outfit you two in?"

Both men looked at me in the dark, and the one mom was questioning came to the recognition that he had shot at me. I was the target. I was the guy he had "killed." He saw blood splatter and my skull blow apart. All he could muster in his amazement was, "How? What the hell?" in his harsh East Belfast accent.

"Strawberry jelly and my good bone china preserve serving jar, you bloody eejit," was mom's explanatory remark.

Mom had covered the gun with a towel or cloth of some sort. I didn't know where she got the cloth. So when she shot him in the foot, the sound was muffled as was the flash. He went down in a heap screaming. She cuffed him on the side of the head with the weapon and said, "Wrong response."

"Who are you and what group are you from?"

He just sat there holding his foot while moaning. She shot him in the knee of the other leg with the muffled 9 mm. He let out with more screaming and she let him have it with another cuff.

"I've more rounds here so you just keep it up and you'll die one slow agonizing death you Loyalist piss ant. You come over here and try twice to kill my son. 'What the hell,' is right you Protestant Pup."

"Mom, slow down. Let him talk."

"He'll talk better with more lead," and she shot him in the shoulder.

His buddy yelled, "Stop. We're in the UDA. His, your name was given to us along with your address by our commanding officer back in Belfast. We are just following instructions."

"What is the commander's name?"

"George Sawyer. His address is, I don't know, in Crimea Street, right off the Shankill Road."

Mom said, "Give me your passport, his too. Is your man George married? Any kids, pets?"

"Aye, he's married with two kids, a boy and a girl, and a dog."

I said, "Help your friend up. I've had enough of your bullshit. You have been found guilty of crimes against me, Humanity, and specifically the Irish people."

Mom moved behind me and I opened up with both 45s. They were dead before they hit the water. Using a flashlight we retrieved the casings.

"Nice touch son. Sort of a eulogy before they died."

The bodies drifted a bit along the shore, but then as they began to sink a current took them out deeper and seemed to be sweeping them almost north towards Canada.

I nodded toward Canada and said, "It would be nice if they washed up over there. That would make the cops think, maybe, that the same one who got these fellahs also got the other two last month. Ah, but that's probably asking too much."

"At least it wouldn't be American garbage, it would be British garbage. They could hardly blame us for that now, could they?" mom asked with irony.

By morning we were home in Hartford in our own beds. By noon my friend Jack called from Washington and said possibly the guy from Ohio intercepted two of the Loyalists and shot them dead last night. "Their bodies were found this morning by fishermen in Lake Eire between Canada and Ohio. We aren't even sure there is a guy from Ohio, he could be living in Canada."

"Who is tipping this Buckeye shooter off, Jack?"

"Damned if I or any one else knows. But he's fast and accurate. I guess this pair were both shot with a 45, and one also with a 9 mm. They looked like Swiss cheese according to the police report.

"I wouldn't want to fuck with this guy. He's probably an old IRA man with a big chip on his shoulder. We had a couple of crack pots like that back in Nam, remember Rudy. Get pissed over something and kind of go nuts. You always used to say that when you said your evening prayers you always thanked God these guys were on our side. You can thank Him again Rudy, you wouldn't want to piss this guy off.

'No one can tell if they were shot in the US or in Canada. Two different calibers. UDA boys. One guy was shot in several joints, pretty painful. We don't know about the third guy maybe dead too. Or if alive. and he's smart he's half way home to Belfast. Who ever is shooting these guys is deadly serious, deadly accurate, and deadly efficient. We'll talk later Rudy."

"Thanks Jack."

That night, out in the yard under the stars, I told a modified tale about scaring the hell out of the would be assassins and turning them over to some IRA boys exiled in Detroit.

Barbrie, Eve and Paul, were enthralled while mom sat inside and watched "her Irish granddaughters" sleep peacefully. She never looked at me as to give anyone a hint that my story was made up. She was content watching her Irish grand children dream of a better world. Amen.

I took the two passports we had collected and shot holes through them with one of my 45s. I put them in a package with George Sawyer's address on it. I also put a note in the packet for George informing him that any more displays of stupidity on his part and his wife, both kids and his fucking dog would be killed slowly and methodically. I put the package in an envelope with ten bucks and a note and mailed it off to a PIRA friend in Cleveland, Ohio, instructing him to mail it for me. Cleveland would get credit for housing an IRA assassin. Another nice touch, I thought.

A week later George Sawyer got his package containing the threatening message and the passports of his men with the obvious large caliber holes in them.

He shared the contents with his wife, but not his kids. He also shared the contents with his lieutenants and waited for their reaction. His wife had shown concern if not fear. After all this was the Shankill. They, whoever they were, wouldn't dare.

The heavily tattooed second in command said, "You got it from Cleveland in the US? It was delivered to your home address? Dickie and Chris must have given him your name and address. If they wasn't already dead I'd shoot em myself."

The other confident reflected, "They have your address and whoever this cunt is he has been quick to deliver, and deadly. I think we should let this drop. The American from Queen's and the guy who got Douglas and McVeigh aren't here and they aren't worth any more trouble.

"We don't even know for sure that the Yank from Queen's was who the authorities suspect he was. Their source has said it was pure speculation. Even Special Branch has backed off. They say this American worked for British Intelligence. It's a fecken mess and a fecken joke. Lets be done with it.

"So the guy has a taig wife from Belfast. That doesn't mean shite. What does make shite is that we are loosing people over nothing. Again, lets be done with it."

"Maybe, but I hate to back off. It looks bad to everybody. Especially anyone who is a good Loyalists," Sawyer reflected.

A few days later both Sean from Chicago and Denny from Belfast called to pass on the news that according to sources the UDA was calling off any action in North America. "Too damn dangerous."

Of course only Denny knew that it was me. Along the secure line I told him he didn't know the half of it and some day I'd tell him the whole story.

He responded, "Jaysus, I can't wait."

"Any thing I should be aware of, new threats, anything at all?"

"There has been some rumblings that the UVF might try to step in where the UDA is vacating in Canada. Nothing specific yet. But the Loyalist community is astir about the loss of four UDA guys in Canada. The word is a secret IRA cell, a murder squad, is just waiting to pounce on any Loyalist who comes over there. Orangies in Canada are nervous too.

"They're all paranoid, but the UVF thinks it can succeed where the UDA failed. I'll keep you informed. I'll especially watch for any thing with your name on it. Slan for now."

"Slan, Denny."

That very evening Jack called again and said the Michigan State Police got their info from the Royal Mounted Police, Canada's finest. "They got it from a Orange Lodge member who is a snitch and passed info to them. So that's that, Rudy."

"Well I sure wish I could know for sure that I was out of the cross hairs of these assholes. You did say they were UDA, right?"

"Yeah. But our source says they're out of the game now. Someone in Ohio is taking care of things before they get to Michigan. Thank your lucky stars, Rudy."

"And you are sure?"

"What do you know about the UVF, Rudy?"

"I'd say they are as bad as the UDA. Why?"

"They may be attempting to fill the void now that the UDA are withdrawing. Our Belfast sources, a couple of them, say the UVF may be making a move into Canada via the Orange clubs.

"There is no evidence that any particular individual, including you, are in their sights. They just seem to want to collect money and watch and learn what Nationalists are doing across the border in the US.

"This is like a new Cold War, Rudy. You certainly know about that. These guys are more amateurish but as deadly. When I get more I'll pass it along.

"Oh, I almost forgot. One of the UDA big wigs got a direct threat on himself and his family, and he supposedly got the two latest dead guys shot up passports. Sent from Cleveland of all places. New York, Boston, Chicago I could see. But Cleveland. What's this world coming to? But he's one mean sadistic son of a bitch."

I thought, *be careful what you call my mom.* But what I said was, "Thanks Jack."

"Great. Just great," I thought. *"We are going from the frying pan into the fire."*

History: 1979-1980

Eleven gang members of the Loyalist murder club known as 'The Shankill Butchers' who picked up at least nineteen random Catholics and subjected them to horrendous torture, often at bars along the Shankill Road, before dismembering and killing them, receive forty-two consecutive life sentences.

A month later in March of 1979, a British report said that injuries received by Republican prisoners at interrogation centers were not 'self-inflicted,' something the Nationalist community knew for years.

The Conservative Party spokesman on Northern Ireland and a close friend of Margaret Thatcher, was killed when a bomb exploded under his car as he exited the parking garage under the Parliament building in Westminster. A month later, in April, a prison officer was shot dead and four RUC men were killed in a bombing at Bessbrook fort in South Armagh. Three more prison officers were shot and one killed outside the woman's prison in Armagh.

Margaret Thatcher of the Conservative Party won the general election and prepared to run the UK in May.

A land mine in August killed two more soldiers, bringing British Army deaths to 301. But this same month witnessed even more IRA firsts: the Queen's cousin, the 79 year old Earl Louis Mountbatten and three others died after the forty foot sail boat blew up at Mullaghmore off County Sligo in the Republic. Within hours of this bombing six members of the Parachute Regiment were killed by a bomb, and as members of the Queen's Own Highlanders 'quick response force' came to the rescue in a helicopter, a second bomb killed twelve soldiers from this unit at Narrow Water near Warren Point, County Down.

These August actions by the IRA were revenge for 'Bloody Sunday.' Shortly, a rhyme appeared on the wall opposite the Sinn Fein office on the Falls Road:
  'Thirteen gone and not forgotten—we got eighteen and Mountbatten.'

As was expected, there was a sharp rise in sectarian murders of Catholics. In the United States 'Tip' O'Neill, Speaker of the House of Representatives, Senators Edward Kennedy, Daniel Moynihan, and Governor Hugh Carey of New York (known as the 'Four Horsemen'), put pressure on the British to take a political initiative in the North. The response by the British was to announce that the RUC would be increased by 7,500 officers.

Pope John Paul II addressed a quarter of a million souls at Drogheda, the scene of one of Oliver Cromwell's greatest massacres of men, women, and children. He called for an end to violence in Ireland. The IRA responded "respectfully" that violence seemed to be the "only means of removing the evil of British presence in Ireland . . . ."

In the Republic, the Gardai (police) confiscated half a million dollars worth of weapons sent from American sympathizers for the IRA. Twenty-four suspected IRA members were arrested across England to stifle an expected bombing campaign.

In December five British soldiers were killed by bombs and a reserve RUC officer was shot dead.

In January of 1980, three UDR members were killed and four others wounded in bomb attacks, while three civilians were killed when a bomb went off on a train between Belfast and Lisburn; the next month a British Army colonel was shot dead in Germany.

Also in February, thirty women prisoners begin their own 'dirty protest' in Armagh Jail over restoring political status. The IRA stepped up attacks on prison officers amid increased street demonstrations.

In late October, seven H-block prisoners at the Maze Prison went on 'hunger strike' over the right to wear their own clothing. Thatcher announced that there would never be any concessions to the hunger strikers. Three women prisoners at Armagh Jail also went on hunger strike. Twenty-three more prisoners at the Maze join the hunger strike.

An IRA prisoner and two others escaped Brixton Prison in London. Several more prisoners joined the hunger strike at the Maze prison. Cardinal O'Fiaich appealed first to Thatcher to intervene in the hunger strike. Then he was instrumental in convincing the prisoners to end the hunger strike after fifty-three days, having suggested that there might be some movement on the issue of political status.

A Loyalist group calling itself the 'Loyalist Prisoners Action Force' shot dead a prison officer in Belfast.

Seventy-six deaths of the 642 people shot were attributed to the Troubles in 1980; of the 400 bomb attempts 280 actually exploded.

Visitors

The next twelve months were relatively quiet. We were all vigilant, but I didn't expect anything to happen really. My calm seemed to pacify everyone. I figured if I went about life at a normal pace and with a casual attitude I could and would relax the atmosphere for every one. It was working.

Paul had fully recovered. People in Hartford, many of whom came from Irish lineage, knew the circumstances of the shooting. "Me" they called "Lucky," Paul they called "Tough Guy." He kind of relished the attention. That was just fine with me.

With peace reigning on the home front, both Barbrie and Eve were pregnant with number twos. Again we seemed to be about a month earlier than Eve and Paul. I accused Paul of having the doctors remove too much 'lead' from him! Eve got the usual, "You have to wait and get instructions from your sister to see how this comes about?" Paul knew enough to let the jibes roll off. Eve was a different story.

It seemed that any spoofing comment just wound her up. She waited for my comments, she expected them, and would have been disappointed if I failed to make them. She'd threaten me, she'd throw things at me, she'd chase me, all in fun, I think. I never let her catch me, deep down she was like my mother and quite capable of harm to friend and foe.

Down towards the do date for Barbrie, I got a call from Denny. It was the usual cryptic message so I went into town to use what I hoped was a safe phone. I called Denny at a safe number as well.

"Well, are you a da again?"

"No, but its getting close. We are all excited. I told you Eve and Paul are expecting too. These Irish can't say 'no' and they are fertile as rabbits."

"Aye, numbers, that's our secret weapon," Denny responded.

"As my mother says, 'They may have beaten us this time, but give us fifty years and we will out number the bastards," I repeated reverently.

"Jaysus, your mom is not only a saint, she is a wise woman. A wise woman! Now before I forget what I wanted to tell you, let me give you the news. Very hush, hush, now, OK? An in-law is making his way to the US in a couple of weeks. Things are getting hot for him down in the 26 Counties. Dublin is making nice with the Brits, so they are cracking down on boys on the run. So, your man is coming to America.

"I knew youse would welcome him. I really don't have much to do with it, but when I saw him last he said if he had to leave it would be to America if possible. Of course with Aer Lingus anything is possible. It is OK isn't it, Rudy?"

"I'm excited and he'll be welcomed with open arms. You say I can expect to hear from him in a couple weeks? He can ring me at home and just tell me a package will be coming from where he wants me to meet him. He can tell me when through our code, the date and the time. Barbrie and Eve will be so excited. Hell, I can't wait to tell them. Thanks Denny.

"Oh, any thing else?"

"An old friend of ours, Sean Green, you remember Sean, a great talker he was, well he died in Birmingham a couple of days ago. What a shame. I was not able to go to the wake, it being over in England and all. You can ask your man when he shows up. He **was** able to **make** the wake, if you get my meaning.

"At the funeral the word was spread that an Australian who passes himself off as an American, was responsible for the demise of Mr. Green. Apparently the Brits and the RUC are reevaluating their suspicions about an American being involved with the RA. They really have their heads up their arses now. They don't know if they are on foot or horse back.

"Now let me think, anything else? No, not much. Oh, wait, those UVF boys have been to Ontario and back here a couple of times. They are just making contacts in upper New York state, and snooping around Ohio, and Windsor, near Detroit. I guess they just watch and listen for any Republican news or people who are hiding out over there. You will have to have **you know who** keep his head down as you like to say."

"I sure will Denny."

"Well, I'm off. Keep safe, Rudy. God only knows when we might need youse again. Say hello to the Misses and your little one, and let me know about the new wee one. Maybe he'll be like his da, a 'true Ulsterman.'"

"Aye, I'll teach him 'The Sash My Father Wore."

"Jaysus, Rudy, not that one."

"Bye the way, Eve and Paul are expecting another in a month or so. You know, copy cats."

"Give my best to them. There are times I feel like you concerning Paul. He's a saint too."

"Slan, Denny."

"Wow," I thought. "This is both exciting to me and fills me with anxiety. Maybe that will be the new baby's name if it's a girl, "Anxiety Castle."

When I told Barbrie that Danny was on the way here, she was ecstatic and could hardly contain herself as we drove over to Eve's and announced the good news. I explained that I would be going to meet and collect Danny from where ever. I also explained that we would have to be careful because of US officials and the Canadian based UVF.

Needless to say these warnings put a bit of a damper on the festivities. But it had to be said and some guidelines set up. In a sense we would all be in a precarious spot if something went afoul. I just hoped and prayed that he would fly under the radar getting here and while staying here. He certainly was used to that kind of existence because of his professional life back in Ireland. His work there for PIRA made blending in a necessity.

Danny understood that, I just hoped his sisters understood it. They were happy that he would be in the US and were proud of who he was and what he did back in Ireland for the cause of Irish freedom.

We had another beautiful baby girl, Emma Mary Castle. Barbarie's only regret was that her brother Danny wasn't here yet to join in the festivities. I explained he would be here for the baptism and he could be the godfather to both our Emma and Eve's baby. That thought satisfied both of Danny's sisters.

I was getting concerned that I hadn't heard from my brother-in-law. He was overdue and I was getting anxious. I contacted Denny via the safe route and he said he had been gone for more than a week. We promised to exchange any and all info on Danny.

Finally, I got a call from Ontario of all places. It was Danny saying that he, and a travel buddy from "up North" were coming through Canada. I could expect him in two days.

Two days seemed like two weeks, but it was the third and fourth day that seemed like years. "Where in the hell could he be?" I kept asking no one in particular.

———————

A full week went by and not a word from Danny. I hid the guns in the car and only packed toiletries and one change of clothes. Only mom knew about the guns. No sense in worrying the others. I said goodby to everyone, instructing Eve to wait on having her baby until Danny and I got home. She smiled and said, "Aye, of course Rudy, like I have control over that."

"Eve, you are always in control, aren't you?"

"If I could get my hand on you Rudy Castle, there would be two hits: when I hit you and you hit the floor." My mother smiled her approval at both the intention and how it was stated by Eve.

As always, Eve's comments relieved the tension as I left for Canada to look for Danny.

Mom had called relatives in Canada to let them know that I was coming there and might need lodging for a night or two. By way of explanation she offered, "Nothing too definite now. He is trying to retrieve somebody who has gone missing for a couple of days. Nothing serious. We expected him earlier in the week. Rudy will be looking for him near Ottawa and Ontario. But he or the two of them might need some lodging for a bit."

She also called some "people" in Detroit for another used car. I had two hundred dollars to defray their costs and to pay my own expenses.

I had explained the nature of my leaving so soon after the baby was born. Barbrie understood. "Serious business," she said. "And family business to boot."

She did understand. She too was a saint.

———————

It was a grey day all the way to Detroit. The boys in the Motor City would only take a hundred dollars for their arrangements, and said, "Good luck Castle."

The border crossing was easy enough and helped lift my gloomy mood somewhat. I headed straight for Chatham and killed time near that Loyalist watering hole where I had confronted the two UDA men.

I followed the bar keep to his house, scoured the neighborhood, made mental notes, and found a cheap motel for the night.

That night I phoned and then stopped by some relatives of mom's, and to my surprise Barb from Saintfield, County Down, was visiting the family. She had been pregnant when mom, Barb, Eve, Paul and I had visited the North. She was visiting family in and around Chatham who were entertaining some of the exiles from Saintfield who were staying in Canada to avoid the Troubles back in the North.

She had her "little Emma" with her. As pretty as a picture she was. I asked, "The second?"

Barb broke up laughing and said she remembered the conversation during our visit. "Yes, the second, sort of."

She was specifically checking up on two young teenage nieces by the name of Emma and Maya. I smiled and asked, "Which number was this Emma?" Then I spelled out 'Maya' and Barb nodded "Yes." "That name is beautiful, but quite unusual."

"Aye, her da wanted to be an archeologist and work in Central America focusing on the Mayans. He said every one seems so interested in the Incas and Aztecs, but the Mayans were traditionally overlooked, but they would be his El Dorado.

"Well, he never got to study archeology let alone travel to Central America. So after he married his childhood sweetheart and they had their daughter, they named her for their new treasure, right there in County Down. They named her Maya"

"What a wonderful story. Is she here? When can I meet the girls?"

"They'll be coming from the store shortly. You will recognize them from when you were at the house in Saintfield. They are getting a bit bored and restless here. Probably too sedate. I talked to Frank and Betty about it. They felt it would be all right if she moved on for a bit. We were hoping to the US. I was going to call your mother and ask her if she would want visitors for a few weeks."

It was obvious that Barb was hoping that she, little Emma, young Emma and Maya could return with me to Hartford and visit. So I suggested it.

She thought it over for at least half a second and said, "Little Emma and I would love to. Just for a week or so. We have to get back and we leave in ten days from Toronto for home."

"Good. It's settled then. You will see the real United States, not just the news reels of the big cities. Real mid-west America. Everyone will be so happy to see you and 'little Emma.' The girls will love staying in Hartford with us too, as will my mom, Barbrie and Eve. They'll keep them busy with the babies and strawberry and blueberry picking, jam making, and the like," I responded.

"They'll be so excited. But I must warn you, Emma is a bit shy. She may hesitate in going and staying."

"That's alright, she doesn't have to make her mind up right now. She can come along to Hartford, and if she doesn't feel comfortable, I'll bring her back when I bring you back in a week."

My mind was racing as Barb and I chatted while waiting for Maya and Emma. I called mom and explained the situation to her. She said that Franklin and Betty could be trusted with information concerning my "quest."

"Mom, its not a quest, it's a rescue mission and it could be messy."

"Semantics, let me talk to Frank."

Just as I was explaining to her that they were out for a moment, in they walked. I handed the phone to Frank while Barb introduced me to Emma and Maya. They both remembered me, as did Frank who studied me while listening on the phone to mom. He nodded and smiled occasionally.

After what seemed like an inordinately one sided and long phone call, Frank said good by, hung up, smiled at me and came over and shook my hand.

"It has been a long time Rudy. You are more than grown up, and you have your own family so I hear."

"Yes, unfortunately I have no pictures with me to show you."

"I understand it's a family matter that brings you here."

Betty said, "Oh. How nice."

Frank explained it wasn't so nice, and looking to me for consent, he explained the nature of my visit. He said, "We will help Rudy, within reason."

"I do not want to cause any problems for any one. I didn't know Barb was here and that Maya and Emma were staying here either.

"I will be gone for a day or two I know. Um, I'm thinking out loud here, on my way home I could possibly bring Barb, little Emma, Maya and young Emma if she wants to go, with me back to Hartford, along with my brother-in-law. We would look like a big happy family. I could bring Barb and little Emma back here before their plane leaves for back home.

"I hope I'm not stepping on any toes here, I certainly do not want to cause any trouble."

Frank exclaimed, "Rudy, from what I hear you thrive on trouble and in the Troubles. You'll have no trouble from us.

"Quite frankly, the girls were wearing us out. Betty and I are just too old for young teenagers. We are both pooped and aren't much fun for the girls. That's the plain truth of it."

Frank's smile was nervous but disarming.

"Barb can sort things out here for a day or so until I get back and then we can decide for sure, OK?" I asked.

The next day after the barman left home, I canvassed the neighborhood on behalf of a "potential supermarket" that was considering locating in the neighborhood. When I hit the barkeep's house and spoke to his wife she provided way too much information to a complete stranger.

She gave me her first name, maiden name, the names of her two sisters and their addresses along with her parent's names and addresses. She provided her husband's parent's names, and addresses and the same information on his sister and her family and his brother.

I filled two pages of my notebook. She said that her husband's family were from Belfast, Northern Ireland. The dad and Will, her husband, were both in an Orange club, and despised what the Catholics (she looked around as if she expected someone of eavesdropping, lowered her voice and said, they call em 'taigs') were doing over there.

After leaving her place, I stopped at three other doors to continue the rouse, then walked back to the car. Seeing her looking out the window, I waived to her and she squeamishly waived back and disappeared behind the curtains.

I went for lunch and while eating I started memorizing the vast amount of info I had collected on Will. After an hour or so, I had the whole family tree down pat.

That night I pulled into the parking lot as the last car was driving off. I adjusted my fake glasses and beard and burst in the door as Will the barman-owner was just about to lock it. The look on his face was worth a million dollars. I used my best East Belfast accent.

"Hello Will, you Loyalist Orange lacky. Lock that fucken door. Then get your ass over here. We need to talk and maybe you will see your wife Ruthie and your daughters . . . ." I listed the whole family, their names and where they lived to complete the shock.

Will was devastated. He started to sob. I cuffed him and told him to shut-up or I'd make him watch as I killed them all. He was completely overcome with fear. I thought of discussions I'd had with the Dark about "fear."

I explained, "We know everything, Will. You are ours or they are all dead. You got it?"

He just nodded his head. His face was wet with tears and sweat, and his eyes registered utter fear. I had only seen one other person so utterly destroyed by fear before and that was back in Nam. That man, a South Vietnamese traitor, became a blubbering idiot by the time we were done with him. We never did touch his family. But he was ruined as a man.

Now it was Will's turn.

"I'm looking for a man. He is from Ireland. Your people have him. I want him back. If I get him back, OK, you get your family. If he's hurt, I kill some of your family. If he is dead, I kill all of your family and you are going to watch it all happen. Then I'll kill you, you fucken wanker. It's all the same to me. I'm a hired gun. You understand, Will?"

He didn't make so much as a sound, because he couldn't make a sound or even nod his head. He just shook uncontrollably. He was clearly scared to death.

"I want my man and I want him now. If you don't know for sure where he is, I bet you have a pretty good idea of where he is. So lets go."

He finally gathered himself and managed, "It's only a guess now, but they probably have him up at a rural and remote place called Shawville, fifty or sixty miles northwest of Ottawa. It's a drive but I suspect he's held up there. It used to be heavily Orange, less so now but still pretty Loyal."

Will phoned his wife, Ruth, and explained that some urgent business would require him to be gone untill tomorrow. He explained that it had to do with the Orange Order. Reluctantly she accepted his excuse.

We drove all night, and Will actually slept, probably from exhaustion. I was getting tired but I simple couldn't afford to sleep because I had nothing to secure Will with, and how might I explain to any police who stopped me why he was tied up.

About nine that morning, Will made a few phone calls from a grocery store's public phone and located the right people. He said he needed to talk to the man they were holding concerning the killings of the Ulster men in Chatham some time back.

About 11:00 we pulled into an old Orange Hall. Two men were waiting outside for us. Introductions were exchanged, Will and me, going by "Sam" from Chatham. We entered the hall and three more men were there just studying us. I explained that our interest in interrogating the "prisoner" was to see if he could shed light on how the IRA got to the two sets of Ulster men gunned down in Chatham and those found in Lake Eire, and who the "bloody wanker" was who shot them and where he lived.

Prompting Will, he finally offered that it was in his bar where the first victims were shot dead. I had instructed Will to stand on my right and a little in front of me at all times, and if I so much as suspected him of doing anything to compromise this rescue, he was dead as was his family. He would just close his eyes when I brought up his family.

I added that Will escaped by the skin of his teeth and that his whole family had been threatened. I instructed Will to show them his tattoo indicating that he was a high mucky muck in the Orange Order.

That seemed to do it, they led us into a back room. Danny Conlon was tied to a chair and there was a car battery and cables in front of him. He didn't lift his head when we came in but his eyes rotated towards me as I exclaimed, "Look at that sorry Fenien bastard. By the way Danny, thanks for taking care of that cunt Sean Green."

He recognized my voice, turned his head in my direction slightly, and concocted that famous Conlon smile.

Without hesitation I shot the two Orngies standing at Danny's side. The surprise look on their faces was complete. Since I had returned from the North of Ireland, I had spent some time on an outside firing range to stay sharp and focused. It paid off. I hit them both in the head. Pure luck. The blood spray went mostly up to the low ceiling and as the light filtered through the dirty windowpane the spray seemed to change to an orange color. Very fitting I thought.

Then I got two at the door as they were drawing their guns from their trouser pockets. Who'd put their gun in their front pants pocket? I thought, *Jaysus, what a way to die, with hands in their pockets.*

The one left, shot Will in the face before I could nail him with three shots in the torso. The shooter gurgled and bled like a punctured pig.

None were breathing, not even Will, and as I got Danny untied I stood him up and asked if there were any major wounds he had that I should know about?

"No. But I'm pretty well burned. I'll probably never father any kids of my own, they fried my balls" he managed with a hint of pain and disgust.

"You'll also need to see a dentist, you've got holes in your grill." He was missing at least two front teeth on the top and bottom of his mouth. *No corn on the cob for Danny, at least for a while*, I thought.

I waited for a moment listening for any noise before we exited the building. I put Danny in the back seat and we headed for Chatham.

I don't know if there was simply an absence of signs or if I was simply missing them, but we ended up taking the long way to Chatham. I was exhausted.

It was early evening when we pulled into Frank and Betty's place. Fortunately they lived on the edge of Chatham and there was quite a distance to their neighbor's houses.

Frank helped get Danny into the house, then he parked the car around back and out of sight from the road. Barb said, "We've a surprise for you, Maya talked her cousin 'young Emma,' into coming to Hartford. Another Emma, also fifteen, who wants to join us going to Hartford, so I called your mom and she said it was fine to bring her."

"Aye, of course, the more the merrier. We'll all fit in the car. No problem. It should make the crossing into the US easier. We'll look like a big family returning from a family reunion or wedding or something. We'll figure that out tomorrow so as to be on the same page in case some one gets nosey and asks."

Danny was bathed, cleaned up, and fed. I called mom to let her know we were on the way home in the morning. We were "all" on the way home and none the worse for wear. We were tired and would need some good home cooking and looking after.

I also explained, since we had a car full, it would take us longer than usual with toilet breaks and having to change "little Emma's nappies."

———————————————

Canada, Oh Canada

I put Barb's and 'little Emma's' luggage in the trunk next to Maya's and Emma's stuff. I had started the car. Maya and Emma hoped in the front seat and as I rounded the rear of the car to return to the house to help Danny down the steps, two men with drawn guns confronted me.

"Where is the Irishman?" one demanded.

"Who? What's this all about? What Irishman?"

"A local barman was shot up in Shawville along with five of our friends. It was reported on the news. A local man spotted you here. Said you were a stranger and acting suspicious. You also answer the description of a man who questioned the local victim's wife a few days back."

"I've been here for several days with my family visiting relatives, so whoever pointed me out to you is mistaken," I said in an irate voice. "Are you police? I'd like to see some identification," I demanded.

The two men just stood there looking at me. A third man came around the corner of the house at this point and said, "Aye, this is the stranger. Let's bring him by Will's house and see if Will's wife recognizes him as the guy who was asking questions the other day."

I had no idea of what I was going to do. My guns were hidden in the auto and would prove more than difficult to get to at this point. I started around the front of the car to turn off the ignition when the two men followed me with obvious violence on their mind. The local man came around in back of the car and met me by the driver's door.

At that point, Maya had slipped behind the wheel and put the car in gear and stomped on the accelerator. She ran the two armed strangers down. I grabbed the local guy and smashed his face with my fist.

Danny hobbled down the stairs and said, "Jaysus, Mary and Joseph, Rudy. What the fuck? Those two cunts were part of the crowd who beat me and shocked me."

I raced to the car and got it in neutral. Then I got Maya out of the car. She was cool as a cucumber. I hugged her and said, "Quick thinking. You saved the day. But now I want you and Emma to go into the house and wait with Barb for Danny and me to return."

The car had dragged the two Orange men about two lengths of the car. Young Emma had picked up their guns and handed them to Danny, two old Webley revolvers. The two casualties moaned and crawled out from under the car. I gave Emma a hug and praised her bravery as she headed into the house with Maya.

"Keep the wankers covered Danny, and the asshole over there."

I went into the house and said, "We need every one to stay put and be ready to leave when we got back in about half an hour. Maya here saved the day. Frank we need you outside."

I searched the pockets of the Orangemen, found the car keys in one of their pockets and drove their car to the back of the house. We loaded the three men into the trunk of their vehicle.

"Danny can you drive that thing?"

"Actually I don't think so. My legs are too fucked up so they are."

I ran up the steps and got Maya and asked with a smile, "Two more favors. Do you have a camera and can you drive a car without running over people?"

"I don't have a camera and I probably can't drive," she answered. But Emma said, "I live on a farm and I can drive all sorts of equipment. I think I can drive the car, even if it is on the wrong side of the road."

Barb hesitatively said, "I have a camera."

"I need to borrow it. I won't take any pictures but I need someone to think I have."

Barb scurried into another part of the house to locate her camera while Emma and Maya went out into the yard.

Frank drove his own car and led us to a deserted area on a lake. I drove my vehicle. Emma drove while Danny rode along in the Orange men's car.

"Frank, you, Emma and Maya should go back now and wait for us, we'll be along shortly." He looked pail as a ghost and sickly. Emma and Maya looked like they wanted to stay, but they didn't say so.

Danny and I each had one of the Webleys and when Frank, Emma and Maya were out of sight I said to Danny, "Do you want to do it or should I?"

"My legs are fucked up not my trigger finger. I'll do it and relish it for what they did to me and my friend. I didn't get a chance to tell you but they killed my friend who I was traveling with. I don't know what they did with his body."

"We'll ask the bloody cunts before you execute them for killing your friend," I said.

We rousted the three prisoners, and Danny asked what they did with the body of his friend? The two Orangies just stood there. One had what I took to be a smirk on his face so I pulled his jacket off of him and used mom's trick of wrapping it loosely about the gun and I shot him in the foot.

He howled like a banshee, and as I turned to the other one he began to describe a hill in back of the lodge in Shawville. We quieted the first man down and we stood them next to the car. I emptied the bullets from the gun and I handed it to the local Orangeman. I told him to point the gun at his two chums and I pretended to take pictures from some distance in back of him.

At that point I retrieved the gun with his prints on it as Danny was about to execute the other two. I interrupted the proceedings by stating in a loud voice, "You two have been found guilty of crimes against Ireland and Humanity and you are sentenced to die."

Danny needed no prompting. He emptied the cylinder into the Orangies. I had the local man stuff the two bodies into the trunk and we sent the car into the lake. Within minutes it sank. I handed Danny's Webley to the local and now had his prints on it too.

We brought him back to Chatham and explained that if he ever talked we would send the photos to the Canadian authorities, and then we would return from Ohio and kill Will's family and then his family while we made him watch. I went through Will's family tree and said we would find out his family tree too. Before we left him, he was clearly scared to death.

We headed out to Frank's, explained that the local man was unharmed and that we had incriminating evidence that he had done his friends in. We explained that the two bodies were in the trunk of their car that had been driven into the lake.

I explained, "Frank, you and Betty need never say a word about this to any one. Everything is deniable on your end, deny everything. You hear, everything. Your local man has been compromised with a serious threat from some wild Irishmen. Believe me, he won't say a word. Ever."

And with that, and some "Thank yous," and "Good byes," we were off for the border and Detroit. It was a piece of cake. Barb and little Emma were up front with me, Danny and young Maya and Emma were in the back pretending to be playing card as we cruised through the check points at both ends of the Windsor Bridge. "Ya, we are all Americans coming home from a vacation."

We switched cars in Detroit, setting the loaner on fire. I was exhausted again, but I knew the way to Hartford by heart.

Eve had a baby boy, Paul junior while we were in Canada. So Danny was the God Father to both Emma and Paul. All the Conlons were happy and proud.

Homecoming

Danny stayed with us for about two months, getting used to American food and customs. At first the small town seemed to fit him to a "T". He learned to drive on our side of the road. He loved American cars and would drift into town and hang around one particular garage, Kelly's Auto Service. Sean Kelly's parents were from Waterford in southeast Ireland and had come to the United States in the fifties with young Sean in tow. Sean had a thriving auto garage and he was willing to allow Danny to hang around and learn a thing or two.

Sean also had a smashing daughter who'd just graduated from high school and was going to attend a local community college while living at home and keeping the books for Sean's business. We all thought Danny was more interested in the bookkeeper than the autos.

Maya and Emma fit into rural Hartford well. Before we knew it young men and boys were stopping by the house after supper for stories of Ireland and desert. The girls were the social hit of the summer in Hartford.

The other Sean, our Sinn Fein organizer and Provo representative, came over from Chicago several times, and finally told Danny he had a place for him, not in Chicago, but in St Louis. That was a little farther than any of us had hoped for but it would be safe for Danny. As it turned out, he got a job in construction and it was not only safe, it was also rewarding for Danny. He made money, gained a Scottish identity, and had made a lot of friends. He would come to Hartford or some of us would go to St. Louis every other month or so. Life was good.

Before Barb and little Emma returned to Canada and then on to the North of Ireland, we all spent a day in Chicago that "wowed" Barb beyond belief. Our Irish girls went back to Chicago with my Conlon girls

120

for an over-night stay in one of the big hotels near the Loop; later they went with us to St. Louis, crossing the Mighty Mississippi River. They were awe-struck by it all. "Everything is so big, even the rivers," they would say.

By September "young Emma" (so designated to keep them all straight) was eager to return to County Down in the North of Ireland and tell her friends about "America." She asked if she could come next summer and stay with us in Hartford. We all agreed she was more than welcome. Maya decided to stay in Hartford. After several phone conversations with her parents, a plan was settled on and she would stay at least until Christmas.

We had a heart to heart talk with Emma about Danny and the need for absolute silence concerning him and everything concerning his rescue in Canada. I explained that it would not only affect her returning to us, but it would jeopardize our family here in Hartford and Frank and Betty in Canada. "Ach, I know Rudy, and I'll not be touting to anybody, ever, promise. I want to come back and I don't want any of yous to get in trouble."

We were all confident that Emma would not say a thing to anyone back in the North of Ireland, family or friends. She clearly knew the gravity of our secret and understood the consequences of saying anything to anyone.

After a year of relative calm, we all began to breath easier and we became more comfortable and carefree. Cousin Maya was enrolled in high school in Hartford, staying the whole year. She was becoming more American than her classmates.

The news from the North was never good, but this year it was deadly. Bobby Sands and the 'hunger strikers' were in the news and on every Irishman and woman's mind. It seemed all hell was breaking loose in the North, and here I sat in Hartford, doing nothing.

We were glad Emma was coming to us out of the North again this summer, and that Maya seemed content to remain with us out of the 'Troubles' in her backyard of County Down. All of us were concerned about the family in Saintfield and about family and friends all over the North.

In the summer Emma did returned to us for three months. She said very little about the 'Troubles' and we did not ask her. We got news regularly from several sources and knew how bad it was. She was just so happy to be here with us again.

She was happy to see her cousin, her aunts-in-law, and she wanted to see Danny again. Both young Emma and Maya had crushes on him. We had talked about visiting him in St. Louis, but there was a glitch, Danny was no longer in Missouri.

We all went to gather her up in Chicago, spending a night in a hotel and most of the next day in the "Windy City." No matter how often we took the girls to Chicago they would start counting cars, then give up after "at least a million." They would complain that their necks hurt from looking up at the tall buildings.

I promised the Irish Colleens (that's "Cailin, in Irish) that I would teach them how to drive an American car on the "right" side of the road. After a week of driving around the parking lot of the local high school, I had to admit they were very good drivers.

Danny had been relocated with his construction company to Atlanta, Georgia. With the Hartford family growing, travel to Atlanta was too far and too expensive, but Danny visited us regularly. We kidded him about calling at Kelly's Auto Service before he made it to our house. He would usually say, with a wide grin, that he hoped we didn't mind but Megan Kelly would be joining us for supper. Megan was such a sweet heart that even young Emma and Maya liked her and were not too jealous.

On a more serious note, he often brought news of the North of Ireland that was not reported on network news stations. Much of it covered explosions with Semtex, C-4, and new detonating devices. Danny would smile and add, "Just thought you might like to know, Rudy."

I also spoke with Denny from Belfast regularly, but he was always cautious on the phone, even seemingly secure lines . . . just in case. I kept inviting him over, but he always declined, "Och, Rudy, bad timing," "Too much up in the air," "Too much happening," or "But one of these days."

I'd usually signed off with, "Aye, our day will come."

His traditional come back was, "Tiocfaidh ar la," Irish for "our day will come," a mantra of Irish Nationalists. Denny always said it as a fact, never a wish or a hope.

Redemption

The phone call from Ireland was a complete surprise. We got calls from Denny periodically, placed from the North and the South. This one came from Donegal; and it was for my mother. It was Sean Keenan on the line. He had information concerning a matter involving my grandfather which he had spoken to my mother about back in Belfast during our visit.

She listened intently and periodically punctuated the silence with "I see," "I thought so," or "of course."

Then after an exaggerated pause, she said, "Yes I can come. I'll try to get Rudy to accompany me. Can you call back in a week? I'll have my plans ready by then.

"Sean, I can't thank you enough. This means a lot to me and my family. Thank you. I sure will. Talk to you soon."

Barbrie and I had left the kitchen so mom could talk in private, but she called us both back in for a obvious conference. We couldn't help but overhear her end of the conversation with Sean. She motioned outside. We walked nearly to the garage in the morning sunshine that filtered through the few fruit trees spread across the backyard.

"Sean sends his greetings and congratulations to you both on your growing family."

Barbrie and I just stood there and nodded acknowledgement, intently waiting to hear what caused her imminent travel plans that apparently included me if she could pull it off.

"Rudy, do you remember Sean mentioning back in Belfast that he was pursuing a matter for me concerning my dad?"

She didn't wait for my acknowledgment, she just barreled on, "Well he has found someone who can put a lot of confusion straight. Oh, I know, there are seemingly more important matters that need attention concerning the war. But this is terribly important to me, and Sean says it's the least they can do for me who did a few things for the Cause over the years."

I finally got a word in edgewise, and it was just one word, "OK. But you understand what's going on in the North. It's a war zone. It's dangerous. And it has spilled over into the Republic."

"If I'm that close I'll have to go North and see for myself. I'll have to see Denny, and check on The Dark. He's the IRA OC, you know, Officer Commanding, in the Kesh, or Maze as they now call it. He called a Hunger Strike with six other guys over the Brits denying Republican prisoners their rights. That one fizzled because of British duplicity. But now there is a new one. I'm nervous about his safety and that of the others."

Mom said, "Let's sit under the trees for a spell close to the house. Little Eoffa can play and we'll be close enough to hear little Emma if she fusses. Ok Barbrie?"

"Of course mom" Barbrie said. She and her sister Eve had taken to calling my mother "mom," or "ma" and that alone would have endeared them both to her. But more than that, much more, they were the "daughters" she never had.

As I gathered up a few folding canvas lawn chairs and arranged them under an apple tree near enough to the house to listen for the phone or little Emma's cry, mom said, "It's too bad your sister Eve is not here to hear this one last saga of our modern family, but you can tell her for me."

As if on queue, Eve pushed a pram up the driveway with her babies. I said, "Jaysus, she's fey I tell you, she's fey."

We all broke out laughing and Eve asked, "What?"

"Mom said she wished you were here, and here you are. Rudy thinks you are fey," Barb explained. Eve enjoyed that.

"Hell, I think you're all fey and possessed," I said.

"Rudy, be careful, the children," mom scolded.

"Aye, I'm convinced they are too, or they will be. I'm sure, and in time I'll be proven right"

At that very moment a large dark cloud blocked the sunlight and cast a really dark pall over the yard, and my mother simply said, "There you are Rudy, now mind yourself and don't make it worse." Everyone looked up and no one laughed or mocked now, certainly not me.

Mom began simply, "I've a story to tell. My da, Rudy's granda, was an active member of the Irish Republican Brotherhood up in the North.

As things were unhealthy for Republicans up there, and especially so for Protestant Republicans and their families who were seen as not simply rebels but traitors to the Crown, the State and the Protestant Faith. Traitors with a capital "T." So he relocated down in the Dublin area where his identity would be unknown and thus protect his family up in County Down.

"My da eventually fell in with Harry Boland, Michael Collin's good friend. He was at the General Post Office during the thick of the fighting and got to know most of the leaders from Pierce on down after the fall of the GPO. He stuck close to both Boland and Collins over at the concentration camp about fifty kilometers southwest of Liverpool called Fron-Goch near Bala in Wales.

"So as not to waste time, Fron-Goch became an unofficial 'university' for the IRA prisoners. Actual subjects like mathematics, book-keeping, telegraphing, and shorthand were taught and taken by prisoners, as well as Latin, Spanish, French and Irish, and Irish History. There were more practical courses like house budgets, dancing, acting and public speaking too. Your granda learned Irish well enough to speak it with Irish speakers later on.

"Courses were also taught on guerilla warfare, military strategy and tactics. There were political seminars of what kind of government would be set up once liberty was won.

"Furthermore, several of Michael Collin's special squad who took out touts, British spies, and military and police personal during the Tan War, were Fron-Goch men. Harry Boland and Collin's groomed granda to be a special currier since he was unknown and unfamiliar to the Royal Irish Constabulary, the Dublin RIC, Special Branch, British Intelligence, the British "volunteers," "auxilaries," and "black and tans." During the Tan war he spent a lot of time on trains between Dublin and Cork posing as a soap and brush salesman. He delivered news and orders, but also spotted and reported on British agents who were posing as salesmen.

"With the conclusion of the Tan War in late 1921 and the peace, Collins, Griffith and others got, actually issued, by the British Prime Minister David Lloyd George, a new row turned deadly with the split of the Irish government and the Irish Republican Army over whether to accept the dictated 'Peace' or not.

"This new round of war was especially horrific because it was a most uncivil 'Civil War.' Families split, father against son, brother against brother, mother against daughter, sister against sister. The treaty signed in London under the threat by the British Prime Minister of "total war" waged by Britain against Ireland, ended the Tan War but kept those six north-east counties of the nine counties of the Ulster Province for, and in, the United Kingdom as we all know, and especially you two girls (mom nodded toward Barbrie and Eve). They were sacrificed for peace.

"Collins was convinced that the lost six counties would in time join the other twenty-six counties comprising the new Free State of Ireland. The treaty was far from perfect, but the IRA was 'exhausted and spent' according to Collins: they had only a few arms, virtually no ammunition, and many men dead, wounded or on the run. Further, the consensus of the people of Ireland was for peace. The treaty would be a start, a beginning towards an all 32 county Irish national state as well as some much needed peace.

"But the likes of DeValera, Boland, and other leaders said the fight should continue unabated until all thirty-two counties were free and independent. They were the anti-treaty faction. Granda, being from one of the six lost counties from the North, sided with the anti-treaty crowd. Because of his experience of working for and with Collins and his allegiance to the liberation of the North, he was utilized as an advisor to Boland, and now DeVelera.

"Just before Michael Collins was shot down in Bealnablath, not too far from Cork, my da was privy to some discussions between the anti-Treaty-Irregular commander-in-Chief Liam Lynch and DeValera over whether or not to continue the Civil War. Lynch was all for it, but DeV was hedging. In fact, these discussions between the two had been going on for some time. The uncivil nature of the Civil War's brutality was a concern to Dev. Da had sought to contact and confide this info to Kitty Kiernan, Collin's fiancée, with the understanding that she would not disclose her source.

"Collins also sought a conclusion to the Civil War. So in August Collins and others set out for a tour of the southwest to get a read on the war with the people there, neutral IRA men and hopefully some Irregulars.

"Da was back in the south by then, and DeValera was also in the south-west and still trying to convince Lynch to consider peace. Da heard lively discussions pro and con about continuing the war. Da also knew there were Irregular units in the area Collins was to visit, and although Collins had a small convoy, the local Irregulars were very adept at ambushes. Da feared for Collins' life. Although da was working for the anti-Treaty crowd he greatly admired Collins and felt enough good men had been sacrificed in this unholy uncivil war of Irishmen killing Irishmen.

"Then on August 21st, da heard comments about Collins being close by in County Cork, and him finding out what the 'Irregulars of West Cork' were made of . . . the usual brag and bluster. But there was an edge to the tone that da feared. He took the chance of his life, he stole away in the night to Cork and contacted Emmet Dalton, one of Collin's generals who had recently set up his headquarters in Cork.

"Da always claimed he indeed met face to face with Dalton to warn him that tempers were hot and not to under estimate the local anti-treaty forces. He could not, and probably would not, give any specifics but said the mere presence of Collins was enough to cause rash comments and possibly actions. Collins reportedly said that the Irregulars certainly would not shoot him in his own county. But in fact da reportedly heard someone of the Irregulars say to the contrary, 'getting Collins in Cork would send a message.'

"Again da told Dalton no specifics, but reported that he had more of a feeling, 'a bad feeling,' and the feeling was the Cork Irregulars would, if they could, do something spectacular."

I broke mom's monologue to ask, "How did granda get to see Dalton? Cork had only recently been captured by Free State forces, not just anybody could get in to talk to a general."

"That has always been part of the mystery. But more importantly, both sides, the Free Staters and the Irregular anti-Treaty folks, in the aftermath of Collins assassination branded my da something of a 'traitor' to their causes. While in Ireland over the years I was held in contempt and mistrusted by some IRA men because of the slanderous label of 'traitor' hanging over da's head.

"That was also the reason he and mammy went on the run, first to Canada and then here. I tried to clear his name myself over in Ireland, but to no avail, and then sought the help of Sean Keenan. Sean says he has found someone who can verify da's side of the story and lift the cloud that has hung over his head and name for all these years.

"Barbrie, I know it's a divil of a thing to ask, but I'd like Rudy to go with me back to Ireland to get this whole mess straightened out," mom pleaded.

Barbrie simply whispered, "Of course, mom, of course."

Eve got up from her chair and came over to my mother's chair, knelt down beside her and before she gave my mom a hug said to her sister, "Good on you Barbrie."

And then turning to my mom Eve said, "And mom, after all these years and after all you gave and did for Ireland, finally some recognition and restitution for your da, yourself, and your whole family. We are all so proud to be part of your family."

———————————————

History: 1981 The Hunger Strike

The end of a fifty-three day 'hunger strike' (27 October to 18 December) in 1980, resulted in a sense of relief in much of the nationalist community in the North, but it left a depressing mood in the H-blocks of Long Kesh Prison. The 'five demands' of the Republican prisoners had not been met, though there was a hint in December of 1980 that some 'movement' might be expected from the British Government. Brendan Hughes, the IRA OC in the Maze had been fooled by the Brits, for Margaret Thatcher was in charge of the British Government and neither hell nor high water was going to budge her towards any accommodation with Republicans, in or out of prison.

In January of 1981, two events triggered a confrontation between various types of Republican prisoners and the British government and their agents. With the enemy in the crosshairs there would be 'no surrender,' an epithet usually associated with Ian Paisley who was pushed from the stage, for being irrelevant, for a time in the North of Ireland.

The first was the attempted murder of Bernadette McAliskey nee Devlin, a Nationalist icon, and her husband as they dressed two of their children in their home near Coalisland. Although shot seven times by hard core Loyalists, she eventually recovered. Nationalists of every stripe were outraged by the attack.

The second were the reprisals in the deaths of a UDR part-time major at Warrenpoint where he worked at a customs post. Five days later the former Speaker of the Stormont Parliament, Sir Norman Stone and his son were shot dead by the IRA at Tynan Abbey, their home.

The IRA stated, "This deliberate attack on the symbols of hated unionism was a direct reprisal for a whole series of loyalist assassinations and murder attacks on nationalist people and national activities." Two weeks later Republican prisoners warned of a new 'hunger strike.'

The new IRA leader in the H-blocks at Long Kesh prison, Bobby Sands, started a new hunger strike on March 1, the fifth anniversary of the ending of 'special-category' status for offences committed after March 1976. Regaining 'political status' was explained in the prisoners' 'Five Demands:'' the right not to wear prison garb; the right not to do prison work; the right of free association with other prisoners; the right to a weekly visit, parcels, and letters, along with being able to organize recreational and educational activities and pursuits; and full restoration of remission lost through the protest.

To focus on the new 'hunger strike' Republican prisoners ended the 'dirty protest.' Rather than have several prisoners go on 'hunger strike' all at once, Bobby Sands organized the new strike so that a new prisoner joined intermittently. Sands was alone on strike at first.

A new wrinkle emerges when the Member of Parliament (at Westminster) for Fermanagh-South Tyrone died, and after some early confusion about candidates, Jim Gibney of the Belfast Sinn Fein, convinced the party to put forward a Sinn Fein candidate. It would eventually be Bobby Sands.

Francis Hughes, an IRA prisoner, joined Sands as a second hunger striker on March 15. Then on March 22, IRA man Raymond McCreech and the leader of the INLA Patsy O'Hara join the strike.

Sands was willing to have other Republican groups join in the strike, and men were chosen from various counties in the North thus ensuring a broad representation so nearly every community and Nationalist constituency were represented and affected. Sands interviewed each candidate so as to make sure they were committed to death and to stay on the strike. There would be no double-dealing, compromise, or false promises in 1981.

On March 26th, Sands was nominated for the by-election for Fermanagh-South Tyrone, and while other Nationalist candidates withdrew, he would face Ulster Unionist Harry West. There was concern over the number of Nationalist votes since the census discloses that since 1971 more than 130,000 people (many if not most Nationalists) had emigrated.

But on April 9, 1981, "Hunger Striker" Bobby Sands won the by-election to Westminster, and on April 11 when the results were formally declared, celebrations turn to riots in Belfast, Lurgan and Cookstown. When Sands election agent requested a meeting with the British Government, Prime Minister Thatcher responded, "We are not prepared to consider special category status for certain groups of people serving sentences for crime. Crime is crime, it is not political."

With that statement, Sands fate was sealed, the bitterness Nationalists felt toward Britain was increased geometrically as it was apparent the British

Government was prepared to let the hunger strikers die along with their replacements.

Sands sister, Marcella, appealed to the European Commission on Human Right to no avail. The North was poised to explode.

On May 5, MP Bobby Sands died after 66 days on hunger strike. Riots sweep across the North and in the Republic. The IRA single out the British Military and RUC. On May 7 100,000 people march at Sands funeral. On May 8 another Provie, Joe McDonnall replaced Sands on 'hunger strike,' and four days later Francis Hughes died on the strike after 59 days. In Dublin thousands attacked the British embassy.

IRA man Brendan McLaughlin replaced Hughes on hunger strike. The English and Welsh soccer teams cancel matches in Belfast. The IRA kill five soldiers with a land mine near Bessbrook, South Armagh. An 11 year old girl was killed by a rubber bullet in Belfast by the RUC. Tension was at a fever pitch.

Raymond McCreech and Patsy O'Hara died on the 61 day of their hunger strike (May 21). Cardinal O'Fiaich condemns the British "rigid stance" and warned that Britain will face "the wrath of the whole nationalist population".

On May 26th, Brendan McLaughlin had a perforated ulcer with internal bleeding and was taken off the strike, but two days later he was replaced by Martin Hurson. On June 8, Tom McElwee started his hunger strike. Two days later 8 IRA prisoners shot their way to freedom from the Crumlin Road Prison using hand guns smuggled in to them and two comrades escaped wearing captured guards uniforms.

Thatcher's government amended the 'Representation of the People Act' prohibiting prisoners standing for Parliament. The IRA just missed exploding Lord Gardner's auto claiming that he was "the political architect of the criminalization policy and the H-blocks."

Paddy Quinn joined the hunger strike and a week later Michael Devine of the INLA, joined the hunger strike. A week later Laurence McKeown began his hunger strike, thus reflecting a new strategy of adding one striker a week. Also, the IRA expanded the 'Five Demands' for all 'political prisoners' including Loyalists, not just Republican inmates.

On July 8, Joe McDonnell died after sixty-one days on hunger strike and was replaced by Patrick McGeown. The British Military disrupted the IRA firing-party at McDonnell's funeral, seizing weapons and making arrests. Major rioting ensued.

Martin Hurston, died on July 13th after forty-five days on the fast. He was the sixth hunger-stiker to die. The next day Matt Devlin joined the strike. Riots outside the British embassy in Dublin cause major injury over *the hunger strike. Republican prisoners on hunger strike refuse to have the Swiss Red Cross, Provisional Sinn Fein, or the Irish Republican Socialist Party mediate with the British.*

On July 31, Paddy Quinn's family request, for medical reasons, that he be removed from the hunger strike. But the next day Kevin Lynch was the seventh prisoner to die after 71 days on hunger strike, and the next day Kiernan Doherty after 73 days on hunger strike, died. The next day Liam McCloskey of INLA joined the strike.

On August 8th, Thomas McElwee died after 62 days on strike, and two days later Patrick Sheehan joined the hunger strike as more than a thousand petrol bombs were thrown at the British Army and RUC on the 8th and 9th, also an anniversary of the introduction of 'internment.'

On August 17 Jackie McMullan joins the strike. Three days later Michael Devine was the tenth hunger striker to die after sixty days. Patrick McGeown's family interceded to save his life and took him off the strike.

In August the second by-election in Fermanagh-South Tyrone was held since the elected MP, Bobby Sands, was now dead. The Ulster Unionist candidate was a member of the Dungannon District Council, Ken Maginnis, a part-time major in the Ulster Defence Regiment and a teacher. Sands' former election agent, Owen Carron of Provisional Sinn Fein ran against Maginnis and not only won, but got nearly 800 more votes than Sands. After these wins Provisional Sinn Fein announced a change in tactics and said it would contest future elections in the North, including those for Westminster.

Bernard Fox, and a week later Hugh Carville, joined the hunger strike. Matt Devlin's family interceded for medical reasons and he was taken off the strike as was Laurence McKeown, the third and fourth men to be taken off the strike by family. But the following day John Pickering joined the strike. A week later Gerald Hodgkins joins the strike. And on September 17th James Devine joins the hunger strike. But clearly with four families intervening to save four lives, there was some question about the continuation of the strike.

Bernard Fox ended his strike because of his rapid decline after only thirty-two days. Liam McCloskey ended his hunger strike when told his family would intervene. And by October the remaining six hunger strikers ended their strike because their families said they would intervene. Although the hunger strike ended on October 3rd, the Republican prisoners in Long Kesh returned to their 'blanket protest.' The British Government, through its Secretary of State for Northern Ireland, James Prior, conceded to most of the 'Five Demands' on October 6, 1981.

Back To Ireland

Mom used some of dad's insurance money to secure Aer Lingus tickets for Dublin during my summer break in the 1981 school year. Being on tri-semesters, I was finished with my second semester classes in late April. We left for Ireland on April 27th. Our man who would clear granda's name was in an old folks home just outside of Dublin.

When I contacted Denny, he suggested that I should try to come North for a couple of days without my mother. He indicated, "all hell is breaking loose with Sands and the new hunger strike. The Brits are fucken this all up. They couldn't have helped us better if they tried. We used to say 'no one ever shoots Paisley because he is more important to us alive than dead.' When people hear him speak, they immediately turn to the Republican cause. Now we can say that about Thatcher. She must have a mental problem. I'm sure of it. It seems your Reagan is her only friend. Maybe he has a similar mental problem.

"And Rudy, I have something of a personal issue you could help me with. It is somewhat important."

I assured him that in spite of "'all hell breaking loose,' a condition I was intimately familiar with," a trip North would be arranged. I had some academic articled for my friend Professor Smyth. That would be my story for mom as to my quick trip North.

Just two weeks later we were in Dublin and mom was making arrangements to meet up with Sean Keenan's man, the authority on granda's secret mission just prior to Collins' death. Sean could not meet with us because of the seriousness of the situation in the North, so we were on our own. He gave us the location and the man's name: Jerry.

Mom set a meeting for the next day. She wasn't just excited, she was nervous as I'd not seen her in a long time. She said, "Let's walk."

We went to some of the regular shrines, the General Post Office, Parnell Square, Bachelor's Walk, and the Shelbourne Hotel just across the road from Saint Stephen's Green Park. After our supper, we walked up toward the Castle and Christ Church, the actual place where Robert Emmet was martyred, not the incorrect one tourists are shown.

We were both good and tired and slept well that night. The next day, after a good hearty breakfast we hired a taxi that delivered us to Saint Brendan's Home for our meeting with the mystery man, Jerome, "Jerry" Clare.

The Home was a sprawling old building in the Classical style dating from the mid nineteenth century. The grounds were spacious with flowering shrubs and flowerbeds of various kinds.

"Nice setting, well taken care of too," I observed aloud.

"Lets hope it offers more than just a nice setting and view," mom added with the hint of nervousness left over from yesterday.

"Aye. No worry. If your man Sean sent for you to meet the man there must be something of substance, not just appearance," I offered.

"I surely hope you are spot on, Rudy. I have high hopes of drawing a sixty year cloud away and setting the record straight."

"You and I know the truth, who else is keeping the record. I never got wind of any concern while I was here. Many knew who you were and that helped me," I explained.

"The history and memory of events is not the only record. Just as in the old Celtic times when the aristocracy was made up of not only warriors but also scholars; the Brehons (men of law), Poets (immortalizers of men and women), Druids (religious leaders), and Historians (recorders of deeds and misdeeds of individuals and families), so there are Historians today, keeping records secretly so that when the hour of Liberation comes to Ireland, all will know the truth about events and people," mom explained.

"In the aftermath of the Reformation and the Elizabethan Settlement of Leinster and Munster, this scholarly tradition of the Historian was kept alive in the Franciscan Friary at Donegal Town between 1632 and 1636 by the 'Four Masters.' They drew on ancient texts and contemporary witnesses to record the "Annals of the History of Ireland" so it would not be lost, or worse, tainted by the conquering English and their perverted slant and rewriting of History.

"In the early 1920s both sides of the Civil War, the Pro-Treaty and anti-Treaty leaders held a secret meeting to establish a new History of

Ireland. It covered the period from the establishment of The Society of United Irishmen and the Risings of the 1790s and early 1800s, through the 1848 and 1867 Risings, and the Dynamite Campaign of the 1880s, then the rise of the Irish Republican Brotherhood and the 1916 Easter Rising, the Tan War and the un-Civil War.

"Each side nominated two men of undisputable integrity who were accepted by the other side, and the four were given the task of recording and writing the history of the last 130 years. Their names were kept secret down to this very day. They took the name of the earlier Historians, 'The Four Masters.'

"Their work is still being worked on since to my knowledge they are all still alive. They collaborate where they can, but each has their own style and insights. It's not so much that each has their own slant, for they are in agreement as to the particulars and the general story, but each has a unique perspective which adds color, different shades, to the same drawing sketched by all four.

"To this day no one except for a handful knows of their existence let alone their identity. It is the one great secret from the Civil War period. The leadership on both sides of the Civil War understood the need for a professional, universal, and insightful rendering of the most recent tragedies of Irish History. When their Annals are released it will cause quite a stir in Ireland and England, not the least from the fact that these authorities have undertaken such a monumental project which they have collected, written up, reworked, revised, consulted the other Masters about, then painted from their palate on the mural of nearly two hundred years now.

"There have been whispered rumors that the Masters have continued the work right down to the present day, and I certainly hope they have," mom said.

"And you want to make sure that they record the truth about granda," I concluded.

"Actually no. It's my understanding that they have da's story right. They have decided to let the truth about da out of the bag without tipping their hat to their very existence. God only knows when the official Annals or History of theirs' will be released, but for my sake they have decided to set the record straight, without showing themselves or the whole of their sacred work. They are going to honor this old woman by doing so," mom explained.

"Honor the 'Hope' of another time that they themselves know so well," I suggested.

"Aye, something like that."

"Why don't they just come out with what they have? Surely enough time has passed since the early stuff for people to deal with the truth of the facts. They could not only leave the later, more recent stuff out, they could not mention their continued work on the recent Troubles."

"Well Rudy, I have no doubt the Masters have considered this very course of action themselves, but I suspect, and it is only my suspicion mind you, that there are some people and families, not to mention some political parties and countries that will be badly depicted and sorely affected by their Annals.

"For example, our own President Woodrow Wilson, members of our Senate and negotiating Peace Treaty team at the Versailles Treaty, so I am to understand, were bought off from dealing justly with Ireland and Sinn Fein by promises and arrangements made by the British in favor of the United States' presence and power in Latin and South America. The Brits were broke after World War I and they had to divest themselves from many economic and trade interests in the Western Hemisphere. They made a deal with the US that allowed the United States to dominate things 'south' of the US border in Central and South America, and they assured the US that Ireland would be treated justly and pacified as far as possible.

"American Anglophiles took the Brits at their word, and the US became the dominant force in much of Latin and South America, and they kept American official interest clear of Ireland."

"Damn. They don't teach that in history or political science classes. And your Four Masters have the facts to back this story up?" I asked incredulously.

"Rudy, as I said, these are only things I have been led to believe. I have no actual knowledge that the Masters are dealing with these matters specifically, but this is the kind of material they would be dealing with, with adequate proof to support their claims.

"I have also heard that your man Winston Churchill's 'heavy handed' dealing with the Easter Rebellion and his threats to seize the neutral Irish ports during World War II stem in part from his disgust of the Irish Brigade's work for the Orange Free State during the Boer War. He hated the Nationalist Irish for siding with the rebel Boers, and personally sought vengeance against Sean McBride who was in South Africa as part of the

Irish contingent. Churchill got his pound of flesh when McBride was shot after the Easter Rebellion," mom clarified.

She continued, "Some will argue that Churchill was not involved in any of the individual reprisals against the leaders, specifically McBride. But when it came to the challenge to the British Empire, Churchill was of one mind to punish and make examples of any and all who were disloyal, especially the Irish.

"Some even claim that after the un-Civil War that Churchill, now out of the British Government, had some incriminating evidence about some great matter that he held over DeValera's head. To DeV's credit he didn't give in to Churchill's threats and demands over the ports in 1940, 41 and 42, but neither did DeV allow the Nazi German air force or navy use of neutral Eire for their benefit. DeV's cooperation with Churchill had less to do with any military threat than the disclosure of some secret Churchill had about DeVelera, so it is said. Maybe a secret about what Dev knew about the death of Michael Collins?

"These are hushed whispers only exchanged by a few conspirators. Who knows for sure either way? But a betting person would be wise to lay money down that our Four Masters know and will eventually expose all, like a dynamite explosive charge.

"But again, Rudy, these are just speculations and suggestions by an old Irish woman. Nothing concrete at this point. Just speculative suggestions, right?"

"All right mom. But I think I got about four layers of answers from you. But where do you get all this stuff, these speculations as you call them? You don't know the Four Masters, you don't know what is in their Annals for sure other than the obvious. But you hint at some pretty explosive stuff. So, from where?" I asked.

"There is an old maxim, German I think, 'Everything comes to he who waits'" mom smiled, or was it a grin? There is a difference, a big difference, between the two, and I didn't know which one I was getting.

Our contact, Jerry Clare, was waiting for us in the Common Room. He was elderly and looked as if he was as old as the Saint Brendan's Home itself. But looks are often deceiving, and he was spry, in good agile health, and as intellectually sharp as a razor. He too had a smile that bordered on a grin that made me pause several times during our visit. He would often grin at me in this hybrid smirk, as if he were patronizing me. But to mom, he was not just courteous and polite, he was clearly cordial and doting.

He addressed mom, "My dear 'Hope', you have been through so much, endured so much. I apologize for our countries clouding your da's reputation. He was neither a traitor nor a coward. Any indiscretions you experienced all those many years ago, or of late, were unwarranted, undeserved and misdirected. I apologize to you and your whole family.

"I fear that there was so much pain and suffering during the Civil War that the survivors needed to take out their misery on someone, namely your da, 'Hope', and then you fell victim to their cathartic release of placing blame for their pain on some one who could not, or would not, defend themselves, or explain themselves.

"Some times being honorable by being silent speaks loudly and in volumes. As I understand it your da, 'Hope,' understood more pain would come from his defending himself than to simply vanish and let the wounded wallow in their misery, that was real enough, and their accusations, that were spectacularly erroneous.

"'Hope,' you tasted some of the falsely placed gall when you came here to Ireland those many years ago, and I hope your present intentions are pure, namely to clear your father's reputation and not revenge. I sincerely hope you are not bent on revenge against those who through jealously, ignorance, or deceit, held you and your father in disrepute."

Then Jerry looked at me and with that holier than thou smirk, and in a very condescending tone said, "As for yourself, Rudy, I wonder, did you ever experience any discrimination by members of Oglaigh na hEireann in your time here? Or for that matter, by any one here in Ireland? If so I apologize to you specifically. I would hope that you were man enough to consider the source, or take into account that the slight to you was probably only 'slight' after all these years."

I smirked back at him, and giving a little exhale puff, I said, "You need not patronize me, I came here as pure as the driven snow, knowing bits of my families history. I got involved in the recent round of the Troubles, mostly through and because of my mammy, I did what I did for the cause of Irish Liberty. If I was shunned or insulted I was as ignorant of it as a baby.

"I frankly don't give a shit whether any one questions my worth, dedication, commitment and loyalty. I did things that I didn't have to do. I'm a second generation American first, and half Irish second. I forged friendships and am loyal to Ireland as the next man . . . and my mom," I said matter of factly, a little tired of his looks and tone toward me.

The smirk was gone from his face and before my mom could chastise me for being rude I added, "I've done things here and in Asia that I am ashamed of and proud of at the same time. I'd match my worth against any man, living or dead, including the likes of you. It's obvious your condescending tone directed at me is a parody of what you claim to be apologizing to my mother for as being directed at our family for a misunderstanding about my granda.

"My mother is tired of fighting the fight under a cloud. Do right by her and that is enough. I certainly have no expectations. This 'Annals' and 'Four Masters' stuff is getting way out of touch with reality, if you ask me, and you are an example of the erudite tradition of these Masters. What is needed in Ireland, North and South is leadership, faithfulness, and less selfishness. Less ego trips, less looking out for one's self, and more doing for Ireland.

"What is needed is a strong dose of 'making history,' not 'writing history.' I teach the stuff back home in America. But I'm telling you an ounce of doing out weighs a ton of talking. It's just that simple.

"There. I'm done. Sorry mom if I embarrassed you, but I've done more than most and I don't care if any one knows the 'truth' or not. I didn't do things for the truth, I did them because they needed to be done and I had no doubt that it was me or nobody.

"So, to sit around and ruminate about what happened by whom is superfluous. As long as it was done, that's the point. Those who did what needed to be done know who did what. Let the rest of them talk. If lies are spread let those in the know sort it out.

"I still can't believe that certain people who knew what my granda did, let him hang out to dry all these years. That's not only a crime, its immoral, unethical and as something of a representative of the Four masters who know what's what, it was unprofessional. My mother has indicated the delicacies of granda's circumstances and the possible repercussions that might arise if the matter is not handled delicately. Secrets might be exposed, like the Annals and the Four Masters themselves. Fine. But let some one get off their arse and do something to clear the air. Do something besides write the Annals. Do something constructive for God's sake, my granda's sake, and my mother's sake."

At that I stormed out of the building and left mom and Jerry to sort out what would and could be done. If it wasn't important to mom I'd have let the whole issue go to hell in a hand basket, as my granny used to say.

It started to rain, but only slightly. Just enough to dampen the mood even more. After half an hour, I was soaked and could feel a chill coming on when mom emerged from Saint Brendan's Home.

She walked to me, then by me, saying, "Come on."

"Lets get a cab. I'm soaked and chilled to the bone," I said.

"And whose fault is that, Rudy?"

"I'd say either yours or Jerry's."

"Nice try. You are striking out in every inning today. You bit on curve balls in there with Jerry, and my change up has you guessing. You are off balance and not helping the team, Rudy. Not helping it at all."

"Well, every one has a bad day. Every team I've played for I've given my all for. In case you didn't realize it Jerry was at a loss for words back there. I think I got some extra bases by landing a few hits."

"Well you've gotten it wrong again slugger. Jerry was not lacking in words. He's pitching your granda's reputation as we speak.

"He knew granda and it was he who granda went to in Cork to get the word out to Collins via Dalton. He was Dalton's aid. He was under orders to keep quiet about what granda did and said for fear of antagonizing Civil War victims and their families."

"All these years he just kept quiet? For fear of antagonizing certain people? What about granda? Wasn't he antagonized? What about you? What about our family?" I asked.

"Apparently granda agreed to take the rap. He was then helped out of Ireland and given some start up money to go on the run. He did it for Ireland."

"Amazing! Did granda ever tell you that's what happened? Is this Jerry's story? You believe Jerry's story? What proof does he offer about his story?"

"Rudy, what does he have to gain in telling me this if it is a lie? But in hindsight what Jerry says makes sense. Things I remember both in Canada and in the early days in Hartford are now clear to me. And now Jerry is going to do some thing about it."

"What is your man Jerry going to do?"

"He has a friend at the paper and he's going to give an account of granda's story. The trumped up reason was a visit by granda's daughter, calling on an old friend here in Dublin. Jerry will take all the heat and glory."

I concluded, "Well, if you are satisfied. All's well that ends well."

"Not quite. We are now going to discuss your rude, insensitive, and brash comments towards your elders, Rudy."

"All right, but did you give him hell for playing me for the fool?"

Mom stopped walking and just looked at me for about five seconds, then turned away and kept walking.

Needless to say, it was a long cab ride back to the hotel. Supper was equally uncomfortable. Bed and sleep came as a relief, not a reward.

I needed to go up North, even though the Nationalist Areas of Belfast, Derry, and dozens of other towns were engulfed in demonstrations and riots because of the Hunger Strike. It was obvious that Thatcher was going to let Sands and the rest of the Strikers die. Thatcher's intransigence ignited and united the Nationalist communities as nothing had since "Bloody Sunday" nine years earlier.

World opinion turned against Britain as much as it Had against the United States because of the malaise in Vietnam. All I could envision was that I was constantly finding myself in worlds of chaos and death. The difference was, in the North of Ireland I knew civilians, soldiers, and prisoners more Intimately. I wasn't simply trying to survive in Ireland, I was committed to long term change.

Back North To Help A Friend

I called Denny and made arrangements to go by train up to Belfast. He said he'd send his usual man at the usual time to collect me at the usual place.

As I disembarked the train in Belfast, I sought out a bearded man wearing spectacles and a duncher standing next to a black taxi. I approached and asked if he still possessed a driver's license, to which he replied, "Fuck off."

As I piled in I replied, "Right."

He peeled out and headed into traffic and before I knew it we were in familiar territory along some back streets off the Falls. West Belfast didn't get better or worse, it simmered like a fine Irish stew, the thick broth, the aroma, the vegetables and meat slowly cooking together to form a lumpy mush in a Guinness bath over a low flame. If the stew could have the meat and veggies form rows like cramped housing terraces it would be Belfast stew.

Denny finally said, "It's good to see you Rudy. You're sorely missed. As usual, things have gone from bad to worse and it's a mess all around. The 'hunger strike,' the demonstrations, the Brit Military and the RUC, and the Loyalists, it's gone from bad to worse."

"The same old shite and new shite, huh?"

"Aye. I'm in a bit of a bind myself. It seems that some high and mighty potentate has accused me of ordering the shite that befell the Officials a few years back. You were turning the O-boys over to that Brit officer who was running you, well thought he was running you. What was your man's name again Rudy?"

"Major Somerville."

"Aye, that's your man. With all that's going on with the hunger strike and the demonstrations and riots, the Army Council has nothing better to do than accuse me of ordering those Officials to be handed over to your Major Summerville for some rough treatment. The Army Council is making nice with the old Officials and as a plum they have offered to look into the selling out of their young toughs to the Major. My name came up so I might be the sacrificial lamb," Denny explained.

"Like hell you will. Get me an interview with who ever and I'll settle this once and for all."

"I was hoping you'd understand and help an old friend."

"It was me who turned the names over, not you. You confirmed that they were all assholes besides being Officials. Get me an interview. I'll explain and leave you entirely out of it. This politics of positioning really pisses me off Denny."

"Aye, it's the stage we're going through at he moment. I fear as we go more political we'll be doing more of it all the time. I can see a day when we'll put the gun aside so the leaders can wear suits, sit at the political table and dabble and doodle in 'politics' instead of making headway towards real unity, liberty and freedom."

"Ah Denny, you always were a smooth talker who beat around the bush just keeping your eyes on the ground ahead of you and not bothering to speculate or condemn. That's why I love Denny," I smiled up at him in the rear view mirror as he wove the taxi down narrow streets making sure we were not being tailed.

Periodically Denny looked up out the wind screen or out his side window, "Fucken helicopters. They are getting sophisticated. The 'eye in the sky,' you know. The Brit bastards."

"Anyone still out of the Kesh besides you?"

"Damn few Rudy. Their eyes are not only looking down from the skies, they have ears in rooms, houses and streets. At times they seem to know what we are going to do before we decide to do it."

"That's the work of spies and touts, Denny. It was only a matter of time that they turned to the clandestine service. The Brits have always been good at it. And Ireland being so poor, a few quid here a few quid there and information can be bought for a reasonable price. It's Britain's virtue and Ireland's vice," I mused.

"Here we are. You'll be hold up here till I can arrange a meeting for you. Keep inside to be safe Rudy. We don't need to lose you now."

I was holdup in a flat with threadbare carpet over creaking floorboards, sooty windows with stitch repaired curtains, paint faded walls with cracks and chips that certainly dated from and witnessed the German bombing of Belfast early in World War II. The furniture was sparse and the place was as rickety as bombed buildings after the Tet Offensive in 1968 Vietnam that I had witnessed. The difference was that Vietnam was actual war, whereas in west Belfast it was poverty. Well, I thought, maybe Marx was right after all, poverty is the residue of class war, sectarian war, national liberation warfare.

I told myself to slow down, to stop getting too philosophical, and get a game plan for meeting who ever from the Army Council to defend Denny.

I found a stained box spring on the floor of a second storey bedroom. I spread my coat over the stains, rolled up a pair of jeans for a pillow, stretched out and promptly fell asleep.

I heard someone enter downstairs and call out my name. It wasn't Denny so I just laid there until who ever started up the steps. I was behind the door, my sound muffled by the visitor's racket on the stairway. With no other sound discernable, I surmised he was alone which could mean one or a combination of things. A whispered "Rudy" distracted my thought.

First he stuck his head in, then his whole body as he saw my coat and jeans on the bed. I had his arm up his back and my free hand at his throat when he said "Rudy, its me Ruairi."

Even though I was behind him I recognized Ruairi. He was one of the regulars working with Brendan back when I was a student here some years earlier.

"Jaysus, Ruairi, I was expecting someone else."

"Aye, Denny. But they have sent me to get you. Denny will be there, he's OK. I think you will clear him of the accusations. It's mostly politics, making nice to the stickies for solidarity and all, unfortunately we have sunk that low," Ruairi explained.

"And how have you been Ruairi? With so many lifted, how are you managing?" I asked. The second I asked it I wish I hadn't. I hoped he didn't take my questioning as an accusation. I quickly said, "I don't mean anything by my question, I just wonder how you are doing," I said by way of apology.

"No offense taken Rudy. The way things have gone the past couple of years you really don't know who to trust. Now they are sniffing around Denny. He is square on. Always has been.

"What have you been up to back home? Denny is pretty tight mouthed. Doesn't say a thing about you or your wife and her sister. What ever happened to their brother? He was the long distance man here in Belfast. Any news?"

"Ruairi, even if I knew the where a bouts of Danny Conlon, you understand I wouldn't tell a soul. I don't think Barbrie or Eve know either. We hear nothing and that is good news. He had contacts in the East, Czechoslovakia I think, but who the hell knows," I shrugged.

"You married Ruairi, seeing any body seriously?"

"Not during the war. Too much can get fucked."

"Aye. Wise man. Go it alone till victory."

"Aye, till victory," Ruairi said without conviction.

My antenna was up and running now and I suspected Ruairi was more than just curious. We had suspected someone close to what was happening in the Falls area to being a tout to the Brits and RUC. You never wanted to be too casual about naming someone or accusing someone, but I just had this feeling. I'd talk to Denny about him, and explain the conversation we just had and explain my gut reaction.

We were in Andersonstown and my memory was trying to process streets, buildings, terraces, stores, and public houses. Nothing was looking specifically noticeable. We turned up a narrow lane while several cars blocked the end of the street we had just come down. We went through a home, emerging in an ally, went down a few gardens, went through another terrace house, entered another car, a taxi this time and went to the end of the block, turned up a couple of streets, turned again went to the middle of the block and I was shuffled out not too ceremoniously into a non-descript terrace house with plenty of armed men watching out windows from behind dirty lace curtains.

The dwelling was again rough. Dingy, not from lack of trying to keep it clean, but from wear and tear, fried food, and poverty. I smelt greasy chips. The odor hung in the air, clung to the surfaces and fabric of the place as if it belonged here. It wasn't the buildings that were depressing, it was the permanence of it all. Not much had changed.

There were several men sitting at a table and I was motioned to a chair on the long side of the table. It was cramped and no one asked if I wanted a cup of tea. This was going to be a short meeting I gathered.

Denny was conspicuously absent. Some around the room I recognized, others at the table Denny would fill me in about later. I recognized Seamus Twomey, Dathie O'Connell and a young man named Martin from Derry recently released from a six month sentence in the Republic. Joe Cahill, who I vaguely knew, presided and came right to the point.

"Did your man Denny direct you to have the Brits arrest certain Officials?" Cahill asked.

Just as bluntly I answered, "No."

"Who did?"

"Look, I will categorically say that Denny didn't, but I will not identify who did. The first group whose names I gave to the Brits I had personal contact with and they were running drugs. Their leader was a man named Eddy and he was a low life ass wipe who deserved much worse than the Brits gave him. The second group, were Officials who were also scum bags who dealt in all sorts of unsavory things and they were not held in high esteem by the Official leadership here in Belfast. I would go so far as to say their removal was if not sanctioned officially by the Official leadership it certainly was quite acceptable to them.

"Mac Stiofain questioned me about handing them over to the Brits back in late 71 or early 72 and he accepted it. He didn't sanction it because he came into it after the fact. He warned me about going it alone. My info strengthened my relationship with a Brit Major whom I was double crossing as I am sure you all know. In the process I removed some scum from the scene if not with the blessing of both the Official and Provisional leadership, then at least their nod in hindsight."

What I didn't mention was that Mac Stiofain's right hand man, Jimmy, gave me the names of the Officials. I assumed Mac Stiofain knew these men and had OKed their sale. But on reflection now, maybe he didn't, and Jimmy did it on his own. That would explain why he questioned me back in the early 70s. Maybe Jimmy was going it alone. Settling some scores, and I was the innocent patsy. I didn't care then and I didn't much care now. I wasn't going to sell Danny, Mac Stiofain or Jimmy out now.

"Denny had no part in it. Period. That is my story, it's the truth, its factual and it's final," I concluded.

Cahill searched the faces of his colleagues, and seeing no signs of questions, he abruptly said, "Thanks Mr. Castle. Say hello to your mother. I take it she is still in the Free State? I also assume she does not know the nature of this inquiry?"

"Correct."

With that, I was whisked away by surreptitious routes out of Andersontown into the Falls and dropped off at Denny's place.

I went up to his door and before I could knock he flung it open and greeted me with a big smile. He yelled to his wife that we were going out for a bit.

We walked past St. Peter's Pro-Cathedral and I told him what happened at the enquiry, what was asked and what was said. My descriptions of the men I did not know were sound enough for him to identify those mystery men. "All the chiefs of the clans," he said. "Let's hope this shite is over."

"Aye. By the way, your man Ruairi picked me up for the meeting. He was awful curious about the where a bouts of Danny Conlon. He used to be sound, but there was some thing about his inquiry about Danny that seemed off. Is he alright?"

"It's interesting you mention that. I've had my suspicions for a couple of years. Nothing specific, just a feeling. I'll have him looked into, he may have turned. There has been a lot of that going around as of late," Denny concluded.

I stayed at Denny's and was planning on returning to Dublin as soon as Denny got the all clear sign from his case. Two days were to pass before the all is well with Denny came down the line.

"Denny, I've felt guilty as hell that I haven't been able to try at least to visit people in the Kesh, especially Brendan. I hope you could get word to him that I have asked about him."

"Aye, I have mentioned you to folks who have had visits there, telling them, if possible to mention you, and your concerns," Denny reassured me.

No Clean Getaway

As I was planning to make arrangement to leave by train, Denny and I were contacted by an old friend, Mac Stiofain's man Jimmy.

"Rudy, how are you? How have you been?" I wasn't given any time to reply. He continued, "I hear you cleared Denny with the Council. Good. I also understand that you mentioned Mac Stiofain's questioning you back in the 70s and didn't mention my name to any one then or now. I owe you Rudy. Those guys were real shite cases. Getting them off the street was a good deed."

"You played me Jimmy. It was all right since I could look them all in the face, back in 1971 or 72 and now and say Denny was not involved. That was the important thing.

"So Jimmy, how are you?"

Jimmy hesitated, looked first at Denny and then took me in and said, "In some ways every thing has changed. Some good people have been killed. Others have been locked up. Some have just been brushed aside.

"The organization looks like a tea strainer, more holes than metal. We leak everything, liquid and leaves. Personally I think everything is a mess. Every one questions every thing, no one trusts any one, and people are sold for a fiver. What a world."

I smiled at Jimmy, then at Denny, finally saying, "Alright, now give me the bad news."

We all laughed. I said, "If it wasn't so damn serious it would be funny. But with so many leaders out of the way it's difficult to settle on a handful of real and legitimate leaders. Denny says it ultimately comes down to attrition. Who ever is left standing is the leader for a day, week or month, regardless of leadership qualities. This is no way to lead the Movement, the war, or the soldiers."

Jimmy smiled and said, "Well put Rudy. Are you available for a year or ten? We sure as hell could use the likes of you. You have brains and understand what is needed. Your activity is legend to all of us, even if your exact identity is anonymous, and your identity is secure with a select handful. We really could use you Rudy."

"Kind words Jimmy. I would if I could, but I can't so I won't. I have a family now and I'm needed back home."

"I know. I hear things periodically, whispered by the chosen few. We all wish you the very best and are truly beholding to you for your participation in the past. We are better off for it."

"Jaysus, Jimmy," I complained, "You are really laying it on thick. Next Denny will start on me and the ambush will be complete."

"Alright. Alright, enough of that shite. But I do have something of interest for you. Are you planning to leave soon. I see your bag here. Back to Dublin, then home?"

"Aye, that's it. Why? What's up?"

"Well, do you remember that academic conference you went to in Dublin a few years back, and you encountered a wanker named Edward Worthington?"

"Aye. I mentioned him not only to our people, but to Major Summerville. I figured a double dose of shit should come his way. Why?"

"He's up here now, at Queen's working with and for people in your old department. Word has it he has his eye on your professor Smyth. He is a graduate student getting close to professors, their files, notes, contacts, etc. You said he was a snake in the grass. He could really screw up Smyth's life. I just thought you would like to know before you left the North.

"I don't know if any one could or should do anything about him. I just thought you might like to know. Denny here might be able to get more info for you should you be interested in looking into this matter before you head home."

We chatted a bit longer, and after Jimmy left, I said that I had no doubts that he was set up with Professor Jones who was a contact for the British Major when I was here. I also suspected Smyth remembered him and was wise to him. But I felt I might just look into the matter all the same.

I called my mother in Dublin and said I needed to stay a couple of days longer. I suggested she could visit the family in County Down without me. If I got back early I could always find my way the twenty miles to Saintfield, where the relatives lived, to find her.

Next I called Professor Smyth and asked if I might have a word with him ASAP.

I caught up with Smyth about half an hour later at Queen's and suggested we go over to the student cafeteria for a drink. Along the way I mentioned Edward Worthington and the word I got from a reliable source that he was zeroing in on him.

Smyth said, "Aye, I'm onto him alright. I remembered Mr. Worthington from down in Dublin, and I remember your comments to me concerning his obvious surveillance of students there who were IRA sympathizers or members. Yes I am quite aware of what he is about and that he seems friendly enough to me. I am being cautious."

"Do you know where his lodging is located?" I said as I smiled at Smyth.

"No, not right off hand, but I can discretely inquire about it."

"The sooner the better. I'll be leaving for home soon and the sooner I can get any information on where he lives the better. I need to check this wanker out. Possibly by tomorrow?"

"Maybe even tonight. He fancies a young student who works a bit in the department. She was in the department as we left for here, I'll talk to her and when I have something I'll call you, where, at Denny's?"

"Aye."

"If I don't see you before you leave, safe home Rudy."

An hour later Smyth was true to his word and passed along Worthington's address. I had Denny drop me off at the corner of University Road and University Street. I walked along University Street untill I came to Worthington's address and I simply killed time till I saw him exit his residence with a young lady in tow.

I waited a few minutes then I crossed over, entered the building. I knocked on the first door and asked the student where Worthington was holed up. Up at number 6 he said. I hoped Denny's fake glasses and hat adequately camouflaged my appearance.

I knocked on the door in the event he had a roommate. No response. Tweaking his lock with Denny's penknife took only a second and I was in. For all appearances it was a typical student's room, maybe a bit neater than most. *Maybe too neat for a student*, I thought.

I immediately went to work. I just looked about, I didn't roust the place. I'd rather he not be aware that anyone was checking him out. I wanted him smug in the feeling that he was above suspicion and too smart for the IRA.

I eventually found a paper taped to the bottom of a desk drawer. There were several names listed and some had check marks. Although I didn't know what the check marks indicated, I did recognize some of the names. Of course Smyth's name appeared followed by a check mark. I recognized a few other names from the faculty, all native Irish that meant Nationalist leaning (though discretely) and Catholic (possibly practicing). Suspected enemies all in the eyes of the authorities.

The name that caught my attention as being completely out of line was Jerry Clare's, my Mother's contact from back in Dublin. Now what the hell was his name doing on Worthington's roster? And up here in Belfast?

I memorized the names, put the paper back under the desk drawer, took a quick look around to be certain that all seemed as it was when I arrived. Then I slipped out and found Denny's cab down a block.

On returning to Denny's, I quickly jotted down the names from the list and said that I would share it with Smyth and leave it up to him to inform the people listed, or not, that they may be under surveillance by the authorities.

I talked at great length with Denny about Jerry Clare, who he was and what he represented. I continued to wonder why his name was on the list. Neither of us could sort it out.

I thought I might contact Smyth and pick his brain, But then thought better of it. Possibly the further I stayed away from him the better for him. My relationship with him had caused him grief in the past and I didn't want to rekindle that inferno for him again.

As awkward as it would be, the obvious thing was to contact Clare when I got back to Dublin. But Worthington was here in Belfast and I wanted to deal with him before I left in forty-eight hours.

I was at a loss when Denny suggested someone I might run this by. "Joe Cahill might have some inkling about this," Denny mused. "I'll track him down and see if we can have a word with the man."

Two hours later we were sitting with Cahill in a house off the Falls Road. I explained how I came to know Jerry Clare, who he was and what he represented. I pleaded with Cahill to keep this information in the strictest confidence. "He has broken the silence about the Four masters to placate my mother. He is going to clear my granda's name for her. It's important to her and she hasn't that many years left. Clare is sticking his neck out for my mammy by possibly revealing the existence of these historians and their history."

Cahill nodded and said he would be discrete.

I also explained how I knew Edward Worthington and what he represented. Then I simply asked, "Do you have any idea why and how this is all connected?"

Joe Cahill put his hand up near his mouth as if he were going to utter something profound that he had drawn from the back of his mind but wished to keep it in a hushed tone. But what he said was, "I have no idea. But I'll check with some people and get back with you. I will be very careful Mr. Castle, so no need to worry, very careful in deed."

I explained that I was due back in Dublin to be with my mother in two days, and then we were off to the States.

He bobbed his head and said, "OK, I'll do what I can."

Denny and I returned to his place and waited for news from Cahill. We had a short wait. About an hour later he called and said the mail had arrived and Denny had a letter. This was a signal that he had some information and to meet him at a pub up on the Springdale Road.

We drove around making sure we weren't being tailed for about half an hour before we sauntered into the establishment and found his table in a secluded niche.

"Boys. I got nothing for you Rudy on Jerry Clare. Sorry. But your Mr. Worthington has made some inquiries about you Rudy and your time here in Belfast a year or two ago. You might want to check up on that before you return home."

I thanked Joe, and Denny and I slid out of the bar and headed back to Denny's place. "I wonder what his infatuation with you is?" Denny asked. It was rhetorical, but I answered non-the-less.

"He must be checking out stuff for my friends at the friendly Belfast RUC and Special Branch. Probably the wankers who I had a run in with back there when Barb, Eve, Paul and my mammy visited. I'm sure they get the word when I enter the country and maybe "Little Eddy" is helping them put some chronology around my visits and some shit we did over the years.

"The Brits are good at keeping tabs on that sort of shit and maybe somebody has given the RUC stooges a heads up on the process and us in general and me in particular. You've got to be really careful Denny. They can pick you up any time, and we sure as hell can't afford to lose you."

"You really think they are on to something, Rudy?"

"Some time back we thought there was a tout, and my man got to Sean Keen. I still think we are correct in looking for another one." Denny nodded. "Now I think we have somebody putting two and two together and adding up to us. The tout, bruised egos at the RUC, some dinged G-men, and now Worthington . . . this is adding up to four in my book Denny. If twos company and threes a crowd, four is a cluster fuck. You know what I mean?"

"It's the same old fecken mess Rudy. We are infiltrated, sold out, betrayed, locked up, and the whole Movement has taken another step backwards," Denny mused.

"Let's try to keep up with the immediate problem. Bring me back to University Street. If you have your duncher and eye glasses with you, I'll need to borrow them again.

Wearing two-thirds of Denny's official disguise I returned to Worthington's flat after checking from the street that no light seemed to be on in his apartment. Using Denny's pocket knife I entered Worthington's flat and began to look around again. I went to areas that I had skipped over before.

I found nothing. I went through his satchel and leafed through some books and came up with nothing. In disgust I returned to the desk drawer, pulled it out, flipped it over and saw that the paper was still taped to the bottom, but clearly it had been tampered with since I had checked it out yesterday.

Retrieving it I opened it and was awe struck. Next to Smyth's name I now found my name penned in parenthesis. *What the hell?*

I returned everything to its place and carefully exited the building without being seen. As I headed down University Street to meet up with Denny, I encountered Worthington coming toward me obviously on his way back to his apartment with a young lady in tow. Whew, I was lucky to be out of there and he was lucky to be going in there with such a cute girl. My only concession to wishful thinking was that I hoped the girl had venereal disease!

On returning to Denny, I exhaled heavily, gave him back his gear, and asked, "You sure this car has been fumigated?"

"Aye, like the Royal Vic Hospital. All sanitary like," was Denny's reply.

"Well, we are going to need some antiseptic cleaning of our own," I commented.

I explained my lone discovery, namely my name added to the list behind Smyth's name.

"I'll warn Smyth tomorrow and contact my mom in person down in Dublin. I'll call the college back home and explain a fantastic opportunity has come up, and then I'll call Barbrie and let her know that I'm staying for a bit longer. I'm sure she'll be thrilled. I'll come back to Dublin as soon as I can wind things up here."

Barbrie was not pleased, but she resigned herself to the stated fact that I was doing a follow up on some folklore research with some storytellers. The college was bought off with the possibility of a travel program for students to come to Donegal to hear the last of the storytellers. It was my mother, Kathryn Mary Castle who was buying none of it.

"What's up, Rudy?" mom asked.

"I'm not going to tell you that 'you don't want to know,' because you really will want to know. But the rules are my terms, no negotiations. You understand?"

Few times in my life had I given such an ultimatum to my mother, any type of ultimatum. This being the case she knew it was important.

This being the case, she hesitatingly agreed.

I explained Worthington, the threat to Smyth, the potentially dangerous identification of Jerry Clare, and the inclusion of my name on his roster of persons of interest, that are 'suspect,' aka, enemies of the British Statelet of Northern Ireland.

If her concern for Clare was great, her alarm for me was palpable, enough so that I feared she might renege on our "my terms" agreement.

"You must go back home to be with Barbrie and the children. While I stay here in Belfast, and before you return home to confirm my Irish Studies story, you can go see Clare and warn him of the potential danger that Worthington poses. Leave out the sorted details, just tell him an acquaintance passed on the info that he was on Worthington's list of persons of interest, along with several names including mine, concerning God knows what. Tell him that through me you know Worthington to be a British spy, a liar, and a government sponsored *agent provocateur.*

"If he doesn't buy it, so be it. We tried to warn him."

Mom was not too pleased, but a deal was a deal, and as I explained to her, her role was crucial for this ruse to be pulled off. She reluctantly agreed to everything and fulfilled the plan to the letter.

Jerome "Jerry" Clare was warned, and mom was able to convince him that the threat was real and truly dangerous to him and his friend and their credibility. She also convinced Barbrie that my extended work for the Irish Studies program was legit. She even contacted the school and gave a glowing report on my efforts to establish a first class Irish Studies Program in Donegal focusing on Story-Telling, what would eventually be dubbed Oral History, and other cultural phenomenon like wakes, banshees, and match makers to mention a few.

———————————————

Speaking of wakes, Thatcher's Hunger Strike policy was resulting in wakes that were indistinguishable from protests, many of which turned into riots. If the Iron Lady was obstinate, the Hunger Strikers were equally committed. However, the Striker's families began to waver in their support of the Strike. Some Catholic clergy encouraged them to intervene to Prevent the death of their loved ones.

Personally, I was torn between support and sympathy. Being in the North gave me a new perspective and a renewed commitment to change.

An Old Adversary

I was reacquainted with some old friends during my extended stay in Belfast. I ditched everything not necessary. I was traveling light, with one change of socks and underwear, my tooth brush and tooth paste, and wearing two shirts that I could inter change for effect. No razor, no after shave, no deodorant; I wanted Worthington, when the time came, to smell the terror that was about to befall him.

Denny found me a bed close to his place so I could have some distance if I needed it, but if I needed him he was close enough to help. We were both right off Divis Street, in the shadow of the Divis apartments.

After discussing my strategy with Denny, I struck out to confront little Eddy Worthington. I was planning to accidentally bump into him and slowly confront him as a British stool pigeon. I figured the shock of seeing me, then my questioning him about his activities and intentions, and finally my accusing him of playing the game of agent provocateur, and in the process falsely accusing innocent people of criminal and treasonous activity, would really rattle him.

I intended to quiz him on not only his intentions, but on whom, besides Smyth and myself, he intended to black list. I wanted to make these accusations as public as possible, to not only discredit him but to expose him to the people he intended to victimize.

I thought confronting him at Queen's would be just the first step in a marathon of misery for the prick.

Denny thought it sounded like a good tactic, but he worried that being in Belfast in plain sight, the authorities might catch up with me.

I said that just about the time people started to focus again as the dust was settling, I would drop out of sight, head for Donegal and try to set up the Irish Studies Program I had used as an excuse for staying in Ireland.

I went directly to Queen's and called on my friend Professor Smyth. I thought I would bring him up to speed on my plan of attack. He was just returning to his office and so we had a minute or two to discuss my plan.

"Well Rudy, there is nothing like a head on confrontation. I suspect your Mr. Worthington will be around shortly. He often hangs around the departmental office. I suspect he scrutinizes the incoming and out going mail for everyone in the department.

"If anything is said, I'm here getting your input on a potential Irish Studies Program for my college. We will be spending time with story tellers and such over in Donegal. A likely cover, don't you think?"

"A tried and true cover story if I ever heard one," Smyth retorted with a smile, then added, "Oh my, Rudy. You are in luck. There is your boy now by the mail slots. Probably checking my mail."

I walked right up to Worthington and before he could side step me, I blurted out, "Worthingham, right? From down in Dublin met at a conference, with Professor Smyth here, right?"

"Its Worthington, Edward Worthington."

"Right. From some where in England, as I recall," I blurted.

"Yes that's right."

"You do remember me, right? We had a bit of a discussion to every ones delight about the Troubles up here. I was somewhat cautious about commenting on the Troubles being an American and all. But you were British to a fault. You mouthed some vague generalizations as I recall. Wouldn't or couldn't get specific on how to address the trouble with the Troubles as I recall. And now you are up here, I assume addressing the Troubles. Are you working with the Secretary for Northern Ireland now? Special Branch? The British Military? The RUC? What in God's name are you doing here?" I asked.

"Working on an advanced degree."

"Well I'll be. Smyth you didn't mention that our Mr. Worthinham, oh, sorry, Worthington was up here now."

Smyth started to answer when I cut him off by turning back to young Eddy and asking, "Was it my wit and charm that attracted you to the North. Certainly it wasn't the friendly atmosphere that seduced you. Or was it Smyth here? No, I suspect that you would find Professor Jones more to your political taste, right? When I worked with Jones he was professionally polite and discrete when it came to politics. I mean he had his opinion of the Troubles and was clearly Loyal in the true sense of the word, but he was not pushy. He didn't inflict his views on me in any way. He even gave me a tour of west Belfast, right down the Falls, to his wife's chagrin when she found out about it. But deep down she was proud of him for doing it and he was proud for having done it. So who are you working with, Jones?"

"Actually I split my time between Professor Smyth and Jones," he explained.

"Ah, still middle of the roading it hey? Not a bad strategy. Pick and choose. See whose doing what. Keep them under surveillance as it were. Are you doing surveillance work up here Worthingham?"

"It's Worthington. And I am a student here, that's all."

"Oh come on, I can see you working for the Brits or their subalterns. I remember how you acted in Dublin. You were scrutinizing everybody and taking mental notes of who said what. Every one down there said you were an informer. I wouldn't think it was for the Republic, you being from England. It had to be for the Brits.

"So you are a student and you keep tabs on people for the Brits. Only students, or faculty too?"

"You sir are way out of line. These wild accusations are unfounded and could lead to misunderstandings and . . . ."

Before he could finish his sentence and train of thought, I blurted out, "You are so correct, unfounded accusations could lead to damaging results. Not just some one loosing their position at a university but possible arrest. And in Northern Ireland mere accusations can lead to more than simple arrest, mere accusations often leads to imprisonment, financial ruin, divorce and worse if possible, suicide.

"So you be careful Mr. Worthingham when you confide in your handlers, be they from England or here in the North of Ireland. You could ruin somebody with a simple accusation . . . arrest, imprisonment, financial ruin, divorce, suicide, or . . . murder.

"I hear, way over in America, that the IRA doesn't take kindly to touts who spy on innocent victims, any more than Loyalists do, whose names are passed on to the authorities after being accused of anti-British, hmmm help me here Worthingham, anti-British thoughts, attitudes, questions, looks, religion, nationality, ethnicity. Which of these is it Worthingham that spikes your curiosity and leads to your accusations?"

Worthington had fled from the office, but several people were standing about open mouthed as it were, clearly in disgust. Whether at me or at Worthington I did not know or care. I concluded for those present, "In Dublin he was reputed to be a British spy eyeing and reporting on both students and faculty. So take care. Especially if any of you are Catholic, Irish, Nationalist leaning, or even Unionists who are open minded, liberal or honest.

"Many of you I've known for some time and I fear for your safety and well being because of this man."

They were all still there, dumbfounded. I turned around, mumbled laud enough for every one to hear, "It's a crime," and walked out heading down the hall towards Smyth's office.

Smyth stayed. He pressed his lips together, shrugged his shoulders and waited to register reactions. Some one finally said, "Whew. We don't need that now, do we?"

At that point every one dispersed. When he caught up with me in his office he told me of the final comment, but said he didn't know if it was directed at my accusations directed at Worthington or the fact that I made such accusations in public.

I said, "Time will tell. I suspect the jury will be split depending on just those factors that I accused Worthington of taking into account as to who he sees as good or evil."

"Rudy, I suspect you are correct on that count also," Smyth commented. "I don't know if you decapitated him or castrated him. Jaysus. It was a real God awful blood letting Rudy. I've never heard anything like it. Simply incredible. I'm glad we are on the same side and that I haven't crossed swords with you."

"Aye, we are on the same side and for that reason you must take special care of yourself with the likes of Worthington around. He is malicious, malevolent, and here in our midst.

"I should think he is only castrated, because I still have work to do with him and I want him alive, for a while at least," I smiled at Smyth.

I informed Denny of my confrontation with Worthington at Queen's. He was physically distraught at having missed that session. I assured him that I planned a few more and said that I would try to see to it that he would observe me in verbal assault mode.

Smyth contacted Denny and reported that the faculty truly appreciated my exposing Worthington as a snitch for the government, security forces, and or the British. I felt exonerated and encouraged.

Denny had a couple of his friends keep an eye on Edward Worthington. They kept track of his movements, especially after traditional university hours. Three nights after my run in with Worthington at Queen's, Denny informed me that Eddy was at an old watering hole near the University with a couple of students.

"Can your friends stick around for an hour or so? I'd like to have another conversation with Mr. Worthington and this time I do not want him walking out on me."

"I'm sure that can be arranged. I would like to hear, incognito of course, your exchange with Eddy this time. You promised," Denny pleaded.

"We'll have your boys go in ahead of time and position themselves to prevent little Eddy's escape. You can go in next and get situated within earshot.

Then I'll wander in, all innocent, and I'll confront the bastard for all to hear. It will be a thing of beauty. Like those two wankers, the one from Special Branch and the other from the Prison Service. Wham. The major difference will be that when I've wounded him sufficiently, then and only then, I'll let him slither away like the snake he is. You'll be comparing me to Saint Patrick when this is all over," I promised.

I had become deadly serious, and since there was no glee in my eyes, no smile on my face, and a hardness in my voice, Denny just looked at me and said nothing for about a minute. Then he uttered only two words, "Let's go."

Denny's friends were in place; Denny himself had gone in about five minutes ago, when I wandered in.

I slowly headed for the bar when I smiled, looked around as if to acknowledge some of the locals, and pretended to be genuinely surprised to see Eddy Worthington sitting at a table with a couple of young men. It was as if he was holding court. He was clearly older than his companions and he stopped talking in mid-speech when he saw me wandering over to his table.

As I pulled a low stool over to join his group, Denny's boys took up positions just behind him without his notice. The students did however. Tension was palpable.

"Mr. Edward Worthing . . . ton, right? **ton**."

"If you don't mind, we are having a private conversation and . . . ."

"Castle. Rudy Castle, from the good old USA. Worked with Professors Jones and Smyth and was awarded my degree a few years ago now. I come back now and then for . . . Hmm . . . special occasions.

"And twice now I run into Edward Worthington. Got it right that time didn't I Eddy? Do you go by Eddy? The more formal Edward? Huh, British and all that."

Worthington started to push his chair back and to stand up when Denny's friends each put a hand on his shoulders and pushed him back into his seat. He was truly astonished as he looked up at the rough unfriendly faces.

"Friends of yours Edward? They don't seem too friendly.

"How about you two, friends, students?"

They both nervously nodded their heads in the affirmative.

I just smiled and said, "Stick around, I want you to hear this." They both sat like scared puppies. I then returned my attention to Eddy.

"He said you were having a private conversation. Mr. Worthington is good at having private conversations.

When I first met him I was a student here at Queen's and Smyth took me down to Trinity to a conference. Worthington here was quite a fixture in Dublin. He was all British, all eyes, all ears, trolling for enemies of Britain's there in the Republic.

"A lot of Catholics, Irish Nationalists, Irish by nationality or ethnicity, critical of what was going on in the distant North, but open minded regarding the Troubles, somewhat Left and honestly searching for truth. I might also add innocent, naïve, trusting.

"Mr. Worthington here worked for the Brits, down in Dublin, finding enemies. They wanted a list of people holding dangerous political sympathies. Hardly real enemies, more imagined enemies. He could just imagine these young students, he could just imagine them in balaclavas, camouflage, and holding an Armalite, holding Republican view and singing Rebel songs . . . you know 'The Rising of the Moon,' or 'A Nation Once Again,' or 'Come Out You Black and Tans.' He could imagine it so he accused these students to his handlers.

"His accusation was enough for the Brits. He sold these young students out. He accused them and that was enough for the Brits to put their names on the list. Can you imagine these young people trying to get jobs in British companies? Loyal British companies, owned and run and operated by loyal British subjects or their lackeys?

"How long have you been here in Belfast Eddy? Can you point out those you know to be treasonous right in this pub? Not all students I'll bet. Some of these locals I can imagine.

"Aye, I know what some of you are saying to yourselves. He was acting down in the Republic just like some RUC act like in the North of Ireland, right here. All it takes is an accusation from the right person and the authorities assume you are guilty. Right Eddy? A life ruined because of your imagination and accusation.

"So I tell you young lads, don't be naïve, and trusting. This man has sold out young students like you, down in the Republic. Can you imagine whom he has accused here in the North? The two of you? How many others do you suppose? This wanker is a cancer.

"Have you turned these students names in, Eddy? What's the matter, cat got your tongue? You are quiet now, but when you report in I'll bet you will have a lot to say. Me for accusing you and the rest of this lot for listening.

"So if either of you two, or any of you others, are Catholics, or have Irish ethnicity, or are Nationalist leaning, or open minded, or Left leaning, and honest about it and have ever expressed anything other than the 'Official' British propaganda, your religion, nationality, ethnicity has condemned you in the eyes and mind of Mr. Edward Worthington here. And his keen sense has discerned heresy, dishonesty, and treason in you and he has accused you to the powers that be. You are gallows fodder; prison fodder at the very least.

"All of you take heed, people in Dublin told me this was his racket, and now he is here. Do you think he has changed? Do you suppose he still works for the authorities? Do you see him studying people and what they say . . . a little too closely? Does he not seem to make mental notes on those who voice an opinion or God forbid, a fact, contrary to the official line?

"And of late it is not just those I've listed so far. His British handlers have expanded his brief to include any one he suspects of political unreliability. A lot of Loyalists, Protestants, and Unionists who haven't cow towed to the British government's ways have been arrested. A lot of paramilitaries from the Shankill Road have been lifted thanks to the likes of you know who? You see, Mr. Worthington works both sides of the street. To him it proves he is impartial. That's your man, a first class tout. Mr. Edward Worthington. What have you to say for yourself?"

"You can't prove anything. This is all just speculation on your part," Worthington pleaded staring directly at me and no one else.

"Well actually Eddy, it was your colleagues in Dublin who said all of these things of you at first. I doubt that you have changed since you relocated up here. If I hadn't run into you how many more lives would you have sorely affected? I can imagine several in this room."

The two students were white with fear, and I dismissed them. They scurried out. I said to an interested crowd, "Not only students, I'm sure, have come to his attention. So be careful of this cancerous snake. He ruins lives on a hunch."

There was an audible stirring among the crowd. I suggested to Eddy that he leave now. He looked up at his guardians who motioned with their heads toward the door. He was gone in an instant.

I said in passing, "Take care my friends. This public service announcement was brought to you by the National Health Service. Get vaccinated early and often from pestilence like that."

Amid the laughter there were many a head that was nodding in agreement. I nodded to Denny that I was headed out. Several locals nodded, some said thanks for the lesson, or thanks for IDing the bastard, and the like. Denny followed about five minutes later.

When he was situated in the car he turned to me and announced, "That was a death sentence. That man is dead. He hasn't a friend in Belfast with the exception of the security services. What a job Rudy. Jaysus, what a job. Remind me to never get on your bad side."

"Let's just go home Denny. I'm tired."

Ian Partridge was at his desk talking to his partner David Potter. "The word came down this morning that the American Rudy Castle has verbally attacked and shattered one of our special agents working in and out of Queen's University. According to the agent, Castle set upon him the other day at the university and then again last night in a pub near the university.

"He exposed him in both places as a agent for the government, and in both cases he was said to have turned in names of both Loyalists and Nationalists for special attention by the security forces and employers.

"As a matter of fact, according to the boss, the agent has only focused on potential IRA members, recruits and sympathizers, not Loyalists. But Castle accused him of listing both sides as enemies of the state. Castle, in effect, destroyed him as an effective agent and possibly endangered his life.

"We are ordered to bring Castle in for a talk. If anything happens to the agent Castle will be charged with conspiracy to whatever, maybe murder if it comes to that."

Potter frowned. "Two questions. First, where is Castle hold up? Second, can the conspiracy charge hold?"

"I don't know the answers to either of your questions, David. It's up to us to find him, and we'll leave it to the legal experts to answer the second question."

"We know that he has used the Europa Hotel. We can start there. If he's not registered there we can go to the university. He has friends and contacts there," David suggested.

"Right."

"Why did he decide to expose the agent? How did he know the man was an agent? Castle seems to have taken on a mean streak since he has married that Conlon girl and gotten himself involved with that crowd."

"He claims he was willing to work for British Military Intelligence for camaraderie, but he sure has no liking for the RUC, Special Branch and the like. Something must have happened to turn him bitter."

"Personally, Ian, I think his brother-in-law, his sister-in-law and his wife are at the root of it. He's probably had no bad personal experience of 'police brutality' as the Nationalists all claim we inflict on them. But he's become a pain in the arse if you ask me. He needs to be put in his place," David Potter concluded.

"Maybe you are right, but what ever set him off he has become a liability to an agent whose cover is not only blown but whose life may be in jeopardy. So lets talk to him and bring him in for a scare at the very least. The boss anxiously wants a crack at him. So lets get this show on the road."

I stopped by the department at Queen's and several people told me in no uncertain terms that they appreciated me putting Worthington in his place and exposing him as a tout for the Brits or who ever.

I was grateful for their kind words and said there was no place for his kind at the university or any where for that matter. "Lives could be ruined by his baseless accusations."

Then several faculty related experiences that they or their students had after being interrogated by the authorities for suspicion of being IRA members or supporters. In every case they said they had been set up by someone. They were not in fact supporters or members of the IRA, but had expressed doubts about the legality of some of the practices that the authorities were using. They had expressed their concerns in private conversations among friends and colleagues who they knew and trusted. But on further reflection, the one new person who was an unknown entity was Edward Worthington. He figured in every case where someone was detained by the authorities.

It had been so obvious that every one had overlooked the obvious. They trusted each other and felt their community of academics could be honest with each other and not have their comments distorted and repeated out side the community. Clearly Worthington was the new man, an outsider, and the tout. They all thanked me again.

I was told that Professor Jones was looking for me so I wandered down to his office. He greeted me warmly and explained that he had no idea that Worthington was on such a damaging mission for whomever.

His assertions were so heartfelt that I almost believed him. Yet there was something that lurked at the back of my mind that said, just as Jones was in on my relationship with Major Summerville years back, he probably had some thing to do with Worthington.

I said, "When I worked for the Major I was always sure of my targets, sure they were dangerous, and never just speculated about a target just to make myself look good. But everything I heard about Worthington was bad. I was sure of my accusations against him. You can check with Major Summerville about my work for him. I prided myself on being accurate You just can't be flippant about accusations in this day and age."

"Do you ever hear from Summerville?"

Jones was nodding his head in the affirmative. "You are correct Rudy. I know you were accurate. You had a sterling record with Summerville. I can imagine that this Worthington, your assessment of Worthington, is also correct and I only hope he has not created too much damage."

"If you have any contact with the authorities, officially or unofficially, I would appreciate it if you gave them the heads up, in case he hasn't turned me in yet and described my blowing his cover.

"Bye the way, once again, do you ever hear from the Major?"

This time Jones was turning his head in the negative as he said, "No I have lost all contact with Summerville. I'm sure he is no longer here in Ulster."

I would have liked to correct Jones by saying, "You mean here in the North," but I let it slide by.

"Well if you can put in a good word for Worthington's victims and me to whomever. I'm sure we all need it."

After a long pause he said, "I will, Rudy, surely I will."

We shook hands, smiled and nodded to each other; I left his office and I headed back past the main department office and saw Smyth at his mail cubby.

"Rudy, where are you coming from and where are you off to?" Smyth inquired.

"I was just talking to Owen down in his office and I was looking for you."

"Aye, I've a beak just now, lets go over and get a tea at the cafeteria where we can talk."

Smyth was very vigilant as we walked over to get our drinks, and so I asked, "John, should I be looking over my shoulder?"

"Aye. Both shoulders Rudy. Your G-men friends were here yesterday and again earlier this morning looking for you. I think your man Worthington has put them on to you."

I described Partridge and Potter. Smyth said, "Those are the boys. No nonsense types. All business, and they clearly have a bone to pick with the likes of you. Worthington has clearly set you up, so take care."

We shared a drink. Mine was not tea, I found an "All American Coke. I wish you guys believed in ice," I commented.

"That's just for whiskey, Rudy."

"It's too early for whiskey. What if I had rum to put in my Coke? Could I get ice then?"

"Probable in high-class establishments, but not here in the student's establishment. Too common, if you know what I mean," John suggested.

"The pleasure and treasure of class. You know the Marxist shit of the Officials might have been on the right track," I said.

"Rudy we have company heading our way. The two gentlemen we were discussing just moments ago. They have you in their sights."

"Be sure Denny knows who I'm with at this point. I'll try to get them to disclose where they are going to take me."

"Mr. Castle, you are a hard one to locate," Ian Partridge said.

"I'm right here in plain sight in a public venue," I countered. "How difficult is that? How hard did you try?"

"We have been sent to collect you regarding possible slander charges against a Mr. Worthington. We need you to come with us, now," Partridge demanded.

"And you are taking me where? Am I under arrest? The charge of slander, is that a capital offense? Where again?"

'Please Mr. Castle, come along now peacefully or we will have to coerce you," Partridge threatened.

"You wouldn't want all of these people here to see us have to bound you up," David Potter added with a grin.

"First tell me where you are taking me?"

"Mr. Castle, if we must . . . ."

"Tell me where and I will come along like a good boy. If you don't, you will see how the US Army manual instructs a good American on how to defend his civil rights and civil liberties. I just hope you don't incur serious damage to your persons. Professor Smyth will you please contact the US Embassy for me?"

"We will be taking you to our boss at Headquarters in Hollywood. Chief of Bureau Ronald Poole will lead the questioning. Will that do?" Partridge asked sarcastically.

"You are so polite when you are faced with a near death experience. Professor Smyth, will you also have some one contact an attorney for me?"

And with that, we left Smyth at Queen's, and the three of us proceeded to Holywood. As we arrived I said, "Our Hollywood is bigger, better, and has more beautiful women."

I got no response.

"Any Hunger Strikers here?" I asked. "I might have to change that. Maybe a blanket protest and a dirty protest to boot. What do you think boys?"

Partridge sneered, "Starve yourself to death, Castle.

It means nothing to us. Join the others in Long Kesh. What's a few less Micks?"

Busted

"Denny? It's John Smyth at Queen's. Two Special Branch men lifted Rudy here at the university about five minutes ago. He has been charged with slander and they said they are taking him for questioning by a Chief Ronald Poole at their headquarters just outside of Belfast in Hollywood. He wondered if legal counsel could be sent there?"

"Jaysus. I don't know of any legal counsel. Do you?"

"I'll check with the university. I'll say he was on official business here setting up a studies program that hoped to tie in with Queen's. I'll get back to you as soon as I learn anything."

"Smyth, were the two G-men the same two he's had trouble with since he's returned here a year or so ago?"

"I'm quite certain that is the case. He knew them both and he got them to identify where they were taking him after some preliminary discussion of self-defense. He provoked them into disclosing the location so I could pass that last bit on to you."

"That's my boy, Mr. Castle!"

"I fear these two could and would like to do him bodily harm."

"They could try. Did they cuff him?"

"They threatened to. But he said he'd come along peacefully if the disclosed where they were taking him. At first they hesitated in identifying where they were taking them, but he cajoled them into telling where and to whom he was to be delivered."

"Well, those two G-men might try to harm him, but they alone, I don't think they could do it unless they shot him. Without using a gun it would four guys to subdue him I think," Denny said proudly.

"This is the North, and they do shoot unarmed people here," Smyth said dryly.

Edward Worthington had reported the incident at the university to his handler shortly after I had confronted him in the department offices.

Peter Jeffries, his handler, had advised Worthington to lay low for a couple of days while he contacted Owen Jones, from the Department of Literature and Mythology where the confrontation had taken place, for some advice and to enlist him in some damage control at Queen's.

Jeffries also said he would report the situation to the RUC as a slander issue, with the possibility of harm to a British national from England.

The RUC recognized Worthington's name and contacted Ron Poole at Special Branch who in turn was to sick Partridge and Potter on "Mr. Castle." While Special Branch was out looking for Mr. Castle, Jeffries tried to reach Jones at Queen's. In both cases, the attempts were futile.

Two days later Worthington reported to Jeffries the confrontation in the pub. "He must be following me," Worthington said. "Isn't that against the law?"

"I'll check for you when I pass this latest incident on to the RUC."

Jeffries had no more than hung up after making his second call to the RUC when Jones called.

"The secretary said you have been trying to get a hold of me for a couple of days. I was out of town. What's up?"

"Your man Rudy Castle is making a real nuisance of himself. He made a scene at the university the other day and again last night at a pub. In both cases he accused Edward Worthington of being a British tout because he has been spying and informing on students and faculty and everyone else."

Jones responded, "Castle was talking to me here not all that long ago and told me Worthington was harming innocent people with his accusations.

"He asked me to contact whomever, presumably at the RUC, Special Branch, or British Military, and report that Worthington was a loose cannon. His accusations were unfounded in most if not all cases. Innocent people were in danger of God knows what, because of his wild imagination.

"The fact of the matter is, I think Castle is correct."

"Well, we'll leave that to the experts. For now we must be concerned with restoring Worthington's good name and position at the university. You will be leading the way at your level," Jeffries said.

"I will need all the good luck I can muster with that. Virtually every one here seems to think Rudy Castle was not only correct in exposing Worthington, but also correct in his analysis and accusations. Castle has become something of a folk hero in the department with his academic research, his personality, and now his portrayal of Worthington's deceit. What you are asking of me will not be easy.

"Also, be careful about the accusations Worthington has made regarding faculty and students. I think Rudy is correct in Edward being, let us say, reckless in his accusations. I heard about his stay at Trinity in Dublin when he working down there. It sounds like his stay in Dublin was counter productive. Up here he could be a real liability to innocent people," Jones said before he hung up.

Jones was upset. First and foremost he was upset with Worthington. He seemed to poison wells wherever he turned up. Next he was furious with Sutherlund for expecting him to undo all that Worthington had done. He knew that he couldn't counter all the harm Worthington had done.

The one person he was not upset with was Rudy Castle. He seemed above reproach. He stuck his neck out to protect others and now found his neck on the chopping block. That was not fair. But what could he do about it?

"Mr. Castle, it seems that when ever you visit Ulster you bring turmoil along with you," Ronald Poole said accusingly.

"I find the North of Ireland a sea of turmoil with sharks just waiting to gobble up whole schools of innocent fishies. Now can you guess who are the sharks and who are the innocent fishies?" I asked.

Poole offered a sinister smile and ignored the question, but offered one of his own. "Why, Mr. Castle, do you call Ulster the North of Ireland? It's Ulster."

"No it is not, unless you include Donegal, Cavan and Moynihan. But there is no chaos and turmoil in those three counties of Ulster. So the six of the original nine counties of Ulster, that is what I call the North of Ireland for lack of a better word or phrase, and these six counties have had constant chaos and turmoil, going back for nearly four hundred years. As of late those in power have renewed apartide here against Catholics. What I've noticed is that what in South Africa is determined by the color of your skin, in the North of Ireland is determined by your religion. But in both places it's apartide."

"You sound very much like a hard core Nationalist, or more precisely an IRA apologist," Poole said accusingly.

"And you sound like Eddy Worthington. I am an Historian and student of Irish Legends, Mythology and Oral Traditions, and I'm just stating facts, not ideology. You might, like Worthington, confuse the two, but I don't.

"And would you be the Poole that Partridge and Potter referred to when they lifted me?"

"That is correct."

"I thought so. That is why I used the sea analogy, you understand, the sea, a big **pool**," I explained.

He was not amused.

"I have another water observation. May I?"

He nodded, clearly upset.

"All you people I've met here at Special Branch, Partridge, Potter, and now Poole, all have names that begin with the letter 'P'. Ah, you see it coming, a lot of 'Pee'."

Partridge took a step closer to me in a threatening way and said, "See, he is a mouthy bastard. Let us teach him some manners."

"I am not a bastard as my parents were married several years before I was born. The only thing you and your lackey Potter here could teach me is some of that North of Ireland hospitality you are so well known for up here. But it might be a two-way learning session. I think I can give as well as receive."

"All right, that's enough. The point of this inquiry is that Mr. Edward Worthington has charged you with slander. In two separate occasions he claims that you publicly accused him of falsely accusing a number of students and faculty of overtly supporting paramilitary organizations here in Ulster.

"Did you accuse him of such action in public?" Poole demanded.

"That's what he does. It will be difficult to get any official security organization to admit that he is their man and that he has turned in names of individuals whom he has accused of being supporters of outlawed paramilitary groups. Certain individuals from Queen's University have been detained and interrogated by the RUC, Special Branch and British Military, having been accused of working for paramilitary organizations, by Worthington.

"All of these people deny such associations, but they claim that their detention was the result of discussions with or in front of Worthington, where they expressed opinions which may have been seen as questioning official policy and practice: searches, seizures, lack of trials, lack of juries, imprisonment without trial and the like.

"After questioning such practices by the authorities here in the North of Ireland, they were in turn hounded by the authorities for simply questioning such practices. But when interrogated they were accused of not only questioning these undemocratic practices, but of actively working with groups seeking to undermine and sabotage the British system in the North.

"These students, faculty, and citizens had just discussed, questioned, and identified certain practices that seem to fly in the face of British legal and civil rights.

"When Worthington showed up, what had been private discussions became the meat of accusations and investigations by the authorities. Worthington defiled the trust of faculty and students; he turned their thoughts and confidential discussions into supposed actions. I think at least some of the faculty will vouch for my accusations against Worthington."

"Mr. Worthington does not work for Special Branch, and as far as I know he does not work for any other branch of Her Majesties Government. So your accusations are false, and have damaged his name, reputation, and possibly endangered his life. That is what you face Mr. Castle. It's more than simple slander," Poole explained.

"An official list of charges will be filed with the court. In the mean time you will be remanded to the Crumlin Goal. Partridge and Potter will see you safely there. Don't do anything foolish or you might find yourself in deeper trouble. They will take none of your attitude, do you understand Mr. Castle?

"Additionally, you should know some IRA scum shot their way out of the Crumlin Goal a short while back and the security people there are in an awful fowl mood too."

———————————————

Two days later I got a visit from a university barrister, Mr. Neelson. He wasn't very comforting.

"Mr. Castle, these are serious charges, and I'm not exactly sure that you are covered by Queen's University's legal services. We are still checking on the matter. Your friend and associate Professor Smyth, claims you and he are exploring a joint study program between your college back in the USA and Queen's, so you should be covered. Some high up in the administration at the university are not so sure."

"The university wouldn't want to run amuck of the powers that be here in the North, right?" I asked.

"You are probably correct in your assessment," he confided. "These are dangerous times."

"Tell me about it. Stay clear of a horses arse by the name of Edward Worthington. He's a security tout and will turn your name in for just thinking the system is rotten," I warned.

"Aye, we've heard of him all right. He is known to be a rotten apple. There have been complaints, but the administration isn't going to cross wickets with the government and their agents. I heard through the fish line that you roughed up Mr. Worthington, or was it 'Worthingham?' Off the record, good job, but now you may pay for it."

"When do you think I will be charged in court?"

"No telling. They may just let you sit for a while. They'll make you uncomfortable. Just hope nothing happens to Worthington," he warned. "You don't have to answer any questions, and do not provoke your interrogators. They might just be looking for an excuse to treat you to a lesson of goal schooling."

"I hear you and I won't go looking for trouble."

"Aye. I bet you won't," Neelson said in parting. "If things are tense out on the street, they are doubly so in here after the incident a couple of weeks back when some prisoners shot their way out of here. Please, Mr. Castle, be very careful. Do not provoke them. You are more or less in this alone. I will try to find out if I am indeed to represent you."

I thought to myself, *On my own, I'm guessing. With so many good friends and family, here I am alone except for certain people who would like nothing more than make my stay here memorable.*

———————————

Crumlin Road Goal

Crumlin goal was what I expected. It was old, chipped walls and flaking white paint, polished tile floors, florescent light in the corridors shining from above, giving off that malevolent prison atmosphere. It also reeked of history. It had housed some Republican heroes before they were moved on to other places, like the H-blocks south of Belfast, or executed, some of whose bodies were still buried in the goal yard, like Tom Williams from the '40s. But the recent shoot out clearly put everyone here on edge. The mood wasn't simply dark, it was deadly.

I was isolated and had my food brought to me by the guards. Prison food. Bad enough as it is, but I was told that the guards periodically took the nice big pieces of fish or meat, or at the very least took a bite out of it, or they spit or even pissed on what was left before they brought it to you. Every meal pretty much smelt like the latter.

When Partridge and Potter came to visit me and inquire how I was getting along, Potter made a special point of asking how I liked the prison rations. He looked at me, and then Partridge, as he waited for my answer. He was sporting a big smile like the cat that watches the pet owner look for the canary that he has just swallowed.

"I figure I can go a week without eating this piss and shit. By that time I think I'll be out. Then I'll make it a point to discuss the catering arrangements with some friends of mine. But it's nice and thoughtful of you to inquire Potter. I'll keep that in mind too," I chirped.

"Is that a threat, Castle," Partridge demanded.

"Heavens no. It's a compliment and a promise," I responded with a shit eaten grin of my own.

"We can see that you get a double helping and some help eating it," Potter threatened.

"Even more thoughtful," I responded. "I'll remember that too."

"Aye, you just keep it up Castle, and your wise-crack comments will land you in some real trouble," Potter threatened again with more vehemence. He just glared at me and it was evident I was getting under his skin.

"Our boss, Mr. Poole, just wanted us to check up on you and make sure everything is alright. It looks like it is, so we will be off," Partridge said cheerfully as they moved off down the hallway.

"See if you can smuggle in some snacks and a beer or two, will you?" I called out. But they were gone and I was left alone for a while, until the next feeding.

Denny was genuinely concerned and he contacted John Smyth at the university. Smyth explained that the university was not obligated to take my case to their legal team. So Mr. Neeson would not be taking my case.

"Good news" always has a shadow, so Smyth also informed Denny that the US Embassy indicated that I was on my own. I didn't expect the US government to get involved, but I wanted to register the fact that a US citizen was being hassled by the Brits in the North of Ireland. When I got home (I was thinking positively) I would also make sure my Congressman and Senators were informed of the trumped-up charges and overt threats. After the next few days, I'd have a whole catalog of things to pass on to my representatives in Congress.

The actual good news came in the form of two guards, one on day shift, the other on night shift, who took a liking to me. Word had filtered down to them that the special segregated guest was an American who was charged with slander. I was kind of a celebrity. On the same day each of them asked me whom I had slandered.

I answered, "A shite who reported to his bosses any suspicion he had concerning Nationalists or Loyalists. He reported on anyone so long as it made him look good. He's a bounty hunter and he doesn't care who he hurts. I called him on it twice, in public. I hate to see innocent people get hurt, I don't care what their background is."

Both guards agreed that Worthington sounded like a "shite." They also said that he must have some connections for me to end up in the "Crum."

It eventually came out that I was a military vet and had seen action in Nam. They both appreciated that I had served my country, as one of them said "like a good Loyalist," and seemed to be an honest bloke, "like a good Protestant."

"My grand father and his family were Methodists from County Down," I offered. Although the guards were both Free Presbyterians, both of them said at one time or another that "we were all Protestant brothers because we all oppose that whore church in Rome." They obviously took Reverend Paisley seriously.

No room for ecumenism or middle ground here, I thought, and just smiled, but keeping my mouth shut.

They each said they would see to it that my food was not tampered with, and that the other guards would not mistreat me. I "sincerely" thanked them.

Half kidding I asked one of them, "Is the food really pissed on? We didn't do that sort of thing to VC or NVR prisoners, no matter how bad we hated them."

The only answer I got was, "Aye, that sort of thing does happen once in a while to some IRA and INLA prisoners."

When I asked, "What's the difference between the IRA and the INLA?" all I got in response was, "Not much, they're all Nationalist Taig murdering cunts."

I just pursed my lips, got a surprised look on my face and nodded my head slightly. "I've heard a good Protestant Loyalist can spot one of them in a crowd or simply walking down the street. Is that so?"

"For some it is so. They can tell by the narrow set of their eyes, their flat noses, pouty lips and greasy skin and darkish complexion and hair. I can't say myself. I can't ID them that easily. Once they are in prison it seems obvious when you look at them."

"Your description almost sounds like the stereotype of a Jew from back in the thirties and forties," I said, carefully leaving out that the stereotype was befitting a Nazi.

They asked questions about the United States: cars, girls, jobs, and beer. The usual stuff guys in their early to mid-twenties were interested in knowing.

I asked them if they knew Partridge and Potter? Neither of them knew them. "Special Branch is in their own world," the day guard said. "Each section of the police service sticks to its own and doesn't mix much with others," the night man explained.

"A lot like the branches of the US military," I commented. "To each their own."

"That is true of every country's military," I recalled one of them saying. *And not just the military,* I thought, *it occurs with different ethnic and religious groups within a country too.* I didn't share that insight either. I was ahead of the game and I didn't need more enemies than the Special Branch goons.

I was lying on my cot one evening when I had a horrible thought that made me break out in a sweat.

What if some how these Special Branch clowns tumble to the fact that a Special Branch thug was paying Mr. Rudy Castle special attention years ago, because he was sure the American was working with and for the IRA.

That thought gave me chills to offset the sweat. That was an ugly thought, the stuff of nightmares.

Edward Worthington supposedly reported to his handler in whatever security department he worked for, that he was being followed by some unsavory types whom he was sure were IRA thugs. He must have been one of the clairvoyant types that my jailer said could identify a "Nationalist Taig murdering cunt" in a crowd, or tailing some one, or simply walking down the street.

The next day Mr. Worthington's handler reported to Mr. Poole at Special Branch that there was an attempt on the life of Mr. Worthington. Obviously my slander was jeopardizing the life of Mr. Worthington.

I was again brought before a judge and formally charged with slander and reckless endangerment of a person's life; I hade made him a target of illegal paramilitary death squads.

When I was allowed to speak in the courtroom, I asked the judge how my actions were slanderous since several persons could and would substantiate my accusations against Mr. Worthington? It would seem that Mr. Worthington's actions and accusations brought him to the attention of certain paramilitary organizations, so how could I be held responsible for any supposed, but unsubstantiated, threats and actions against Mr. Worthington by those paramilitary organizations. He falsely accused innocent people of working for and with these groups. I didn't put any organization onto Mr. Worthington. Indeed, how could I orchestrate such a deed from my confinement in Crumlin Prison. Further, as an American here in Belfast, in pursuit of an academic arrangement between my college in the United States and Queen's University, how would I know or have time to contact any paramilitary death squads.

Before I could muddy the waters any further, the judge interrupted me and said I would have my day in court to argue my case. In the mean time, formal charges would be drawn up and filed with the court. A barrister would be sought for me, and I would be remanded back to Crumlin Goal to await all of the above.

Things were not looking good, I was sure my wife and my mother were fit to be tied; if they were concerned with my safety, they were I was sure equally upset with me for bringing this upon myself.

Like I did it all on purpose. No matter how hard I tried to explain this mess to the women in my life, Barbrie, my mother, and Eve, I was guilty as far as all of them were concerned. I always seemed to go out of my way to stir things up and get into trouble.

The reality of it all was that deep down I thought it was worth it.

While I sat in Crumlin Prison with my unsoiled food, events on the outside were starting to witness the formation of three diverse, yet connected forces, that would eventually collide and bring my saga to a satisfactory conclusion during this stage of my life.

As one could imagine, the first force was centered on the accusations of Mr. Edward Worthington and the two fastidious G-men of Special Branch, Partridge and Potter, under the guidance of their supervisor Mr. Poole. They conspired to compose a series of fake threats to the life Mr. Worthington that were supposedly the direct result of my doings. Their object was to punish me for exposing Worthington as a fraud and danger to innocent Irish citizens, and for embarrassing the security service he worked for as an agent. At the very least, Special Branch accepted his false accusations as true, causing innocent people, both Nationalists and possibly Loyalists, plenty of discomfort, trepidation and misery.

The second Force was called into play by the totally surprising intervention of my old Loyalist Queen's University professor Owen Jones. Quite frankly, Owen Jones was the last person I thought would intervene on my behalf since I had cozied up to Professor Smyth over the past several years. But Jones acted for me; he was motivated partially out of loyalty to me as a former student and, more importantly, also for what I did in the past of a subversive nature for the British Military to which he was in part privy. He called upon now "Colonel" Summerville to intervene on my behalf, to explain the role I had played for the then "Major" Summerville in sniffing out "real enemies" of Her Majesties' Government. Summerville would explain the care I took to ferret out only real persons of threat, taking care to report on facts, not figments of my imagination, and how I was frank and open as to whom I would and would not spy on. He always admired my honesty, accuracy and loyalty to him.

As one might expect, the third force centered around my brother in arms, my closest Irish friend and comrade, Denny, who sought to have those who threatened me pay the ultimate price. The irony of ironies was that he found help from a distant yet familiar source that I had freed from the Troubles in the North of Ireland. I had sought to divert attention away from this very person by assuming his role in a series of actions that were intended to mimic him and draw attention away from him. These actions were performed in such a way that they did and did not appear to be the work of my brother-in-law Danny Conlon. My actions were to allow him first to flee Ireland and later to save his life in Canada. And now in my hour of need, Danny, at great personal risk, returned to Ireland from the US to punish the people who sought my demise.

These three threads, involving key persons and events that were to change my life, were quite unimaginable to me as I lay in my Crumlin Prison cell. My concern was my wife and our children primarily, and my extended family coming in a close second. I was incommunicado, and I had no knowledge of how much Denny was communicating with my family. I could not have visitors so my isolation was complete.

I resigned myself to wait and see what would unfold.

There was nothing I could do. Next to my family I wondered if my job would be waiting for me when I returned home. I just hoped family and friends would find a way to help me.

Peter Jeffries of MI5, Worthington's boss, decided to "bury" me for causing his man so much grief and setting back his operations at Queen's University.

He informed Worthington to sit tight while he put a new scenario into play. He explained to Worthington that some "dangerous types had been following him," which he in turn duly "reported" to Jeffries. Worthington nodded his understanding. A classic setup.

Then three nights ago some of these imaginary "thugs attempted to grab him and force him into a car." Worthington smiled and nodded his head again. *Perfect, a perfect setup*, he thought.

Again he "reported" the incident to Jeffries who in turn passed it and the earlier stalking incidents, on the RUC and Special Branch. Then tonight, Worthington would be shot at outside his flat, which he would "report" to the RUC. Jeffries, who was meeting with Poole, would thus get the reported shooting at the same time.

Worthington was concerned about being shot at, but he understood the staged drama that was unfurling with him as the star and me as the villain.

After the mock up shooting and a personal visit by Jeffries and Poole to the crime scene, Worthington was placed under a protection order and closeted by MI5 for safekeeping. Jeffries accompanied Poole back to the Special Branch headquarters.

"I think the man you have in custody, Rudy Castle, has placed our Worthington in the line of fire. Obviously we at MI5 cannot file charges against him, so I hope we can work behind the scenes to protect our man and punish Castle for targeting Worthington," Jeffries said in a matter of fact tone.

"Quite right Mr. Jeffries. We explained to Mr. Castle when we detained him for slander that if the situation escalated into just the situation that has arisen, he was in for more serious charges.

"We explained that he has no one to blame but himself," Poole emphasized.

"We must keep MI 5 entirely out of it, and that extends to Worthington's role in MI 5."

"Of course. We specifically told Castle that Worthington was not employed by the RUC, Special Branch, British Military, or any other government agency. We will hold to that," Poole offered.

"The detectives you had working on Worthington's case from the start must be kept in the dark as well. They must just be told that being an American, he is a special case for Special Branch."

"Detectives Partridge and Potter have no love for Castle. They see him as an arrogant American who comes over here and makes constant trouble," Poole offered.

"They've had run ins-with him before?"

"Aye, several times over the years. He's even related to Danny Conlon, the IRA sniper. Castle is married to one of Conlon's sisters. Some time ago we contacted him asking him to inform us if Danny tried to contact his sisters who were on a visit here in Belfast with Castle. The word we had was that Castle had done some work for British Military several years ago when he was a student here. We hoped for his cooperation.

"He told us to 'fuck-off' in no uncertain terms. Then he showed up at Queen's University when some oceanographic equipment he sent over here was stolen. He accused us of being inept."

"So it won't take much to keep your boys on top of Castle as his court case unfolds. I suspect they might find some incriminating evidence of involvement with brother-in-law Danny's IRA friends. You don't know where he was staying here in Belfast do you?

A search of the place by your two boys might turn up some incriminating evidence, if you know what I mean," Jeffries smiled.

"I'll put Partridge and Potter on it immediately."

"Don't have them search the place until we've had an opportunity to check it out," Jeffries smiled again.

"I'll need your number and I'll call you the minute I find out where he was staying."

As Jeffries sauntered down the hallway to the exit, Poole had a thought. Castle had been here as a student and apparently had worked in some capacity for the British Military, but he ended up marrying a Conlon girl, the sister to a well-known IRA sniper. Castle worked for the army but clearly had a problem with the police. Maybe Castle had a run in with the police, the RUC or Special Branch many years ago. Maybe he had a history that was worth checking into.

I was returned to court and informed that with the attempt on the life of Mr. Edward Worthington, I was now under arrest for colluding with paramilitaries to kill Mr. Edward Worthington. I was an accessory to the fact.

Denny decided that getting an obvious Nationalist solicitor would be blowing any cover I had as a simple academic doing work in the North of Ireland without any ties to the Provisional IRA. So he got the Provies to front some money for a secret operation known only to Sean Keenan.

The money was to be used by a well-known "Nationalist-IRA" attorney to contact, and hire, a discreet "neutral" (Nationalist) attorney, without any blatant ties to the IRA, to handle my case. As Denny explained to me once, in the North of Ireland even non-committed neutrals are either Nationalist, Catholic, Republican neutrals, or they are Loyalist, Protestant, Unionist neutrals!

So the solicitor, John Britton, approached me as I was about to enter the court, introducing himself, saying all was paid for in advance, and not to worry. He asked for a quick run through of the facts.

I explained the bare facts of the situation and the charges leveled against me, as I understood them. Again Britton said not to worry; this would all be over in a week.

I didn't really believe him at the time. But truer words could not have been spoken. Forces greater and mightier than the law, judges, and lawyers, were at work behind the scenes, that neither Mr. Britton nor I were aware of.

Getting Framed

Owen Jones stuck his head into John Smyth's office and asked, "Heard any more about Rudy? Is he still up at the Crumlin Goal?"

"Yes. I was on the phone last night to his wife who is worried sick. Fortunately she and Rudy live with his mother so the two of them can comfort each other somewhat. But the stress must be hellish. They cannot contact him nor can he contact them. And all of this for exposing that worthless Worthington. Is there no justice?"

"Well I'm working on a ploy that might just help him. It's a long shot, but if I can pull it off it might turn up aces," Jones said confidently.

He returned to his office and was immediately lost in pedagogical pursuits and the problems of Rudy Castle were out of sight and out of mind for the next two days.

But then he got the call that he was pretty sure could change every thing for Rudy Castle. The ace he was holding on to was none other than the former Major Summerville who had used Rudy's surveillance and reports of actual threats to law and order in and around Queen's University some ten years ago or so.

Now a Colonel, he was currently overseeing training of jungle warfare in Belize. Jones gave the gist of the situation and described the fix Rudy was now trapped in.

The Colonel was dismayed that "young Castle" had been charged with such unwarranted accusations. He remembered Rudy's conversations with him regarding Worthington's reckless actions down in Dublin those many years ago. "Rudy felt he was counter productive and dangerous then. It didn't sound like things had changed regarding Worthington, only the venue."

Summerville explained he was due to return to Britain shortly, as a matter of fact, in a couple of days. He said he would try to bump it up and he could possibly fly out tomorrow or the day after. He would make it a point to stop off in Northern Ireland before putting down in Lancashire. "I'm sure I can swing that sort of diversion. Rank has its privileges."

For the life of them, Partridge and Potter could not locate where Castle had been staying. The only conclusion they could come up with was that he had been staying with a friend. But as to whom it was with and where it was, they were in the dark.

Poole accepted their report and when he passed it on to Jeffries, he was not pleased one bit.

"This is going to complicate things. We need a place that Castle has frequented so we can provide evidence that he is, or was, out to do Worthington serious harm, preferably with help from the IRA."

"Well I can tell you he spent quite a bit of time at Queen's with his old pals Professors Jones and Smyth. Maybe that will be your best bet," Poole offered.

"Yes, maybe you are on to something."

"I may be on to more than just that. I had a hunch that Castle was up to something when he was a student here back in the early 70s. We had a detective that kept and eye on Castle back then. Nothing concrete, but our Detective Ivy was sure Castle was up to criminal activity of one sort or another.

"Ivy was killed during a riot up near the Ardoyne in 1973, so nothing ever came of his hunch. But he kept notes on what he considered suspicious activity."

Jeffries had better things to do than listen to Poole's histrionics, so he said, "And your point is . . . ?"

"My point is that possibly we could present Castle with Ivy's old notes and suggest that there is incriminating evidence against him from back then, and that if he cooperated with us now we would forget about the past transgressions."

"What kind of cooperation? Do you suspect him of IRA involvement or something?" Jeffries asked now becoming more interested.

"His brother-in-law is Danny Conlon! Maybe there is something there," Poole responded.

"Right. You boys run with that angle and let me know if anything comes of it, OK?"

On that note the conversation ended. Jeffries felt Poole was grasping at straws. Jeffries would look into the offices at Queen's though, that might be operational. Maybe something could be planted that would incriminate Castle and keep him behind bars for a while.

Denny was on a secure public phone to the United States and was reassuring Barbrie that I would, should, be out of the Crum in a week and on MY way home. She was nervously hopeful. He also tried to reassure my mother, Kathryn.

He had hoped that Eve would be there because he wanted to ask a favor of Eve that he did not feel comfortable asking of the other women. Fortunately, Eve was there and wanted to talk to Denny too.

After her questions, Denny said in a low flat voice, "I need to talk to Danny, Eve. Here is a number. It's safe. Tomorrow between 8 and 10 PM our time. Thanks Eve. Slan."

What had gotten Denny into a lather was the word that two Special Branch men (he was sure by the description of them it was Partridge and Potter) were snooping about asking if any one knew where Rudy Castle had hung his hat recently. Denny recognized the names and knew they were trying to find who I had been with and where he had left his belongings. Not just to go through his stuff, but probably to plant shite, too. "The bastards."

Denny gathered up my belongings and stashed them in a safe place just in the event he was singled out and his place searched. He wasn't going to turn over my stuff to be cultivated with poison fruit. "Fuck em," Denny said to himself.

Partridge and Potter conducted interrogations of me during lunch time, exercise time, and attorney visitation time. Anytime to harass me and take time away from breaks in the monotony of the routine. They also hoped to place doubts, make threats, and ask questions meant to cause confusion on my part.

Fortunately my military training had included sessions on interrogation techniques that would be used against me in the event he were captured by the enemy, indeed an enemy that was much more aggravating than these two locals were handing out.

I either remained silent or barraged them with questions so they couldn't get a word in edgewise. Some days the interrogators were there three times during the day. It was becoming annoying, boring and tiring.

One day during an interrogation in the afternoon session, Mr. Poole joined the routine. He had a notebook in his hand and a smile on his face.

"Mr. Castle, how are you today?"

I decided not to answer him but to simply smile at the man.

"Can you guess what I have here Mr. Castle? No? Well let me tell you Mr. Castle. Back in the early 70s a Special Branch detective by the name of Ivy was on to you. He spotted you straight away when you got off the boat from Scotland and England to make your covert contacts. He was on to you Mr. Castle. You thought we'd forgotten, didn't you. But we don't forget anything Mr. Castle.

"It's all here Mr. Castle. He didn't miss a thing. He followed you for three years Mr. Castle. As I said, he didn't miss a thing. You thought we'd lost his report, didn't you Mr. Castle? But he didn't miss a thing and we didn't loose his report on you Mr. Castle. So what do you think of that, Mr. Castle?"

"I think you're repeating my name over and over because you might forget it, or loose it, Mr. Poole.

You could fool some of the people some of the time Mr. Poole, but you'd have to pool your resources to fool the whole pool all of the time, Mr. Poole," I joked.

"You play your games now, but we have you and Danny Conlon working together in Ivy's report," he said with a sneer.

"Aren't you going to say, Mr. Castle?" I asked.

Potter jumped up and swung at me catching me on the side of the face with his right fist. Partridge caught me under the chin with his right fist, before Poole intervened, purposely late.

"Both of you are right handed, I'll be sure to remember that," I said.

"What the fuck is that supposed to mean, you fucken wanker?" Potter chimed in.

"You've got to say, 'you fucken wanker **Mr. Castle**," I demanded with emphasis.

Partridge went to land another right handed blow on my face but I blocked his fist and quickly slapped Potter with my right hand. "That was open handed, but I'm going to say we are even for now Potter. But Partridge, you've got one coming."

I no more than got the last word out to Partridge when out of the blue I got whacked and went out like a blown light bulb. I even heard the "pop."

When I came to, I was slouched in a chair with my hands cuffed behind my back. My head throbbed. There were tears in my eyes, but I did a tongue check and I had all my teeth.

As I focused on Poole standing in front of me, all I could muster was, "Hi there!"

I didn't see the next one coming and I don't know if it was from Partridge or Potter. It didn't really matter, but it was like getting hit with a Tennessee tire thumper.

When I came to I was back on the chair with a repeat of the last scenario: head ache, tears, all my teeth, and looking at who ever was in front of me, I couldn't tell from the tears, "Hi there."

Wham. This time when I came to I was in my cell. I had one hell of a headache and the side of my face hurt from the abrasions caused by the object that was used to club me. I wondered if it was what I said that brought out the best of the Special Branch boys.

Shit, I thought. *I'm sure as hell glad that's over with.*

When my jailer friend stopped by to check on me he peered through the opening on the door and winced.

"Make some new friends, did you?"

"No, the same old friends. But our friendship is being tested."

"In a minute I'm to take you to the doctor down the corridor. You be sure to tell him what happened, I mean why they did it to you. Why did they do it to you?" he asked.

"Being a smart ass I guess. Oh, ya, I also tried to defend myself from a blow by blocking a punch, then slapping the other guy for sucker punching me," I quipped.

"They could give you more time for that you know. Any time you have a punch-up with any of us boys you put yourself at our mercy," he explained.

"I figured as much. But the next time they will be a little leery. And knowing that I was in the military they might figure I could do some real damage."

"That being the case, they will probably bring help to the next session. They could bring some of their own or get a few warders to stand around you and glare down at you as you sit on your chair. So be prepared," he warned. "I mean be prepared for the worse. Don't antagonize em when you are hopelessly out numbered. These boys aren't fooling around."

"Thanks for all the advice. I'll be sure to mention my bruises came from Special Branch and not you fellahs," I said by way of thanks.

The doctor didn't ask any questions beyond "where does it hurt?"

I volunteered that what was special about Special Branch was their hospitality to the presumed innocent. I couldn't wait to see what would happen to me when the Kangaroo Court they had up here in the North found me guilty. I planned to write a book about my experience. I planned to name names. If he doctored me up well I would mention him in the book as one of the few good guys. I also mentioned that the beating was from Special Branch and not from the prison staff here in the Crum.

"You work here doc, are the Special Branch all psychopaths? And how about the prison staff here, are they all charitable and helpful Christians?"

The doctor didn't answer nor did he supply his name.

When my solicitor, Mr. Britton, came to visit me, he was physically shaken by my appearance.

"If this is what they give to foreign academic guests, I can only imagine what they hand out to the local population who has no voice except when they say their beads. I'm going to write a book about this adventure. I can't decide if I should name it 'Britain's Uncommon Law Enforcement,' or 'Britain's Magna Crapa,' or 'Britain's Practice of Criminal Law,'" I said with loaded irony.

All Mr. Britton could say was, "Who? Why?"

I specified Special Branch and gave my rendition of the events. I explained the new "evidence" Poole had in the form of Detective Ivy's notebook. Then on a lighter note I added, "Maybe on second thought the title of my book should be 'Britain's Special Truncheon Branch.' What do you think?"

He couldn't take his eyes off my cuts and bruises and black eyes. I broke his trance with a request: "Can you get a camera and get back here soon to get some snaps of my condition?"

'They won't allow that," was all he could muster for the moment.

"Then request the prison authority take pictures. They were not involved. They might like the idea that Special Branch was going to take the tumble for abuse, not them. They might be willing to help under those circumstances," I suggested.

"I'll request it," he finally agreed. "We are scheduled for a hearing, the day after tomorrow. I wouldn't be surprised if Special Branch got it moved back to next week so you can heal some and not be an embarrassment in the court."

"Aye, you wouldn't want some cockeyed hanging judge to be embarrassed by the prisoner's appearance in his court now would you," I said full of sarcasm?

Then I said, "Listen, you've got to call this number and tell the party on the other end of the line what's going on so he can call my family back in the US. Also tell him that the Special Branch men who are working me over are known to him. Ask him for a small camera so you can get some pictures of me."

I could see Mr. Britton was uncomfortable with this last request. Can you bring along another attorney, maybe the one who contacted you, so he can photograph me?"

He said he would think about it. I could see he was working mentally trying to remember everything I was requesting. Unfortunately, I had one more item I needed for him to tell Denny.

"Lastly," I said, "tell him about the old G-man who tailed me years back. They have his notebook and they claim he had incriminating evidence against me. I can't imagine what it is they are saying is incriminating, or they would have lifted me way back then. It must be nothing, only a bluff. But they keep referring to my brother-in-law. Hell, I didn't see him untill just before I left with my wife back then. So it's all BS. A bluff. He'll understand. Have you got all of that? Write it down if you need to. It's important that he get all of this. My wife needs comforting and assurances. He'll know what to say. Thanks. You are my only link with the outside."

Britton recounted, "Call the number. Tell the party on the line what's happening legally and physically to you. Identify that it is Special Branch people doing these things, and he should know the detectives involved.

Lastly they think they have something from a notebook from a detective who followed you many years ago, and they indicate that it has something to do with your brother-in-law."

"Aye, good job. Tell him the last bit is all BS."

"Got it," Britton said, still fixated on my injuries.

"And if the locals won't photograph me ask about the camera, and ask your solicitor friend if he will do it, OK? He'll also need a newspaper from that day, just the first page."

"Oh, ya, also contact Professor Smyth, he'll know those willing to help with my case. They claimed that they were harassed by the RUC after they voiced opinions questioning police and court practices in private conversations where Worthington was present. They suspect him of turning their names into the police. So they will be key to our case."

When he left me he was quite shaken by my physical appearance, and when he stopped by the administrative offices to request a photograph of me. As was expected, the request was denied.

When Denny got Britton's call, he also called Smyth and warned him about MI 5 planting something on me at Queen's, "maybe in your office."

Jeffries and another agent walked down the corridor of the Literature Department at Queen's University. They stopped by the secretary's office, identified themselves as security people and asked to see my office. The secretary informed them that I did not have an office, but that I used the mail room when I wasn't with Professor Smyth in his office.

They asked to be directed to Smyth's office. He was with a student and they had to wait about fifteen minutes. They were clearly uncomfortable since all the students had them pegged as police of some sort. Word got around to the faculty as well by the time Smyth let them into his office.

They questioned Smyth about me, but he stopped them and asked to see their identification. He was interested in the specific department they represented. They told him it was classified.

"So I take it it's not the RUC or Special Branch," Smyth concluded out loud. "My lord, such attention," he said to Jeffries.

Jeffries suggested that they should step out and have a talk with the head of the department. As they left for the department heads office Smyth noticed Jeffries assistant was lagging behind in his office.

Smyth, no one's fool, inquired of Jeffries, "Is your man looking for something in my office or is he planting something there?"

Jeffries over reacted, "What? Of course not. What cheek."

As they passed the department secretary Smyth whispered, "Have someone check on the man in my office."

The meeting with the department head was a bust.

"Of course everyone here would cooperate with the authorities, right Professor Smyth?"

"Of course sir. But exactly which authority are these blokes representing. They won't identify themselves or their agency."

"Is that the case Mr . . . what was your name again? And while we are at it, who do you represent exctly?"

At that point the department secretary came in with a student. The student claimed, "This man's friend was putting papers in Professor Smyth's desk drawer, under some papers in the top drawer. The secretary sent me to check Professor Smyth's office. I came in through the back door of Professor Smyth's office. I just watched through the crack in the door and I saw the man putting papers in Professor Smyth's desk."

The department head said, "Let's go to Smyth office and sort this out."

Jeffries friend was gone. But the student went straight to the top left drawer and said, "Right here. This one."

Smyth sat down, opened the drawer and pulled out a stack of papers. The bottom papers were some crude Republican propaganda sheets along with some instructions for "Rudy Castle" from an IRA commander and something concerning "Danny Conlon."

"These are not mine, nor were they here ten minutes ago when I put my last students tutorial paper in that very drawer. This has to be what you friend was planting in my desk. I want the RUC and Special Branch called immediately," Smyth demanded.

An hour latter Jeffries was sitting uncomfortably in Poole's office explaining what had gone wrong.

"Smyth sent that damn student who snooped and caught our man planting the evidence. What should have been so simple went all wrong. I passed it off as testing Smyth to see where his loyalties were located."

"And how did that go over?" Poole asked.

"I really don't care what they think or whether they bought it or not. And that Smyth character, he insisted that the RUC and you people get involved. He was belligerent from the start. What do you know about him?"

"I know that he and Castle go back about ten years, to when Castle came here as a student. Then some time back they cooperated on an oceanographic research project. Smyth got funding and Castle got some equipment but it was stolen from the university. If I'm not mistaken it happened twice. I don't know if they ever replaced it and got on with their project."

"So you are telling me they are as thick as thieves, pun intended. What is Smyth's background?" Jeffries inquired.

"Academically?"

"No, no. His religious and political affiliation."

"He's a Roman Catholic as is his whole family. I believe I saw somewhere he was involved with the SDLP," Poole said helpfully.

"So he's Catholic and probably a closet Sinner, or sinner," Jeffries said and smiled at his pun on the nickname for a member of the Republican Party, Sinn Fein. "What about Castle?"

"He's married to a Belfast Catholic. He took his wife and her sister back to America, and you know his brother-in-law is Danny Conlon. I wouldn't be surprised if Castle helped Conlon slip out of the Republic where he was last seen and into America."

"Why do I have the feeling all of these loose ends are tied together with Castle?" Jeffries mused. "If we keep him long enough maybe his brother-in-law will show up to help him. Wouldn't that be something?"

"Aye, that would be something," Poole commented. "It would be more than we could wish for."

One or two should be careful what they wished for.

———————————

An Old "Friend" Gets Me Out

"Jones? Summerville here. Just landed outside of Belfast. I thought I would come by the University and pick you up. Then we can head over to see the Special Branch people and straighten this mess up. Have you heard anything from Castle?"

"He's in Crumlin Goal. Some security people were here and got caught planting some incriminating evidence against Rudy in a professor's office. Very disturbing, sloppy, unprofessional, and illegal. I suspect it was to discredit Rudy so the accusations of Worthington would be substantiated if it comes to trial. They identified themselves as government people, but refused to identify themselves specifically. Probably Worthington's associates."

"Sounds like the spooks or witchdoctors at MI 5," Summerville reflected. He hung up and boarded his military vehicle for Queen's.

After Denny got the call from Britton, his "concern-o-meter" spun out of control. He was just walking out of his home when the phone rang. He nearly kept walking, but he was expecting a very important call.

Indeed this was the call he was waiting for. "Denny? You know who this is. Can we talk?"

"No. Not on this line. Give me a scramble and I'll call you."

Denny got Danny's scrambled number and ten minutes later he was reconnected with Rudy Castle's brother-in-law.

It took ten minutes for Denny to fill in all the parts he knew for Danny. Danny was silent for about ten seconds, then he said in a very low

Belfast accent, "This calls for people to be punished. See you in two days. Have hardware ready."

The phone line went symbolically "dead," Denny thought.

Returning to the moment, Denny headed for a rendezvous with a Republican solicitor; Denny was carrying a very small camera in his pocket.

Denny explained that the camera was a point and shoot. No flash, no noise, no expertise needed. The solicitor nodded and said, "This could cost me my license and jail time."

"I'm sure Rudy has a plan to save you from all of those concerns."

"He said he wanted me to bring the front page from today's news paper, I almost forgot it. What's that all about?"

"I've a hunch, but only Rudy knows. Good luck."

Poole was all smiles, as always. "Mr. Castle, how good of you to join us again today. We brought some friends along in the event that you decided to be difficult. I won't take the time to introduce them all to you; you wouldn't remember their names any way. So let's get to it shall we?

"Before you became uncooperative the last time we informed you of Detective Ivy's notebook wherein he describes your habits and acquaintances. Neither are particularly pleasant.

"For expediency sake, let's cut to the chase, and why don't you save yourself some trouble, and tell us about your dealings with Danny Conlon. Please."

There was nothing awkward about the pause. It was calculated. This time silence would signal no head and facial blows, rather body blows. The kick came from a new man on my left side and he delivered it to my kidney area with devastating accuracy.

Since I, like everyone else I knew had two kidneys, I fully expected to get the next kick on my right side. I was not disappointed. But I did not cooperate, for I twisted the chair to the left so the back of the chair took the brunt of the kick.

I smiled and said, "Sorry."

I shouldn't have turned and looked at him because the next kick from Potter came at my groin from straight ahead, but the seat of the chair absorbed much of the force.

Since my hands were secured behind my back, I could not defend myself or use my hand and arms to deflect kicks. Partridge pulled me from the chair onto the floor and said he was going to "polish his shoes on my prison uniform."

After a time, I was returned to the chair, and before Poole could start the questioning again, I looked straight at him and said, "There now," and smiled.

I was off the chair and getting a stomping once again.

Just when I was getting used to it all, I was pulled up onto the chair again. I really felt like shit, but I still had some moxie and said, "My shirt should say 'Welcome' because you are making me feel like a doormat."

I was back on the floor and I was coughing blood and gagging on it to the point that they stopped "polishing their shoes" on me and let me lay there while they filed out. Poole was the last to go, and as he left he said, "You can make this easier on yourself by stop being a mouthy cunt and telling us what we want to know."

I smiled and said, "I thought you already knew everything from Ivy's notebook."

He started back over towards me in a threatening fashion, but stopped, smiled, and left the interrogation room.

I didn't know how long I was on the floor, but the doctor showed up again. I smiled and said, "I'm still having problems, but no longer on my head. Now its on my torso and extremities. I think it's from the same cause though. What do you suggest?"

"I'm here to treat not prescribe."

"Did you only complete half of medical school? And to think, I was in favor of socialized medicine. I thought it would be just the thing for poor souls who found themselves in a British Goal or prison. But you are a real disappointment doc, a real disappointment.

"I intend to get your name. Oh, nothing physical will harm you, but your name will be remembered by certain people."

"I am required to report that kind of threat. Probable new charges will be filed against you for making it."

"It's not a threat, it's a promise. As I said, no harm will come to you, physically. But should I publish a book covering my time in your care, I'll have to mention you by name—that is being honest and professional. Are you ever professional," I asked?

He just gathered up his equipment and left the room.

I hoped I rattled him.

As I was being dumped unceremoniously into my cell, Mr. Britton and another attorney showed up and I was told to pull myself together for certain visitors. I'd just had the shit kicked out of me and I was supposed to receive visitors. *Some body was fucking nuts,* I thought.

Guards half carried me down to the room again for legal visitation. Mr. Britton was again physically shaken. The first thing I asked about was if they had brought the camera. The second attorney shook his head in the affirmative. I took off my shirt and the bruises were purple, black and blue. I stood there and had my picture taken. I said, "Get some close ups."

The solicitor took photographs of my head, arms, legs, and torso. I spit up blood on the floor. I then pissed blood for some pictures. In each shot I held the paper so the date and the headlines were visible. I made sure no furniture was included, to protect the attorneys, so the shots could have been taken in any of a half a dozen different rooms. I stood close to the door with the bared window and held up the paper. I made sure blood was coming out of my mouth too. I'd seen a lot of movies, so I knew the angels and poses they needed for the best effect.

After about fifteen minutes I folded the paper and told them to take off, as I needed to lie down. I was really feeling terrible.

I was led back to my cell and the solicitor got a photograph of me hobbling down the corridor.

I was not acting; I was not in good shape.

I was nicely lying on my cot when I was again called to get up and return to the visitor's room. I thought I was in for another round of "door matting." I thought, *enough of this shit, I'm done with mouthing off. No more wise ass cracks. I'm going to say nothing.*

As I approached the room I noticed a guard and a bucket and mop being wheeled out. I was also not hand cuffed. When the door opened

I saw the two solicitors and thought they got caught with the camera. I couldn't straighten up and the two guards were holding me up when I saw Professor Owen Jones and the Major, "Major Sommerville."

I could hardly get my breath as I slumped onto the chair. I wanted to shake their hands, but I hurt so badly and the tears were clouding my vision that I couldn't even make out where their hands were.

"My God, who did this to this man?" Summerville demanded.

The prison administrator said, "Special Branch has been interrogating him. We have had nothing to do with it, they have been in charge. As a matter of fact they are just leaving the prison now."

"Get them," Summerville ordered.

Jones leaned down and touched my shoulder and said, "I summoned Colonel Summerville to come to your aid Rudy. The Colonel will get this mess straightened out." I tried to smile, but it was a wince.

Colonel Summerville turned to me as if I were his son and said, "Rudy, what they have done to you is a crime. I am so ashamed of what has been done in the name of Great Britain. I apologize."

I was going to explain that this sort of shit goes on all the time in the name of "Great" Britain. Because this sort of abuse happens frequently to a multitude of people in the North of Ireland, there is nothing Great about Britain, and since it's the British who call themselves Great, maybe that is a tip off that there is something phony in the name. But I had decided that I was going to keep my mouth shut, so prudence got the better part of my "smart-ass-ness."

Poole and his gang of cut-throats came into the room. The Colonel just glared at them. The Special Branch men were clueless. Summerville asked, "Who laid a hand on this man?"

I couldn't help myself and shouted, "Those three laid hands on me the other day, but today the whole gang kicked me, and kicked me, and kicked me." Pointing at Partridge I said, "That one said they were going to polish their shoes on my shirt."

"This man, this decorated American soldier, worked for the British Military here in Ulster. And this is how you have treated this distinguished soldier? Your careers are through."

Pointing at Poole, Summerville bellowed, "You were in charge? You will collect their weapons, badges and ID cards. Governor, call the RUC and get a ranking officer over immediately. Get the prosecutor's office and get someone involved with this case over here, NOW."

As I slumped in the chair, Jones tried to comfort me. The doctor returned and was offering me more help in the way of meds than he had on all the other occasions. The Colonel was in deep conversation with the two solicitors, and Poole stood alone, his minions all having been dismissed.

All I wanted was some painkillers, a bed, and some peace and quiet. Colonel Summerville said he had to leave shortly but that he was promised that he would be kept informed of the investigation of this "affair" as he called it.

As we shook hands, I thanked him for "saving my life." I also added: "I hope you can muzzle Worthington once and for all."

The Colonel said he was going to try to do just that.

I managed a smiled and said, "I should get a medal for that, Colonel, and so should you."

The Colonel just nodded his head in consent. He thanked the solicitors and glared at Poole who was still just standing there looking like a whipped puppy.

"Mr. Poole is it? Well, we have some work to do before we contact your superiors. Let's get a move on," Summerville said sternly, as they both exited the room.

Feeling as I did, I could only imagine the condition of the prisoners in Long Kesh prison. I was thinking of not only the Hunger Strikers, but the prisoners who had endured the beatings and mistreatment for so long. Those thoughts alone made me nauseous and added to my miserable feelings of despair.

Any profit made by the Hunger Strike was made at a terrible price. Denny had explained to me that neither Sinn Fein nor the Army Council of the IRA called for or sanctioned the Hunger Strike. The prisoners themselves decided on the action. Certainly PR and political gain was to be made from their decision, but what a price was being paid.

I now had an inkling of that price, but it was only an inkling.

Some Last Minute Details

There was some official court work in the form of papers being filed. I was taken to the Royal Vic Hospital for examination and a night's observation. Denny came by and arranged for me to call home.

The arrangements for my return home were being taken care of by Denny, who said I'd be home in Hartford by the end of the week.

John Smyth also came by and told me about the chaos that unfolded at the department when the boys from MI 5 tried to "plant" some incriminating papers at Smyth's office. We all had a good laugh. I asked Denny if he knew if Poole and his dogs, Partridge and Potter, were going to catch hell over the whole incident.

"A fucken slap on the wrist if I know the Special Branch. They'll just be transferred somewhere."

"What about Worthington and his boss?" I asked.

"Probably a fucken citation and pay raise," he said sarcastically. "We don't even know Worthington's boss's name. But I bet Poole does, and where he hangs his hat; that would be useful information."

"That's a shame. Those lads should get some real shite for all of this. Not just what they put me through, but for what Worthington put a lot of others through," I confessed.

"Well, you never know what might come out of the blue, you know," Denny said cryptically. "Life is full of surprises, then you die," he added with a smile.

"Actually they should get a double helping of shite; one for what they did to you and another for who they are. Maybe a third for dessert."

I squirmed and said, "Dammit Denny, don't make me laugh, my ribs really hurt. They really hurt me."

I was released and Denny took me to his place to wait for the transfer to Dublin and home. It would be a day or two wait, then a train south to Dublin and jet home. I was anxious to leave.

In the mean time, I just lounged around Denny's place enjoying his wife Mary's cooking. Finally I asked him chidingly, "Denny, why is it that every time I leave this place there is a rain cloud hanging over my head?"

"Rudy, you are a fecken trouble maker. Then you leave and the rest of us have to clean up and live with your mess," he said, quite amused at himself.

"Fuck off, you wanker. I try to help the Movement and I inherit all the shite you guys have let slide since I was here last. It will be a cold day in hell before I come back the next time."

"Right."

"You'll have time to grow a real beard by that time."

"Where is my beard? What did you do with it Rudy?"

"I threw it in the dust bin. The last I noticed several Tom cats were cozying up to it and were looking at it very romantically."

"If you weren't so beaten up and lame I'd be giving you a good hiding myself, Mr. Castle," he said with a vicious grin.

"You'd better try it now because this is the closest you'll ever get to making the odds somewhat even."

"You ought to be thinking of getting even with those Special Branch boys and Worthington."

"I'm surprised you would say that. Your man Mac Stick was always against any personal vendettas."

Denny looked at me, not smiling but with a sparkle in his eyes, and said, "Mac Stiofain was correct about that, but times have changed and this situation is different. They should not be allowed to get away with this sort of shite."

"Maybe if I felt better. But I just want to get home. You're not just enticing me to come back and wreak some havoc, are you Denny?"

"Maybe, just a little. I would like you back sooner rather than later."

"You know we can't stay away very long. Eve and Barbrie need to come back just to see what they are missing and not missing."

The day Denny brought me to the train for Dublin, Mr. Poole was in front of a committee of Special Branch Operation heads, who were not pleased with his performance and that of his section. More precisely, they were upset that he had gotten so caught up in this embarrassing "affair."

Partridge and Potter were in for unpaid time off. Poole was going to get at least that same punishment and possibly more for being in charge.

"Mr. Poole, how could you let this situation get out of control?"

"Mr. Castle would antagonize Partridge and Potter to the point that they wanted to do him serious harm. When he started on me I hoped to put him in his place without the need for real serious theatrics.

"As you know, I was in liaison with another security service, they were pressuring me to step up the pressure on Mr. Castle and to protect their man Mr. Worthington. I felt I could play a low key-role to and with the London people."

Another member of the panel said, "That didn't work at all."

Another member said, "Why didn't you seek out council from those above you?"

"Mr. Jeffries, (I can use his name can I not?), of the London service that I will refrain from calling by name, said I should reign in all action concerning this situation. 'Keep it close, even secret from your Branch, you understand? Cover, keep it all under cover from everyone, including your own,' that's what he said. When it came to his suggestion that it might be a legal case, then I felt there would be time to inform and include the upper reaches of our Branch. I didn't tell Jeffries that mind you, but that was my intent."

The chairman at this hearing looked around the table, then asked, "Any further questions?"

All remained silent and seeing that there were no intentions to probe further, he said, "Mr. Poole, we will deliberate and let you know our decision concerning your future by the beginning of next week. We will take into account your record as well as your testimony here today.

"In the mean time you remain relieved of your duties. Do not, I repeat do not, discuss any of this matter with any one. Also do not go to your office. You are to be incommunicado and confined to your residence untill you are summoned next week. Do you understand these directives?"

"Can I go to church on Sunday?"

After a furtive glance along the table the headman nodded in the affirmative, but cautioned, "There and back."

"And my wife? What can I tell or explain to her?"

"Nothing. Tell her what you like, but do not under any circumstances say anything of this matter. Do you understand?"

Poole once again took the posture of a whipped dog.

An Unexpected Visitor

That same day, Danny Conlon slipped across the border into South Armagh in the early hours while it was still dark. It took him four more hours to get settled in Belfast; after Denny hustled me off on the train to Dublin, he made contact with my brother-in-law.

"How is Rudy?"

"Well he can walk on his own, but not much more. I just stuck him on the train for Dublin. He probably looks a bit like you did when he found you in Canada," Denny explained.

"That bad?"

"It's his pride as much as his body. He's not used to taking a beating without some retaliation. He told me he simply wasn't sure he would survive if he attacked the Special Branch men. I didn't ask him if he meant he wouldn't survive the beating he'd get after he laid them low, or if he meant the jail time for doing it."

"Do you know where they are all put up?" Danny asked.

"Aye, my boys have located all three of them. Of course, none of them are together. But they are also not that far apart; it will just be a matter of luck and timing. There will be three different cars with three separate weapons. They are all the same kind of weapon, but three separate guns for three separate drivers and cars."

"Fine. When do we start? The sooner the better."

"First thing in the morning. I've a place for you to stay the night. See you in the morning."

Denny showed up shortly after ten and was all business.

"I've called for a taxi. He'll drop you at the first car. He'll point it out to you. Danny, be careful. It's not worth getting caught or killed over. We can get to them if it proves impossible for you."

Danny paused for a second or two, and then said, "Nothing is impossible. You should have seen your man in Canada. Walked in cool as ice and just shot them, shot them all. He's why I'm alive. And now I will have the opportunity to avenge his tormentors today. If people saw him onto the train then he has an alibi."

"Aye. True enough. And in this world you need iron clad alibis. What was strange though was that he took no baggage, not even his toothbrush. I thought it strange. He said to give his extra clothes to the needy. I sure as hell hope he isn't up to something. He's noticeably beat up. He limps, moans, and staggers. He stands out like an 'All Black' rugby player from New Zealand with a free shot against our Belfast club," Denny said.

"He's on his way home to my sister, he won't do anything . . . rash . . . I don't think," Danny Conlon hesitantly concluded. After a rather long pause, he looked hard at Denny, and asked, "Would he?"

"Shite. I should have waited till the train actually pulled out. Just to be sure. It's too late now. Your taxi is here. See you in a couple of hours."

The day before I had watched Denny walk away from the security gate. I waited until Denny was gone then he took a couple of slugs of the coffee, disembarked and seemingly threw up at the edge of the train.

An RUC man came over and I said, "I'm sick. I can't stay on the train today. I need to change my ticket for a later train, maybe for tomorrow. Where do I go to do that?" I kept my hand over my nose and mouth to hide my appearance.

The RUC man pointed to an office. He remarked, "Now don't go getting sick in there. If you think you may throw up again get into the toilet, do you hear me?"

"Aye." I was using my Belfast accent.

I bought a ticket for a train leaving the next day, covering my face with my hand as I coughed. Then I walked out of the station and entered a taxi. I was dropped off near the university. I didn't have time to seek out the Special Branch men. I had no idea of where they might be. But I did know where Worthington's apartment was, and I felt I owed him a visit before I headed back to the United States.

The first taxi driver was all business, just like Denny was, no small talk. "Your man Potter spends time at that betting office. On days he doesn't work he stops in just about now. Then he crosses the road and goes onto that bar. Its toilet is out back, and there is a clear shot at it from that low building's roof.

"I'll go in and ID him for you. Just get out and wait near that store. I'll be back straight away."

A wirery guy came out of the betting parlor, looked around, crossed the street and went into the bar. The taxi driver got into the taxi at the same time as Danny.

"You got him?"

"Aye, pull into that side street and wait."

Conlon exited the taxi with his coat covering the rifle as he made for the low garage. He hoped he wouldn't have to wait long because he was mildly exposed.

Danny no more than got into position when Potter came out the back of the establishment, lit a cigarette, drew in a mouthful of smoke, and just stood there.

Without hesitation, Danny raised the rifle and pulled the trigger. Potter dropped like a bag of potatoes. Conlon was off the roof and in the taxi in a matter of five to ten seconds. The rifle was stowed and they were on their way to the second waiting taxi.

I loitered out side of Worthington's apartment house. It was too light to check movement in Worthington's apartment, so I simply went in and approached the apartment. Listening outside the door produced no evidence of any one being home. So I simply knocked on the door.

That produced a shuffle of objects within the apartment and a female voice calling out that she would be right there.

I called out, "Sorry. Wrong address," and I hurried away before the door swung open. I was already gone before I was seen.

I worried that Worthington had already vacated the premises, and possibly Belfast. That would really be a shame.

I decided to look at the mailboxes in the vestibule. Worthington's name was not on the box corresponding to the apartment number. But I noticed that more than half of the mailboxes did not display names.

Exiting the building I just loitered along the block and could do nothing but wait. To my advantage it was beginning to get dark earlier than normal because of impending rain.

I hoped the rain would hold off, as I had no rain gear. I just kept moving up and down the street periodically crossing over to the other side, but never taking my eyes off the entrance of the building housing Worthington's apartment.

The best scenario would be to catch him on the way in, that way the young lady in his apartment would not be a possible witness.

I knew the chances of catching him without a witness was slim. There had to be eight to ten apartments in the building, and being so close to the university there was potentially a virtual traffic flow in the early evening. Students coming and going, meeting up with other students, this could be a nightmare.

Then all at once there he was, going up the steps to the foyer. He stopped to check the mailbox, and that was his undoing. I came up behind him and put a bottle's neck against Worthington's back while grabbing his arm.

He was totally surprised. I said, "If you yell or make a false move you are a dead man. We are going to go for a walk and have a heart to heart talk. Now come along. I have people outside keeping their distance but also keeping an eye on us. A false move on your part and they have been ordered to simply shoot you. Do you understand? Will you cooperate?"

Worthington was scared shitless. He nodded consent.

We walked along the street, I had his arm by my left hand and kept my right hand in my pocket obviously holding an object that I hoped he continued to believe was a gun.

"Is it MI 5?"

He said nothing.

I stopped and yelled over my shoulder, "He is all yours Mick. Do what you want with him."

He stiffened and tried to look back in the direction I had turned my head and yelling in. I gave him a jerk that sent pain down my arm and through my side. I winced but kept him walking.

"Alright, alright. Yes, it was with MI 5, just like down in Dublin. I was an *agent provocateur* and a spy gathering names for them."

"We know that much. Who do you report to?"

It was obvious he was not going to give up that information without some serious coaxing.

It has started to rain and the lights from traffic and shops and restaurants were reflecting on the streets.

A bus was coming up fast along the tree-lined road splashing water from the puddles along the gutter of the street.

I had used a bus years earlier to cover a mishap when a potential assassin was pushed off a second story porch, killing him. I hid, holding his body behind a tree along a street not too far from this very spot, and then threw his body in front of a bus to cover what really happened to him and involving me in the episode.

Now I had a live tout who needed serious treatment. I jammed Worthington against a roadside tree. "You are a worthless piece of shit, you know that Worthington? You put people in dangerous positions just to make yourself look good.

"You are dog shit in my book. If the authorities aren't going to do anything about you, I am"

As the bus approached, I pulled my right hand out of coat pocket and I hurled him with all my might in front of the bus. Neither Worthington nor the bus driver had a chance to react.

Worthington's body went smack and crunch under the bus and was nearly under the rear wheels before the driver brought the bus to a stop. As before, I crossed the street in back of the bus and just walked away.

About a block away, I caught a taxi back toward the train terminal. I put up in an all night café, making sure to keep my head down and collar up.

After a long night I was just about to head for the platform when I caught sight of Denny slowly walking about and clearly searching for me.

I walked up behind him and grabbed him, scaring the hell out of him.

"Did you come to see me off for a second time, Denny?"

"What the fuck's going on Rudy?"

"Don't you know that I must be about my country's business?" I had used that line once before, and I liked it.

"In all the confusion I forgot to tell you that your hunch about Ruairi turned out to be correct. He was picked up by our people, and under interrogation he admitted being a tout for money. Money is the root of all evil Rudy."

"Aye. I'm inclined to agree with you. It's like you say, money is the root of all-evil. You never have enough, and the things you do to get more. Now just walk me to the train. You'll read about my last twenty-four hours tomorrow in the paper, and tell Mac Stiofain's man Jimmy thanks for the tip on Worthington, and tell him that problem is solved once and for all," I said with a smirk, as I limped in an exaggerated fashion for effect.

Denny looked at me with a slight smile on his face. He had a surprise too, but he decided not to tell me.

The second taxi had delivered Danny to a Loyalist housing estate in the Greencastle suburb of Belfast. Partridge was an avid dog walker. He walked his mutt mornings, noon and night, if his schedule permitted.

The taxi driver pointed out Partridge's house as they circled through the neighborhood. "Give him half an hour, he'll make his rounds with his dog then. He has been moping about for the last day or two. He actually has been taking the dog out more frequently. You should have no problem lining him up."

About twenty minutes later out he came with the dog on a leash, heading for some open ground. As it was midday, on a school day at that, there were not many people out and about. But what was unsettling was the amount of vehicle traffic; buses, cars and lorries.

Partridge was heading for a piece of waste ground, with little dumps of building rubble and trash heaped about. Danny had the driver wait until the dog had to take a shit and then directed him to proceed at a slow but steady pace.

The back window was down and there was plastic draped all around Danny and his compartment in the back seat. "Wham." One shot. Down he went. Off they drove. No one seemed to be alerted by the shot muffled as it was.

The rifle was stowed away once again and Danny was transferred to another taxi near the city center. The drivers had a clear knowledge of security checkpoints and they avoided them like the plague.

The train got into Dublin exactly on time. I called Barbrie and I said I was in a Dublin hotel and that the flight was scheduled to leave at 1 PM tomorrow. There would be a stop in Shannon, then on to New York. After a two-hour layover it was on to Chicago and then by car to Hartford.

I told her he wouldn't be able to sleep he was so excited to get home. She explained that besides her and mom, Eve insisted on coming too.

"Who will watch the babies?"

"Don't worry Rudy, it's all arranged. They will be safe. The cousins look forward to playing together. I can't wait to get my hands on you myself."

"You'll have to take care. In some spots I'm still bruised and sore from my stay in the Crumlin Goal."

"Oh, I'll be careful all right. And you will tell me all, everything, this time Mr. Castle. Everything, do you understand?"

"Jaysus, 'all' what? It was all just a big Special Branch misunderstanding," I teased.

"We'll see," Barbrie said. "See you tomorrow. I love you."

"Aye, and I love all of you, especially you."

Once in my room I took off my only shirt and pair of pants. I was going to shower, but I just stretched out on the bed to check out its softness and firmness and fell instantly asleep.

When I had told Barbrie that I wouldn't be able to sleep, I knew it was a lie. I was good at lying. I was exhausted and I could totally relax because there would be ten to twelve hours I could sleep.

The third and last taxi ride that day for Danny Conlon was out to Holywood, a few miles outside of Belfast on the south shore of Belfast Lough. Suitably Loyalist, it was obviously the correct spot for a supervisor in the Special Branch. Mr. Poole's red brick semi-attached home was very respectable in every way. Out front there was a bit of green lawn with two large trees for shade on a warm day. You could smell the salty sea in the breeze from the lough.

Poole was out in the yard working with rose bushes along the front of the house. He seemed quite calm considering everything that had happened over the past week resulting in his being relieved of his duties untill further notice. It was just after lunch, and again there was virtually no traffic, nor people out.

Danny rigged his plastic curtains, instructed the driver to go by the house slowly. Danny put the rifle in place to make the shot when a woman came out of Poole's house and stood very close to him while they discussed something.

Just as Danny was about to tell the driver to pull away, the woman returned into the house and left Poole standing alone. He slowly turned to look at the taxi loitering in front of his home when Danny made the shot. At that very instant Danny saw in Poole's face the recognition of what was happening. It was not a look of surprise, simple recognition.

They immediately drove off. Danny did not look back to see if the woman emerged from the house. The shot was loud in the taxi, but again was somewhat muffled to the outside world.

Danny repeated the process of hiding the rifle in the taxi. At the arranged spot Danny was picked up by Denny and transferred to the road heading south toward Newry. They only went about fifteen miles before Danny was handed off to men from Camlough, South Armagh.

Denny had decided to tell Danny about his brother-in-law turning up at the train station this morning.

"Rudy was up to something yesterday or last night. He said I'd hear about it in the news today. I wonder if he visited that shite Worthington. I'm just glad he didn't decide to try to get to the three you got. That could have really caused a fecken problem."

"For being such a planner, some times Rudy is very impulsive. Is there such a thing as an impulsive planner?" Danny asked.

"Aye it's called Rudy," Denny said. "Oh, by the way we are pretty close to the Kesh. Would you like to drop by and say hello to any of the boys?"

Danny grinned and said, "Not on your life. Take care Denny. Till the next time."

And with that exchange Danny Conlon was on his way to Dublin and home to his new home, the good old USA.

Surprises All Around

I slept until after ten in the morning. I quickly washed up, put on my shirt and pants, turned in my key at the hotel desk and caught a taxi to the airport.

"Two stops and home," I said to no one as I got my boarding pass. I cleared security and only after I had cleared it, did I stop and think that possibly there could have been a problem there. The Republic was cooperating with the Stormont government in Belfast on security issues.

I was glad I hadn't thought of that before. I would have been a nervous wreck. I only had half an hour wait at the gate and I could board. I took my seat next to the window and asked a stewardess if it was a full flight.

She said there would be a few empty seats; so once aloft it might be possible to switch seats.

I closed my eyes only to be rudely bumped by a passenger slamming into the seat next to me.

I wasn't going to let this clown spoil my flight home. As I looked at the man, I paused for an instant, not believing my eyes.

"You don't mind if I sit next to you, do you brother-in-law?"

"Jaysus, Mary and Joseph, what the hell are you doing here Danny?"

"Returning a favor," he said in a strong Belfast accent.

"What kind of favor, and for whom?"

"After we are in international air space I'll fill you in. I hear you limp, moan and stagger after spending time in the Crum. But I also hear you stayed around another day in spite of your injuries. What's with that?"

"Over international water," I smiled. "What a surprise, I'm really glad to see you Danny."

"Believe it or not I didn't plan this. I had no idea you were on this flight. The luck of the Irish, hey?"

Over international water, we both told our stories, telling it all as it happened, only leaving out details we simply didn't remember. Neither of us laughed, but certain aspects did bring smiles to one or the other of our faces.

With no one sitting behind us and only an elderly woman in front of us, we felt safe enough to tell our tales. The fellah across the isle was talking up a young blond, so he was paying neither me nor Danny any attention at all. In fact he was entertaining the people around him with his blather. At one point Danny said, "Your man is spewing blather, not blarney. I hope she isn't buying any of it."

I grinned and nodded. "Aye." Then on a more serious note I said, "I'll not be returning to the North for a while, Danny. This one really got to me. And although I don't limp and moan as our friend Denny suggests, I don't want a repeat of that North of Ireland hospitality either. I'm getting too fucking old for this sort of shit."

"You **are** getting old, and I hope you can keep up with my sister. The Conlon women are good for about a dozen babies Rudy, and I've a feeling your return will bring out the best in Barbrie. So if you need to sleep, go at it. I'm tired of talking myself."

The rest of the flight was relatively silent between the two of us. As we put down in New York, I said I wanted to see if I could afford a little something for the girls. So the two of us went looking in the duty free shop.

A big hour later they were on the plane heading for Chicago. I asked, "How long can you stay with us Danny? You know the women will want you to stay a while. They will also demand a full report, and I'm not up to it alone."

"I'll stay a few days. I'll have to check in on my job in Atlanta, but all should be well."

"That's great. All the wee girls will be pleased to spend time with uncle Danny."

"I must admit, I also want to spend some time with Megan Kelly, Sean's daughter. We've kept in touch and I, we, would like to see each other and talk over some things."

"Good on you Danny. I had Sean do some work on my car at his shop. She came out of the office and asked how you were keeping. I told her we were trying to get you to visit, but she might have more luck getting you to Hartford. She actually blushed.

"She is a beautiful girl. No, she is a beautiful woman now. She would look good in our families Danny. I wouldn't wait too long if you really like her. The guys have got to be lining up around the block for a date with her. She's one of the best."

Changing the topic, Danny said, "Aye, it seems like I was with you all just yesterday and at the same time it seems like it was all so long ago. I must be getting old too."

"Yes you are, Danny, just like the rest of us. Don't put off till tomorrow what would be best done today."

"Thanks for the advice Rudy."

History: 1981 Post Hunger Strike

Chelsea Barracks in London was bombed by the IRA, Major-General Sir Stewart Pringle, the Royal Marines Commandant-General was nearly killed by a bomb, and the busy shopping district of London, Oxford Street was targeted for bombing, killing the police explosive expert who tried to defuse it.

At the Provisional Sinn Fein Ardfheis, Danny Morrison, editor of the Republican Newspaper (An Phoblacht), addresses the delegates by stating the obvious new Provisional dual tactics: "Who here really believes we can win the war through the ballot box? But will anyone here object if, with a ballot paper in one hand and the Armalite in the other, we take power in Ireland." The die was cast for the next twenty years at least.

The Methodist preacher, Reverend Robert Blanford, the Ulster Unionist MP for South Belfast, was killed at a community center in Belfast. The IRA issued a statement saying he was "one of the key people responsible for winding up the loyalist paramilitary sectarian machine in the North." Reverend Ian Paisley fired back that "the blood of the murdered not only lies on the skirts of those who did this evil deed, but on the British government who by political and security policies created the circumstances in which such a crime can be done with such impunity."

For statements like this and provocative protests, Democratic Unionist Party MPs Paisley, Peter Robinson and John McQuade, were suspended from the British Parliament. A month later, reacting to just these types of statement, pressure from both US Senators and US Congressmen moved the US State Department to revoke Reverend Ian Paisley's visa to the United States.

Home

You can't imagine the surprise and joy had by all when uncle Danny came off the plane with me. Eve flung herself on him nearly knocking him down. Barbrie was laughing and crying at the same time. My mother was the only composed one of our group.

"Well Rudy, you certainly know how to make an entrance. How did you swing having Danny along? Next you'll tell me that your sidekick Denny will be along in a minute," mom chided.

"I wish he was, for his sake. He's one of the few who have sidestepped the chaos in the North. I fear for him and his family. He was instrumental in everything Danny and I did as of late in the North."

"Danny, you were in the North?" Barbrie asked with alarm. That brought a serious hush to everyone, even Eve.

"We'll explain everything, in detail. But first, I need a hamburger. An All-American hamburger," I said while handing the women some Irish liquor.

"Where is Paul, Eve? He hasn't left you for one of his old girl friends has he?" I chided Eve.

"You mind your manners Mr. Castle. He is babysitting the brood back in Hartford, and just because I might be expecting again doesn't mean I couldn't or won't beat you to a pulp. I should any way for probably endangering my baby brother over in Ireland," Eve threatened with a smile.

The levity returned as I hoped it would and we headed for the exit. Danny had a carry-on, but I had nothing.

Mom asked, "No baggage Rudy?"

"I've less baggage than a week ago, but none that I brought home. I've been traveling light. I left quickly and made it by the skin of my teeth."

"I understand son, and can't wait to hear all about it."

The ride to Hartford was long, but it went by quickly. Mom drove, Barbrie, Eve and I sat in back. Danny sat up front with mom and they chatted about what else, Ireland. Periodically Eve would lean forward and get her two cents worth into the conversation. Barbrie and I were content to just hug in the back seat, even if certain spots were still tender on my body. Actually I felt good all over, I was safe and sound and home.

The next day we had a picnic outside on a beautiful sunny day. The light filtered through the trees in the back of the house and I was content to just sit in a canvas lawn-chair watching the kids play.

Paul had joined us, so I began my saga. I didn't romanticize anything nor did I mince my words. The children were busy playing, and when my daughter Eoffa came to crawl on my lap to make sure I was really there, and not leaving again soon, I simple hesitated for a minute because I knew she would be off and running about soon enough. Then I would pick up the story from where I had left off.

I talked at length about the hunger strike, the 'five demands,' the support for the strike, Bobby Sands' leadership, Margaret Thatcher and the British response. I spoke of the riots and the RUC reaction. My talk became emotional and I had to stop and regain my composure several times. During my pauses it seemed even the birds stopped chirping and whistling, and even the crickets out by the garage went silent. There was a deliberate hush that came over everything. Even the little girls stopped playing and squealing, and looked over to us as if something was seriously out of sorts. They actually came over once and asked, "What's wrong?"

Next I gave a cleaned up version of my escapades and experience in the Crumlin Road Jail. I commented on my concern for Smyth and Denny and their families, as it seemed that the North was sliding further and further into chaos.

Danny then accounted for himself; he adapted the Americanism for shooting the three Special Branch men: "whack"! He identified each of the three Special Branch men who had made life miserable for me, thoroughly explaining where each had "gone to his maker."

When we were both finished, there were no congratulations, just a sense of relief. It had been a terrible set of circumstances that hopefully had ended in a satisfactory way for both Danny and myself. Granted there was a widow in Holywood, a dog without an owner in Greencastle, and a bar minus one patron in east Belfast. But that was the price they paid for what they had done.

As for Worthington, Rudy felt that some family members back in Hertfordshire, England would mourn his passing, but Belfast and Ireland in general would be a better place for their collective grief.

As I looked around the gathering in the back yard, no one here cheered their deaths, but no one mourned them either. I only wished I could have gotten to one more of them. What did Denny say his name was? *Jeffries, Jeffries from MI5*. That was a shame, but John Smyth had got to him. Maybe that was enough . . . for now.

Just then a car pulled into the drive and I scowled. "Who the hell can that be?"

Danny was on his feet and moving toward the car as Megan Kelly got out with the biggest grin I had seen since I saw Barbrie at the airport yesterday in Chicago. They didn't simply meet and greet each other; they hugged and kissed like lovers.

I took Barbrie's hand, looked at her, smiled and nodded toward Danny and Megan and thought, *Jaysus it's good to be home. A home away from home for some here, but home none the less.*

Family came first, and a close second was home, and everything that was associated with that loaded term.

What also came to mind was that for all of us here, since we all could claim two homes, was that we could all agree to something that seemed physically distant, but in reality, was embedded in our hearts and minds: **Erin go Bragh**.

CPSIA information can be obtained
at www.ICGtesting.com
Printed in the USA
FFOW04n0658181214
9670FF